I0787984

WARLORD OF THE SPINWARD REACHES

CORSAC FOX

BOOK 4

BLAZE WARD

Warlord of the Spinward Reaches
Corsac Fox, Book 4
Blaze Ward
Copyright © 2024 Blaze Ward
All rights reserved
Published by Knotted Road Press
www.KnottedRoadPress.com

ISBNs:
Paperback: 978-1-64470-405-9
Hardback: 978-1-64470-407-3

Cover art:
Jay O'Connell https://www.jayoconnell.com/
Illustration 108050035 © Raffaele1 | Dreamstime.com
Illustration 22850687 © Seamartini | Dreamstime.com

Cover and interior design copyright © 2024 Knotted Road Press

Reviews
It's true. Reviews help. Even a short one, such as, "Loved it!" So please consider reviewing this book (and all of the ones you've read) on your favorite retailer site.

Never miss a release!
If you'd like to be notified of new releases, sign up for my newsletter.

http://www.blazeward.com/newsletter/

Buy More!
Did you know that you can buy directly from the Knotted Road Press website?

https://www.knottedroadpress.com/shop/

ALSO BY BLAZE WARD

The Jessica Keller Chronicles

Auberon

Queen of the Pirates

Last of the Immortals

Goddess of War

Flight of the Blackbird

The Red Admiral

St. Legier

Winterhome

Petron

CS-405

Queen Anne's Revenge

Packmule

Persephone

First Centurion Kosnett

Encounter at Vilahana

Consensus at Aditi

Hegemony at Dalou

Princes at Ewin

Empire at Gloran

Domain at Yaumgan

Additional Alexandria Station Stories

The Story Road

Siren

Two Bottles of Wine With A War God

The Science Officer Series Season One

The Science Officer

The Mind Field

The Gilded Cage

The Pleasure Dome

The Doomsday Vault

The Last Flagship

The Hammerfield Gambit

The Hammerfield Payoff

The Bryce Connection

The Science Officer Series Season Two

Alien Seas

Buried Among the Stars

Captain Navarre

Last Stand

Lost Dreams

Ghost Towns

Games People Play

Prophet and Loss

Dandelion

Emergency

Warchild

Moot

CONTENTS

BASTION

ISANN

VATAZHKO

KARAŊGILIKKA

NUBIA

FIRE DIAMOND

For Coop and Surly

BASTION

ONE

"All hands to action stations," the call came over the speaker.

Conductor Ulysses Fortier—Uly—was in his office, mostly reviewing paperwork. He exploded into motion, slipping around his desk and opening the hatch to the bridge before pausing to see who had been on duty at the moment.

He hadn't been paying attention—autopilot was like that—but the voice had been Haydar Ramezani, the ship's Data Officer and somewhere between Second- and Fourth-In-Command, depending on the day and the mission. He was Mazhin, so all his tentacles were currently in motion, seething like a ball of seaweed that locked on Uly as he entered.

"Someone thinks they are being sneaky," Haydar said without turning eyes to look, instead focused on his screens. "They have just launched a raid on a ship in harbor. Figured I'd interrupt them and maybe get a little rude in the process."

Uly nodded and moved to the conductor's chair as Haydar stood up and slid over to where he normally preferred. Off to one side and handling data duties instead of at the center of things.

More than sensors, because he had a particular genius for extracting information from raw output.

Sometimes, the little things that made the difference between victory and defeat.

Uly buckled himself in.

Bad day for pirates to attack, no two ways about it. Sterling Huff was aboard the *Watchtower*, supervising crews assembling and completing the new station. And learning how to be an officer without Uly or anyone else close by. But he was nineteen years old now, and had been with Uly for four years of intense training.

And had the makings of a fantastic commanding officer one of these days. He'd just needed seasoning.

Similarly, Drew Roscoe was elsewhere, currently working with some of the civilian vessels that had accumulated at this moorage and organizing them into a small surveying force that would follow the courses Drew plotted in order to see what was out there.

That left Uly without his primary Gunner and his favorite Pilot, but he had Yuriy Kovalchuk on Guns today, an Ononguli pirate who had broken out of an Auga prison with him, and Yaqub Zobo, a Khet pilot who had helped steal the *Watchtower* at Ixtin.

And, as usual, Yaqub was technically out of uniform, today with a purple headband above his eyes and below his headcrest. His surname was derived from a type of plant with purple flowers, and no amount of discussion would get him to not have something purple on, so Uly had suggested the headband.

And it let you always know who he was from the back, given the large number of Khet crew that Uly had also accumulated.

"Data Officer, give me a sky view of the moorage on the main screen," Uly said, even as Haydar did so.

He had named the system and the planet Bastion, the ancient French word for a stronghold, just as his own surname, Fortier, meant someone who had lived in or near such a place. It was a pleasant world in many ways. Uninhabited when he arrived, but it showed indications that someone had lived there at some point, but left long enough ago that any investigations would be archaeological in nature.

Two moons, a larger one and a smaller one, like a cat and a mouse. More ocean than land.

Perfect for him to establish a new star nation, drawing folks from everywhere else, rather than forcing locals to adapt to his needs.

Uly was already at war with the *Auga Empire* over their intended goal of eventually conquering the entire galaxy.

Watchtower Bastion was the name of the almost complete station nearby, with the ship that held all the parts also being the *Watchtower*, though Uly intended to sell the vessel or trade for something more useful once it was completely empty. The other immense-though-smaller transport *Wren* was close to the *Watchtower*, as was the chartered Ononguli cruise ship that held most of the workers assembling the station.

Beyond that immediate zone, a number of signals indicated smaller ships. Almost all were armed to some degree, but none of them were anywhere close to as large or dangerous as the *Corsac Fox*, his heavy Interceptor ex-pirate gendarme vessel.

Haydar had highlighted four ships with blue rings on the screen.

"These four are up to no good," he announced, voice turning professorial as it did when Haydar got going on the topic. "They have, like most folks, absolutely no understanding of signals encryption, so I have been listening to what they thought were private conversations between conductors. At the moment, they are working themselves up to launching an attack to cut out the freighter *Hansa* by sneaking over boarding parties."

Uly absorbed all that, then turned to look at the man. Mazhin. Something. Ex-pirate scientist.

"And you were going to tell me when?" Uly asked.

"They haven't committed any crimes yet, Uly," Haydar

nodded. "Yet. They have, however, launched their shuttles with boarders and are about to engage in overt piracy."

Uly nodded. Technically correct was still the best way to do it, and he was intending to build up an entire star nation built on laws and order. On universal citizenship, regardless of species, if you were willing to work for the common good of all beings.

Even if he had taken to referring to himself as Warlord of the Spinward Reaches in the meantime.

Nobody lived out here. Or rather, individual planets existed, but no larger nations. Mostly folks hiding in the galactic darkness.

Not necessarily primitive, as galactic technology had been around for millennia at this point, but civilizations rose, spanned, and fell. He was trying to create something that would live long after he died of old age, though at age twenty-seven he hopefully had most of a century in front of him yet.

"Understood," Uly agreed with Haydar. "Have you notified anyone else?"

"Dan and her team are on the *Bastion* itself," Haydar replied. "Not immediately available because I hadn't expected to need communications that secured at the moment."

Uly nodded. He already knew what Haydar would likely stay up all night tonight doing. Either inventing exactly what he should have had available, or adapting something, so that he could put it into Uly's hands in the morning. He was like that.

Haydar and Roshan had originally been Mazhin slaves of the *Combined Crowns of Danumash*. *Technicals*, using their term for scientists, just as most of the rest of the Mazhin prisoners had been *Mechanicals*, tasked with building the things designed.

If Haydar had largely given up the competition with Roshan to invent new control systems, he still dabbled. And had a much more focused intent.

It would get done. Uly only had to step back so he didn't lose fingers or get pulled under by that tide.

It was good.

Uly studied the plot. Noted the vectors of over one hundred ships, most of them at rest to one another and the shell that would become Uly's new...base? Palace? Hall of Government?

Something.

The core of that thing he intended to build, such that it would outlive every person in this system and be handed down to their grandchildren if he could make it work.

First, however, he had to deal with some pirates.

"Mr. Kovalchuk, arm your systems and prepare your teams for combat," Uly ordered, turning himself back into that young *Batyr* officer he'd been, once upon a forever ago. "Mr. Zobo, engage Electroshield Array and plot me this course and stand by to engage the Variable Pulse Spatial Generators."

"Sir?" Yaqub Zobo asked, looking back over his shoulder.

Uly had sent him a rough line. The distance was hardly anything, as it went, but Uly wanted surprise.

"Just a blip, Zobo," Uly nodded. "Then they're trapped in here with us."

"Oh, right, sir," Yaqub nodded, clicking buttons. "Course laid in and ready, sir."

Uly missed Drew and Sterling. They'd have already plotted something even bigger, meaner, and better, just waiting for Uly to approve it.

But his current crew were shaping up nicely. And Uly knew how to fly and fight a ship himself.

"All hands, stand by for combat," Uly announced on the intercom. "Mr. Zobo, charge."

TWO

Uly barely had time to register the Variable Pulse Spatial Generators ramping up and creating a bubble around *Corsac Fox* before they were gone again. To the naked eye, it might have looked like the ship teleported across the orbital distance, but the *Bastion* wasn't complete enough to have its own such generators turned on and running at a low, background hum to keep other ships nearby from doing such a thing.

Yet one more project that probably needed to be accelerated. There was never enough time, enough people, enough anything, even though they had completed more work in the last six months than he'd originally planned for his first year out here.

And now, some punks had decided to try their luck. And his wrath.

He supposed that not everyone this far off the beaten path might have heard what he'd done in Imperial Sector Fifteen, between Z'Gosza and *Taeli Station*, to clean up piracy.

This was, according to almost every map he'd inherited, the middle of nowhere. The place where all the big trade routes turned into side alleys before petering out into nothingness in the wilderness.

Uly would have to remind them. Or educate them.

Lessons would be learned. Hopefully, these four ships and crews would survive. If not, the word would get out some other way.

Hansa was a medium-sized cargo vessel. Built on a hull roughly comparable to *Corsac Fox* in size, but with a small crew and large cargo bays. Many of those bays were filled with supplies to be sold to various folks shortly.

A bright, shiny bauble for pirates to pounce on like kittens.

However, a bobcat had just arrived.

A shuttle had docked with *Hansa*. A second had docked with the shuttle in a chain, presumable to feed a mob of boarders in to overwhelm the crew.

Hopefully, they'd been armed with stun weapons, or Uly would tack a lot of ugliness onto their punishment. The terminal kind, if necessary.

Lessons would be learned.

Four pirate ships. All small. Seeker class, but it was hard to distinguish them as Cargo Lighters, Ultra-Bombers, or Probes. None currently had wavebolts mounted externally to fire in a hurry. All had at least one turret pointed at *Hansa*.

Corsac Fox had appeared behind them, as it were.

Uly didn't even bother with names. Haydar had them available if he cared, but on the screen they were numbered from the left, one to four.

Number three slewed a wavebolt turret about and fired.

"I have a 2dm bolt incoming," Yuriy called. "Gunners, put a 1dm into it. Neutron Omnipulsar teams, stand by to receive more fire."

Uly nodded. Two decimeters in diameter when leaving the tube. A ball of plasma wrapped up in a small electromagnetic bubble by a control system, it bled some of the energy off for speed.

The farther they traveled, the weaker they got. Plus, you could damage them defensively with various weapons. A 1dm would kill it dead, long before it got close.

"Sir, do we return fire?" Yuriy asked, fingers poised.

The Ononguli were almost as savage and violent as Humans. Almost.

Plus, he and Sterling had trained the crew to use violence like a jeweler's tools, rather than a big hammer to crush anything before them. Neither the *Ononguli Confederation* nor the *Auga Empire* were known for subtlety.

"Give the one who fired first a six," Uly replied.

"More fire inbound," Haydar interrupted as the other three unleashed bolts as well.

"Yuriy, *break* them," Uly said simply.

Yuriy Kovalchuk gulped once and nodded, his horns only wavering a moment as he turned back.

"Gun team, give me the second bolt here," he said. "Lance this time, because I want that ship shattered."

Uly almost stopped him, but held back. A 6dm set to lance mode might punch starlight through number three if it hit. It would certainly get their attention.

"Defensive teams, engage on your usual vectors and let me know if you risk overload," Yuriy continued, his voice only rising a little.

But he'd been on the bridge several times when Sterling had fought this vessel against worse odds. And had been taught by Sterling Huff to do it right. Professionally.

Corsac Fox spewed defensive wavebolts at incoming torpedoes. 1dm was sufficient to shatter anything inbound. The Omnipulsar beams would weaken any until someone else could help.

"I've got a runner," Yaqub called, highlighting number one.

It had fired one 3dm, turned, and was accelerating away, obviously trying to get out of the sphere of space interdicted by the Spatial Generators so they could escape.

"Keep with him," Uly ordered.

Sterling would have already pounced, but he had a killer instinct that Yuriy was only slowly discovering.

"Gun teams report a kill," Yuriy announced.

Uly looked. Number three had taken that lance. It had penetrated their shields with enough energy left over to blacken the hull. No lights remained, and plasma and atmosphere were venting through the holes on both sides.

"Uly, we're getting surrenders from two of the ships," Haydar announced.

"Ignore them," Uly ordered, turning to look at the Mazhin to make his point.

You didn't get to start something like this, then step back and say sorry when it turned against you. Lessons needed to be learned, as taught by the Corsac Fox. The man, and not just the ship.

The Warlord of the Spinward Reaches.

"Yuriy, kill number four," Uly ordered. "Yaqub, keep number one from getting away."

There was a moment of stunned faces looking back, then everyone sobered and went to work.

The forward turret was a twin-barreled 6dm. Far heavier than a ship like *Corsac Fox* needed, and even exceptional for pirates, which it had used to great advantage when the ship was the Ononguli raider *Iron Wasp*.

Uly watched the Gunner and his teams coordinate. A 6dm to distract the defenders, while a pair of 1dms raced in right behind it. It was the sort of thing that was becoming a signature Sterling Huff move. The pirates had to choose between stopping the one that might rupture their vessel entirely and the two smaller ones that might do the same thing in smaller bites.

The defenders tried their best, but their best was only sufficient to stop two wavebolts. A 1dm impacted, blasting their Electroshield Array into vapor trailing away like a comet's corona.

The other 6dm raced after number one. That ship appeared to

be nothing more than a Cargo Lighter, as it fired a single 1dm defensively, then focused their only Neutron Omnipulsar.

It wasn't enough to stop a six, but it did weaken it enough that the ship merely tumbled out of control after taking the explosive impact.

Yuriy had hit them with a hammer instead of a shiv, but they were still done.

"Uly, number two is greatly sorry for causing you any problems and offers to make it right, if please you won't kill them," Haydar spoke up. "I gather that number three and four had the two conductors responsible for everything."

"Yuriy, cease fire," Uly ordered, nodding. "Let them surrender. Haydar, contact Dan and ask her to send combat teams over to remove the crews of all four ships and put them under arrest on the station. Have Drew round up scratch crews to get the ships stabilized and moved to a safer orbit, assuming none of them explode at this point."

Haydar nodded, already typing messages.

"Uly, what do you intend to do with the prisoners?" he asked.

Uly shrugged.

"That depends on *Hansa*," he replied. "If everything was polite and safe, throw the raiders in prison for a while to rethink their life choices."

"And if not?" Haydar asked, lips pulled tight.

"Hang them."

THREE

Commander Sheridan Chastain was working. Had been. As Uly's Chief of Staff and Second-in-Command, Dan had responsibilities far beyond the ship *Corsac Fox*, even as she was recruiting and training people to handle things. Just as Uly had done to her, back when she was a mere enlisted boarding grunt that had drawn the short straw to be sent with a young officer the others disliked.

Distrusted.

Mostly because Uly was better than any of them.

As Commander, she wasn't supposed to lead teams into ground combat anymore, but she'd gotten the note from Haydar that Uly seemed exceptionally pissed at someone or something, so she'd dropped everything, asked Suka Kuri to take over for a while, and grabbed her team.

One Human. One Mazhin. Two Emro. One Ononguli. One Khet. One Guezal. At least in the order they had joined. All were equals today. Experts at close combat, boarding actions, weapons, tactics. All female.

Several somebodies apparently needed to have their heads cracked together. Dan was going to handle it personally.

Dan and her team were on a shuttle blasting madly across orbital space to take charge. Four ships, already lined up like ducklings, though two of them were apparently scrap iron at this point.

"Pilot, time to contact?" she called.

"Ninety seconds, Commander," the man replied. "Corsac Fox wants us securing *Hansa* first, then moving on."

"Understood," Dan replied.

She'd grabbed boarding armor, weapons, and her women, running to the flight deck without bothering to get a full update from Haydar.

The situation was stable. Now, she needed to own it.

Dan turned back to the others. Nasrin. Yanouk. Anari. Katya. Ciah. Yeong-Suk.

Grim smiles greeted her. Like they'd all gotten that same vibe that something was wrong and needed to be dealt with by dropping overwhelming force on it up front.

"We going in hot?" Nasrin asked.

Her name meant Wild Rose. No longer the second best warrior of the group, but only because the others had mostly caught up with the Mazhin woman. They were all deadly.

"Ready for lethal, but we'll keep it polite for now," Dan replied. "I got the impression that the boarders were far more polite after Uly stomped their ships into the mud. Doubt they'll give us trouble now, but we need to be ready for it."

Nods. All of them studied close combat. Taught each other. Learned from one another.

"Seal it up," Dan said, pulling her helmet on and checking everything.

For now, she'd leave the faceplate and louvers open, but both could shut in the blink of an eye.

Everyone did the same, then checked one another for green lights on the outsides of their boarding armor. Ready to go.

"Docking imminent," the pilot called from up front.

Dan moved to the hatch and drew her Heavy Exoripper pistol.

One of the few things she still had from her days on *Marshal Castillon*, a lifetime ago. New uniform. New rank. New everything.

New star nation in the process of being born, as much her work as Uly's, because he trusted her to simply handle vast swaths of things.

Trusted. Her.

That still brought a smile to Dan's face, even as the airlock began to cycle open and she followed her pistol into the next chamber.

And trouble.

FOUR

Dan found five people in the mud room on *Hansa* as she boarded. Behind her, Nasrin first and then the rest shifted in and slid sideways along the bulkheads, weapons pointed out. A Khet male in civilian clothing was out in the middle, with a second Khet guarding three other folks she didn't recognize by species.

Hands clenched on the backs of necks was a pose she did recognize.

"Commander Chastain?" the Khet asked, waiting for her nod. "Conductor Rolle Qevin. I've got more prisoners surrendered and locked in a cargo hold, but these three insisted on surrendering to you personally. I've had no other trouble at all from them since the *Corsac Fox* blew up their ships."

Dan nodded, unsurprised. It was one thing to raid. It was something else to be on the short end of Uly's temper, and that was apparently what had happened today.

She studied the prisoners. Upright bipeds, as was common everywhere. Humanoid enough to pass in the dark, though all three looked shorter and wider than Human. Not muscles, just wide frames. Males, at first glance.

Smaller eyes than hers. Huge nose that was almost more of a snout like you might find on a hound. Ears on the sides that came to slight points.

It was the skin she found interesting. Dan had described herself as Afro-Siberian more than once, a dark, rich brown with curly black hair. These three aliens had silver skin. Not reflective, but that polished gray that she'd never seen on a person before.

"You speak Standard?" she asked in a hard tone, Exoripper centered on the middle one.

Dan was pretty sure she could take all three of them herself, if they were only as strong as they looked.

"Some," the middle one replied. In a hard, clipped accent. "Not well."

Dan nodded.

"As long as you understand me," she said slowly, giving him time to parse her. Then she turned to the Conductor. "Nobody hurt here?"

"They had stun pistols and wands," Qevin replied. "One of them had a small cannon for blowing bulkheads if they'd needed, but the battle outside was over so fast that they'd already lost by the time they got to my bridge and pointed guns at us."

"How many pirates?" Dan asked.

"These three are the leaders," Qevin said. "I have another fourteen aft for you, disarmed and behaving."

"Excellent," Dan said, then focused on the three, especially the one in the middle. "You have made a dreadful mistake, attacking the Corsac Fox. You will board my shuttle and be my prisoners. Do not give me a reason to kill you. Am I clear?"

"You are," he replied, still sounding like Standard was a foreign tongue.

Even when she'd been with the *Batyr* Navy, over in the distant swamps of Imperial Sector Seventeen, her accent had been better.

"What species are you?" she asked, which was usually the first thing others asked her, but she had the guns today.

"Isann," he replied, pronouncing it like *YEE-san* and looking like that was supposed to mean something to her.

didn't , but she had to look up a lot of things that folks from around here took for granted. Dan turned to Anari and Katya. Emro Sabre School and former Ononguli pirate made good.

"Put them on the shuttle and lock them down while I retrieve the others," she ordered. "Conductor, let's go find their friends."

didn't take long. The first three had been peaceful. The others were still shellshocked. Lost ducklings who followed Yanouk politely and never spoke.

Everyone got back aboard the shuttle and settled into chairs. Then locked down with safety belts controlled from the cockpit.

Dan was not messing around.

"Pilot, connect me to *Corsac Fox*," she said.

"Mr. Ramezani is waiting on channel five for you already, sir," he replied.

Dan swapped over.

"Haydar, what's the wider status?" she asked immediately. "I have seventeen prisoners locked down here."

"We're making arrangements to gather up the rest," he replied. "Uly said that he found it necessary to make examples of two of them."

Dan winced. She had a better idea than even that old pirate what *making an example of someone* meant. At least to Uly.

"Do I need to supervise that task, or deliver my prisoners to you?" she asked.

"Personally, I'd like you here," Haydar said. "Sterling and Drew have the rest in hand, but this smells bigger, if I can say such a thing."

Dan understood just how broad the sensory range the Mazhin's tentacles allowed. If Haydar had a bad feeling, she needed to be talking to Uly as soon as possible.

"Understood," she told the man. "I'll route there."

"Thank you."

Dan cut the line.

"Pilot, take us directly to *Corsac Fox*, shortest flight possible," she ordered.

"On it, sir," he said. "Stand by to detach and accelerate."

Dan found a seat and strapped herself in.

Time to see what was up.

FIVE

Haydar had dragged Uly aft and pinged Vahid to deliver fresh cookies or something to the conference room. Wonder of wonders, The Spatula hadn't even complained, but had brought a plate of things that Dan and Kolya had both compared to oatmeal-blueberry cookies, still warm.

Uly chewed a second one with a mug of coffee in one hand and Haydar watched some of the stress bleed out of his friend's shoulders.

He had nibbled on his own cookie, mostly buying time. Dan was coming. Her mere presence improved Uly's humor in ways that he doubted his friend noticed. Even Uly.

"Better?" Haydar asked after a time.

"Still pissed," Uly replied in a calmer voice. "No longer carnivorous."

Haydar was willing to take that much. He could read Uly's scent already and see how raw and angry it was, and this was *after* two cookies.

Haydar hadn't been certain that those four pirate ships were going to survive, right until the end.

"I'd ask if there was anything I could do," Haydar offered, "but we're all stretched a little too thin doing too many things at once. What loads can we take off your shoulders to make it better?"

One of the biggest reasons all the Mazhin had elected Uly to *Speak* for them was that in moments like this, the man paused before he gave a thoughtful answer.

"If I said I woke up on the wrong side of the junkyard this morning, would that make sense?" Uly asked.

It took Haydar a moment to parse that. A weird fusion of several Human idioms, but mostly an upgraded version of the *wrong side of the bed*. With all the additional problems inherent in being The Corsac Fox.

"It does," Haydar nodded, head as well as tentacles.

"How many more times are pirates like that going to emerge from the darkness and pull stunts like this?" Uly asked. "Who else is out there that we don't know about, lurking with a knife in one hand?"

That made even more sense. Haydar had been such a pirate in his younger, more raucous days, though he wouldn't discuss that with anybody but Uly. And maybe Dan. If they got him slightly drunk first. Okay, more than slightly.

Then he had an idea so utterly ludicrous that his tentacles gave him away. Uly sat up, not primed for combat but with that immense charisma locked onto Haydar like a turret.

"Yes?" Uly asked.

"We're close to done here," Haydar offered. "The station could be at least ready to turn on all the defensive systems in not all that long, though the crews would still have to finish a lot of other systems if we juggled things around. Why not go look?"

It wasn't often that he could surprise Uly. That anyone could. That was who Uly was.

So it was extra nice to watch the man's face fall slack for a long moment. For his mouth to open and his eyes to get almost as large as a Mazhin's.

That extra blink was just icing.

Haydar grinned.

They stared at each other for a long moment, interrupted as Dan arrived.

She entered in a rush of adrenaline and competence like spring flowers, coming to rest just inside the hatch and surveying the two of them.

"I've got the initial load of prisoners detained," she said, then petered down to nothing. "What am I missing here?"

Haydar laughed. As amazing a being as Uly Fortier was, Dan Sheridan was only perhaps a quarter step behind him. She simply didn't recognize it like Uly did.

Took an outsider like him to see, but Dan preferred it that way.

Quiet. Calm. Professional. Uly's signatures as well, but he also had to charm people.

Dan *intimidated* them into behaving.

"Haydar's up to no good," Uly offered quietly, even as Dan took a chair on Haydar's side and grabbed a cookie.

"And the sun rises in the east," Dan nodded, causing Haydar to laugh even louder.

Hopefully, he wasn't growing predictable in his middle age.

She turned those dark eyes on Haydar and he felt his tentacles flinch back a shade.

"We're in a rut," Haydar replied, skipping over all the bits in the middle. "I had an idea for breaking us out. Uly isn't necessarily arguing with me, either."

And she turned her attentin back to Uly. It was like a cloud crossing the sun on a planetary surface. Haydar breathed.

"He suggested we reorganize the moorage here," Uly explained. "Then take *Corsac Fox* on a survey mission deeper into the interior to see what's there. And who."

"Yes," Dan nodded, surprising Haydar with her terseness. "We have a group of prisoners from a species I don't know, and haven't had time to research."

"Oh?" Haydar perked right up.

He couldn't help himself. Data nerd. Not as big a map nerd as Sterling Huff, but not that far behind, either.

"Call themselves Isann," Dan replied, describing them.

Haydar let himself pick up all the secondary bits in her posture, as well as identifying those new scents she'd brought with her.

Interesting. Not anyone he knew, either. He turned back to Uly.

The Corsac Fox would decide. The rest of them were there to get things done once he did.

"It feels delinquent," Uly noted. "At the same time, it feels right as well."

He paused, deep in thought, as Haydar watched all that anger bleed off even more and turn into...something.

Intent? It was Uly.

The man hit the comm button in the middle of the table.

"Bridge, this is Havrylyuk."

"Vitali, I need to speak with Maks Sobol as soon as possible," Uly explained. "Call him, then route him here, please."

"On it, sir."

Uly leaned back and watched. Haydar saw triumph added to the intent, so it must be good. And Uly wouldn't want to explain it twice.

He could wait.

SIX

Maks Sobol wasn't entirely sure how to describe the last couple of years. From First Mate on *Compass Rose* to owner/conductor of *Scavenger Angel* to...

He supposed that he'd become some sort of agent/troubleshooter for the *Vatazhko* herself. THE Lord of the Endless Plains. Business partner twice over now, since he was also a minority shareholder of this cruise ship *Treta Envoy* she had hired and supplied with workers to build Uly's new base.

At least he'd managed to avoid being appointed her Ambassador to the pirates. That would be her niece, Chervonya Borisov.

Almost a year later, Maks still wasn't sure exactly what Chervonya's intentions towards him were. Flirty, but always with a bright, obvious line in place that kept things safe. She didn't have a spouse, mate, or even serious interest in anyone, at least as far as she'd mentioned, but Maks had also not probed too closely, even after six months out here in the darkness with Uly and his people.

A chime interrupted his daydreams of pretty girls, bringing Maks back to his office.

Conductor of *Treta Envoy*. Pretty white and teal uniform

deeply at odds with the sorts of things pirates habitually wore. Paperwork, but not a lot, because he'd inherited one hell of a crew when Anna Shevchenko, the *Vatazhko*, put him here.

Maks drew a breath and got back to work.

"What's up?" he asked, keying the comm button.

"The Corsac Fox wants to talk to you, Maks," Eugen replied.

First Officer. First rate. Would likely inherit this job when Maks went back to whatever Anna wanted him to do next.

And the crew, while they had relaxed some, still differentiated. THE Corsac Fox meant Uly in conversation, while *Corsac Fox* alone meant the ship.

"Put him through," Maks said.

"Maks?" Uly asked a moment later.

"Here," Maks replied. "What can I do for you, Uly? And thank you for stomping the pirates."

Maks had been a pirate. Not that level of rank amateur dumbass, but not all that much better. He'd have been in just as sorry a position when he'd been young.

"I have a construction schedule question, Maks," Uly said. "How quickly could you rearrange things to bring the wavebolts online and turn on the local Variable Pulse Spatial Generator to protect the station?"

Maks sat back and thought about that twice before answering.

"You expecting trouble?" he asked.

"No, but I'd like the station to turn into the fortress it was intended to be," Uly said. "And sooner rather than later."

Maks had lots of information at his fingertips. And most of it in his head, because his job had been something of a bridge between Uly and the construction crew. Not the contractor in charge, but the guy who ran interference both ways, so that Uly didn't have to yell at anybody when things didn't get done on time.

Though they were well ahead of schedule today.

"What am I missing, Uly?" Maks asked.

"Secured line, Maks," Uly noted, telling him that Haydar had encrypted the shit out of it. "We're planning to take the *Fox* into the interior. I want to know who this batch of pirates are and where they came from."

"Something new?" Maks asked.

"Locally unknown species called Isann," Uly told him. "I need to secure my flank better, obviously. I need the *Bastion* anchoring things."

"Let me talk to Chervonya, Uly," Maks replied. "I think we can adjust things here pretty easily, but I don't make all the decisions."

"Understood, Maks," Uly said. "Keep it quiet for now, since us departing increases your risk. I'd like a pattern of 12dm launchers handy to protect folks. That's my anchor to leaving."

"I'll get back to you soonest, Uly."

"Thank you, Maks."

Maks was alone again, the line dead. He keyed the comm.

"Yo?" Eugen replied.

"Where's Chervonya?" Maks asked.

"Stand by. Last check in was her cabin on deck three. Need me to call her?"

"Negative, Eugen," Maks replied. "I'll go knock."

SEVEN

Chervonya found that she'd enjoyed this vacation from the cutthroat politics of the palace. Almost everyone here was afraid of her on some level. Afraid of her power. Of her aunt. Of something.

Almost.

She smiled at Maks, standing in the hatchway with a bit of a forlorn smile.

"Come in," she gestured, stepping to the side.

As Ambassador, she had the best suite on the ship, even if it was far more than she needed. Except when entertaining Uly and lots of friends.

She moved to a chair in the front part of the main room and sat. Maks took the couch nearby, though he only perched on the edge, as though expecting to flee.

It couldn't be that bad, could it? Hadn't *Corsac Fox* just crushed a small pirate raid?

Or, what was Uly up to that Maks was nervous?

"You look like you need some coffee," she noted.

He bounced up and moved to the machine like she was chasing him with a whip. Far out of character.

What was going on?

She waited on pins and needles for him to sit again.

"Uly would like to rearrange the construction schedule," Maks began without prelude. "Specifically, to bring all the defensive systems online tomorrow, if possible, then get back to the rest afterwards."

Chervonya considered Maks's words. On one level, perfectly normal, especially considering that Uly had just seen off a small raid.

But Uly didn't ever do the obvious. That was what made him dangerous.

"And?" she pressed.

"And a lot of secondary implications that I don't think he or anyone else has nailed down in their heads yet," Maks said. "They will, but this was spur of the moment."

That was why Anna had sent Maks here. That ability to understand what the Corsac Fox had done, was doing, and was about to do, better than just about anybody save Lukyan Chayka, who Aunt Anna was using in other roles. Less diplomatic ones.

"Such as?" she asked.

"Uly wants to take the ship and scout the interior behind us," Maks said. "That is a secret at current, so please don't share it around. Doing so leaves the system at risk, but if the guns are working, we can stand off anybody wanting to be a problem."

Chervonya nodded. She could see that.

"Who'd be in charge with Uly gone?" she asked.

Maks chewed his lips and his horns went back and forth.

"Honestly?" he asked. "I think Uly might ask me to take over as governor until he got back."

Chervonya blinked and felt her brain reset. Not many people could do that to her. Her aunt. Her mother.

Maks.

It was an alien thing, but Uly was alien. Human. The Ononguli would never trust someone else like that.

But it was Uly. And Maks was more like the Humans than an Ononguli these days. That was why Anna had sent her. To keep an eye on Maks, as well as Uly and his people.

To make sure things stayed on the straight line.

And to understand the aliens. All the aliens.

And Maks would do it. Would take that responsibility seriously. Not that Chervonya would undermine Uly. Lock him out of his own station while he was gone.

On the one horn, utterly rude to a national ally.

On the other, it was Uly. She'd seen the things he'd accomplished in his short time. Making him an enemy was about the dumbest thing she could think of. Certainly, among the most suicidal.

"Implications?" she asked, skipping around preliminaries.

"I've got a pretty good idea what he needs," Maks replied. "And honestly, it all has to be done. This just changes the order but doesn't impact other things. Folks will still keep searching the local system for mining claims. Or starting farms and ranches on the surface below us. Ships will come in to trade. This is a place, and it won't turn into a pirate haven anytime soon."

"What do you need from me?" Chervonya studied Maks closer.

She'd teased the man. Flirted with him. He was easy to flirt with, so much more polite and thoughtful than the average Ononguli male. But most of them wanted to grow up and be pirates.

Maks Sobol was an interesting person.

Anna had, however, warned her not to burn him as a contact or agent. Critical, since he had such a solid personal connection to the Corsac Fox.

Thus, they hadn't ever gotten personal themselves. Merely professional.

"Permission, as much as anything," he fired back at her. "I work for Anna. Which means I work for you at the end of the day. This moves me out of that, until we're peers across the table from one another. Things would have to change. Maybe for the better. Maybe not. Different."

And yet another reason she found him so fascinating. He didn't assume gender superiority, like so many Ononguli men did. That was the alien part of Maks Sobol. The influence of Uly, but also of Dan and her people.

Competence wasn't limited to men, though most never got that.

Not like Maks.

"Would you become a threat to the Horde?" Chervonya asked, turning a little more serious.

"Not at first," Maks replied in a sober voice, causing her to catch her breath.

Again.

He wouldn't start anything, but her being Ononguli wouldn't stop him, if she decided to.

She'd make Maks an enemy only because she'd be doing something to make Uly an enemy. And he was warning her as politely as possible ahead of time.

Drawing a line in the dirt.

They studied each other for a long moment.

"Subject to Anna overruling me, I don't see that being a problem, Maks," Chervonya decided.

He nodded and sipped coffee.

She watched him, noting how much the man had changed, just in the time she'd known him, and then, far different from the man the files had painted from prior to that.

Uly.

How would Fortier change her?

EIGHT

Uly knew he'd set in motion an avalanche. Couldn't be helped.

At the same time, he found a spring in his step that had been missing. A smile that wasn't just Vahid's cooking or Omid's perfection of laundry and cleaning.

Dan just entering his office improved his day that she stopped suddenly, watching him, before she smiled back.

"I feel like we just snuck out after curfew," she observed, slipping into the chair across the desk from him.

His office was large enough for a mob. It had been a conference room before, but he'd needed space for people. Especially since some of them were Emro.

"Going to," he replied. "What did you find about the Isann?"

"Not a damned thing," Dan huffed. "Even Suka Kuri was hard pressed to recognize the name. They really aren't on any map or in any database we have."

He nodded.

"That is why we chose this region to build in," Uly reminded her. "Imperial Sector Fourteen as the *Auga* see it. The Spinward

Reaches to everybody else. A big dark spot on the map where there aren't any trade routes of note. Obviously, somebody lives here."

"I was just about to go talk to my prisoners," Dan nodded back. "Did you want to come?"

He almost said no, but changed his mind.

They'd been polite, once he'd crushed them, and no innocents had been hurt so hanging everyone was unlikely at this point, though Uly wasn't sure what he would do.

New alien species from the distant darkness. Where had he heard that before?

"Yeah," Uly decided, rising and shutting off his screen. "There's something to learn there. Especially if we're about to go locate their homeworld."

"I've got Drew and Marlowe stripping their computer systems for information," Dan said, falling into step beside him as they headed aft. "We'll have coordinates soon enough. Do we go visit?"

"That depends," Uly told her. "I want to know who they are and how powerful before I antagonize them. Piracy is one thing. Were they scouts for some invading fleet nobody knows about? I need actionable intelligence."

"The ships were pretty primitive, according to Drew when he boarded," she said. "Even more so than you'd expect civilian *Batyr* ships to be."

Uly paused in the middle of the corridor and turned inward to look at her. Helped that she was his height when he remembered to stand up straight. And she still outweighed him, but Vahid had given up trying to fatten him up.

"Remind you of anyone?" he asked.

Her eyes blinked, then got big.

"Maybe," she hedged, saying it in about six syllables.

He nodded and started walking again.

When this ship had been the pirate raider *Iron Wasp*, Uly had been a prisoner in these same aft bays. He'd upgraded them some, just in case he had to hold other prisoners for a time, but the interior was generally unchanged. Bunk beds that could be detached from the deck and moved around to cluster better. A couple of tables with a variety of chairs. More entertainment slabs and books to read.

And Vahid was in charge of feeding everyone. His people cooked to his standards, or moved on to other jobs. Or other ships.

Emil Beranger and Gennady Travers were guarding the hatch. The Dwarf and the Troll. One of the strongest Humans Uly had ever met, standing next to one of the ugliest. Emil's left leg from the knee down was mechanical these days, but you had to see him in shorts to know.

Both had been with Uly from Day One, when he'd first met Dan. And Kolya Roux, currently Assistant Chief Engineer of *Corsac Fox* because he'd won the coin toss, making Marlowe Michaels become Chief.

Engineers were weird.

"Gentlemen," Uly said as he came to rest. "How are our prisoners?"

"Shock's wearing off, sir," Emil replied. "Might start to feeling feisty by tomorrow. Figure Yanouk and Anari should have this duty for breakfast."

Uly laughed, imagining a pair of Emro women—those exceedingly big, beautiful, and *dangerous* Emro women—taking charge.

"Her responsibility," he said, pointing a thumb at Dan. "Let's go chat with them, shall we?"

Travers moved to the door, Heavy Exoripper in one hand. He opened it and surveyed the room.

"Prisoners will line up for inspection," he howled in an ugly voice that echoed off the distant far end of the room.

Took those folks a moment to understand, but they were pirates, not proper sailors. Quickly, they got in four lines. Roughly one hundred prisoners, but well behaved since they had been removed from their vessels under angry, armed guards.

Gennady and Emil went in first, pistols in hand and pointed

generally at the Isann. Dan went next. Uly was last, coming to rest about five meters from the center.

"I am the Corsac Fox," he announced quietly. And slowly, as Dan had said that they might not speak Standard at home.

Those men stirred. All men. Even the Khet and Ononguli would have a few women pirates in a force this big.

Not the Isann. Uly filed that for later, understanding that Dan had already understood and needed him to imprint them hard before they would accept her authority.

Shitty, but sometimes necessary.

"Did you have any greater plan than stealing a ship from my system?" Uly demanded, focusing on the two men in the middle.

Apparently, the other two conductors, the ones generally in charge of the raid, had died with their ships. As had forty or so of their comrades.

Lessons had needed to be learned.

"No, sir," one of the conductors spoke quietly.

Hangdog look. Vessel Number Two, who had gotten away physically unharmed, when the other three had been beaten into submission.

Carrots now, after Sticks had been necessary earlier.

"What is the punishment for piracy in your home system?" Uly asked slowly, looking around the room.

From the faces, less than half even understood him.

Truly, isolated somewhere.

The conductor down front who had spoken earlier muttered something.

"Speak up," Uly said.

"Prison, sir," he said louder.

"Nothing worse?" Uly asked.

"We didn't kill anybody, sir," he replied earnestly. "Tried to take the ship. That was all."

Uly nodded, hoping that the body language would be similar.

Ethics. If nothing else, it would set these men apart from rabid animals that needed to be put down. And they'd all been armed with stun weaponry they'd acquired from somewhere.

"What will the authorities say, if we returned you to serve your sentence at home?" Uly asked, still speaking slowly and clearly, like he had a classroom of recalcitrant children.

He saw surprise on a few faces. Hope here and there.

Had all of them consigned their souls to whatever hell their kind believed in?

Uly focused on the conductor who seemingly spoke for the others.

"Prison for us, sir," he said forlornly.

"But your families will be able to visit," Uly said. "And presumably you'll get out eventually."

"Maybe, sir," he acknowledged.

"We'll find out soon," Uly informed them. "I'm getting your navigational data from your ships, and intend to sail over and chat with your people. And turn you over to them for punishment."

It was revealing, watching them translate that, then comprehend it. A few whispered to others that didn't necessarily speak Standard, spreading the word.

How remote did you have to be from everything that you didn't speak Standard? Even Humans had adopted it as a primary language, way the hell over at the far end of Imperial Sector Seventeen, in spite of not really understanding anything about the wider galaxy.

"Your ships are forfeit," Uly explained. "Personal gear will be stripped and transported with us. That is all."

He nodded at them and withdrew first, with Dan and her two following.

"Gear, sir?" Emil asked.

"Sort it for anything dangerous, then let them have it in there," Uly decided. "Maybe deliver a few foot lockers or bags or something. I'd rather them be content while traveling."

"On it."

Uly started to walk, Dan falling in on his hip.

"Now what?" she asked.

"We don't know enough about the region, obviously," he replied. "Can you find us folks who might be able to fill in some gaps?"

"I'll talk to Maks and see if he has anybody," she said. "None of the Khet have been this far from home, from what I understand."

"Not surprising," he smiled at her. "Kinda why we chose it. Now I need to talk to Suka Kuri."

"I'll go bother Maks," she said, cutting off and heading down a side corridor.

Uly felt better already, but he needed help.

NINE

Suka Kuri liked to joke that she was an old woman. Technically true, as the Emro measured things, but she was also at least as healthy as she'd been two or even three decades ago.

Having brilliant students who could challenge her mentally and physically on a daily basis did wonders.

Today, she was in one of the smaller training gymnasiums, working on a new open-handed combat form she was inventing. One that combined elements of Dan's *Tai Chi Chuan*, Nasrin's *Sunflower Fist*, and Ciah's *Terrible Gaff*, along with bits and pieces she had picked up from both Moss and Sabre Schools across a lifetime of training.

The hatch opened and admitted Uly, but he was by himself and didn't seem to have nearly the excitement he'd been facing twelve hours ago, so she continued flowing from posture to posture as the form unfolded.

He moved to one wall and watched, silent. Suka Kuri ignored him and focused on letting her hands and feet tell her what the next movement should be. Where it should go.

How she should strike.

Eventually, she came to rest. Uly had waited patiently for nearly twenty minutes, but he was the youngest individual she had ever met to have developed that level of calmness.

She bowed to each wall, then grinned at Uly and walked closer.

He was tall for a Human and she was short for an Emro. Suka Kuri still towered over the man.

Physically.

"How may an old woman assist?" she asked.

He grinned up at her.

"I've seen Dan and her women practice enough to envision that at high speed," he replied. "Deadly. And Ciah is less than half your size."

"She is," Suka Kuri acknowledged. "And much, much faster."

"I have just spoken with my pirate prisoners," he continued. "Told them that we are taking them to their home system and turning them over to justice there."

Suka Kuri nodded. She had helped shape some of Uly's legend, but he was also something utterly special in her experience.

Dan Sheridan might turn into an Exemplar of the Arts like her, one of these days.

Suka Kuri wasn't sure there was a term to encompass Uly.

She smiled as a prompt.

"They don't speak Standard, many of them," he said. "How do we communicate with their people in a polite manner?"

Yes, that fit the man. Everyone understood violence. Few would immediately grasp that he was capable of terrible violence, while still choosing to withhold the blade.

"Who are they?" she asked, probing far beyond the obvious.

"They call themselves Isann," Uly said. "I presume species rather than world, but the two might be one. Their tech is extremely primitive, so they are not trading with the Khet or the Ononguli, who are the largest, closest trading blocs."

"Nor, likely, anyone else," she pointed out. "Do you understand how old the galaxy is, Uly?"

"Probably not."

"Come," she said, turning to where chairs were stacked on another wall. "Let us sit and I can give you a brief history lesson."

They got settled and Suka Kuri took a deep breath, using certain techniques to reach deep into memory and find the thing she needed.

Scholars learned many things. One needed a good filing system.

"I believe—and mind you, I am uncertain—that the region today known as Imperial Sector Fourteen was once home to the Yarikh," she began. "That was the name of the civilization. Republic. Empire. Autocracy. They had tried many things, evolving as their needs evolved."

He nodded, silently absorbing everything like a sharp student did.

The sharpest students, anyway.

"Today, all we have are ancient legends," she continued. "Long lost and conveyed orally for the longest time, until someone wrote it all down. Mostly their greatest adventure stories. The ones that they used to tell themselves who they were. Like your *Iliad* and *Odyssey*."

More nods. Absorbing.

"They spoke of Yarikh in the grand terms of sailors daring the darkest night, Uly," Suka Kuri said. "Going out into the great beyond, from which many or even most never returned."

"Thinly populated region of space," he replied. "No other major nations, especially if these Yarikh chased them all off or conquered them. Exterminated?"

"Possibly," she acknowledged. "It was a long time ago, but you've noted that there hardly appear to be any inhabited worlds around here, for all that they are habitable without much work."

"Everyone moved on and left the worlds behind?" he asked.

Suka Kuri nodded.

"Withdrew slowly as the Yarikh collapsed inward on itself is how I understand some of those stories to translate," she explained.

"Terrible civil wars that grew savage. Then time and entropy, as these stories, to the best of my knowledge, date back at least three millennia to when they were first written down, trailing at least another millennium or more after the events they describe."

"About the time Humans supposedly discovered mechanical technology," he nodded.

Suka Kuri took a moment to process that bit of information. Primitive, but aggressive in many things.

"Are these their descendants?" he asked simply.

"It is entirely possible," she agreed. "They might know the old stories. Or versions of them."

"I'd like you to inquire with them," he said. "To find out if that's who they see themselves as, regardless of the actual truth. The culture is more important to me than the biology."

And that, there, was what made Uly so powerful. So dangerous, at least in the eyes of the *Auga* and others. She smiled. Uly cared about you as a person, not a species. Could you join a greater thing as an equal?

"I will do what I can," she assured him.

"Thank you," Uly said, rising. "That is all any of us can do."

Suka Kuri watched him depart without another word and gave thought to how she might reach these pirates.

Then she thought of Nasrin, and smiled.

TEN

Nasrin studied Suka Kuri's face and didn't bother letting her tentacles hide her shock.

"You want me to do what?" she asked. Confirmed. Something.

"Sing," Suka Kuri nodded with an enormous grin.

"And you expect them to know ancient Mazhin love songs, old woman?" Nasrin asked, grinning back at her.

"Where did your people learn them?" Suka Kuri shot back at her.

Nasrin started to reply with something tart and caught herself.

Mazhin culture was old. And stellar. Most of her kind preferred traveling. Either on one of the greatships that were mobile colonies, or the trade vessels that knit everything together.

Or the pirate ships that occasionally preyed on folks they encountered.

She'd never been a pirate, but that was because she'd been a bright, precocious child on the day that *Danumash* had smashed the ship her parents had been on.

Nasrin hadn't seen any of them again, though the Humans of

Danumash hadn't taken the step she'd been expecting when a bunch of men had a pretty female slave.

They'd classified her a *Social*, and presumably expected her to service the other Mazhin men she'd been tossed into the cell with.

Because *Danumash* had absolutely no clue how any other civilization but theirs worked.

Suka Kuri nodded at Nasrin's introspection.

"The galaxy is a wide, ancient, and decadent place," the old woman reminded her.

"And you want the Songbird to charm them," Nasrin completed the thought, flashing back to that cell on an *Auga* prison barge, where she'd done the same to all the Ononguli pirates—and everyone else—that had been in the block with them.

And it had worked.

"I do," Suka Kuri nodded. "I think that they don't necessarily speak Standard, but will react well to the song itself. And I want to know if some of the most ancient ones are the same here as they were elsewhere."

"Why?" Nasrin asked. "According to Dan, Uly intends to haul them home, then convince the locals to throw them in prison if that's possible."

"Because I want them to walk voluntarily," Suka Kuri replied, voice suddenly deadly serious in ways Nasrin didn't see all that often. "I want them to tell their jailers what happened, and convince them to support Uly's cause, even before they truly understand it. This will do that."

Nasrin wanted to reply with something rude and pungent. Would have, were it someone like Haydar asking. Except that Haydar tended to be an old, wet hen, and this was Suka Kuri.

Exemplar of the Arts.

Literal *Living Legend*.

"Okay," Nasrin agreed. "But I think it might be rude to only do this sort of thing for the pirates."

"Oh?"

"Let's set up an auditorium, either here or use a large space on the station," Nasrin suggested. "Get several of us together to perform, and have the pirates in person live to watch, along with whichever crew members on the other ships win a lottery. Then broadcast it live to the entire system."

Nasrin liked the way Suka Kuri's eyes took on a distant look, as though seeing a thousand light-years away. Or a thousand years into the future.

"Yes," she said simply. "I will speak with Dan. Maks Sobol has exactly the perfect space on *Treta Envoy* for my needs. And that lets the construction crew also be involved."

"Declare a holiday?" Nasrin offered.

"Even better," Suka Kuri smiled. "Everyone has been working too hard lately. Uly has grown almost grumpy. This is necessary, Nasrin Monfared."

Nasrin shivered under that tone, but understood.

This woman was building Uly up into the sorts of demigod whose name would live down the centuries.

She nodded, then found herself alone as the old Emro woman departed, almost perfectly silent for all that she claimed not to be a dancer or warrior.

Nasrin wasn't fooled.

Suka Kuri was a dangerous, *dangerous* woman.

ELEVEN

Uly had slept in. Holidays were supposed to be like that, though starships in service never took a day off. He had, however, put down his foot and ordered that there would be no training today. No drills. No alerts to test people.

Assuming no dumbass pirates felt like pushing their luck.

Then they'd discover just how badly Maks Sobol had been sandbagging things.

In just a week, three of the 12dm wavebolt mounts were live, as were a half-dozen 1 and 2dm defensive turrets. Gravity was on. Generators were maintaining a bubble around the ship, keeping anyone from transitioning to FTL.

Bastion itself was still ugly. Unfinished, save that the four decks Uly needed were complete and working well enough. The rest was personal space, storage, and all the support services that could be provided by Maks on his cruise ship for now.

And Maks's ship was central to the day.

Uly watched *Treta Envoy* grow larger as his shuttle approached to dock. Most of the cruise ship's transports were tiny affairs. Six seats and a small space for cargo, because they were for hauling tourists around. About half had lost the rear four seats so that eight workers could fly together quicker.

Today, Uly was in one of his own. Him, Dan, and her team, including Suka Kuri because Uly liked having that many smart, dangerous women at hand.

Dan smiled at him when he looked over at her, but he shook his head to her unasked question.

Today, he was enjoying himself, and it took Uly a bit to remember the last time he'd said that.

Years, honestly, because so much of the last four had been wrapped up in the raw struggle to survive against a hostile galaxy, then attempt to carve out a space where he could feel safe.

12dm guns ready to pound fools helped.

"All hands, stand by to dock," the pilot announced.

Uly waited through the noise and vibrations as the two airlocks connected, then followed the rest out.

Even on a safe ship, Dan's team were professional, and that meant they entered any room first.

It made Uly feel safe. And loved.

And today was a great day.

Dan walked beside him as the team circled up around. Suka Kuri set the pace with her long legs, but wasn't in a great hurry.

Maks and Chervonya met them quickly.

"All the prisoners are seated and under guard," Maks nodded. "Haven't given us any troubles, though they are still utterly confused about what's going on today."

Uly laughed.

"So am I, but I have bright people telling me that this was the right thing to do," he said.

The larger group split, and his fragment filed into a box overlooking the auditorium. Expensive seats for folks with money or power back home, but Uly supposed that nothing changed in the galaxy except the shapes of the players.

Him, Dan, Suka Kuri, Maks, and Chervonya rattled around a bit, because the space could hold more than dozen.

Uly found the best seat and claimed it before anybody else. Then he sat and watched.

One hundred prisoners, give or take, plus their guards. Another couple hundred lucky souls, everybody whispering and chatting with neighbors.

Then the lights dimmed and everything fell to silent stillness.

There was a curtain across the middle of the stage, but Nasrin emerged from a wing in front of it, carrying a stool in one hand. Tyberiy Petrenko, an engineer who was bridge-qualified, joined her, also carrying a stool he set off on her rear flank and carrying an Ononguli instrument similar to an acoustic guitar.

Both sat. Petrenko focused on his instrument. Nasrin studied the crowd.

When she looked up at him, Uly felt the hypnotic draw of those tentacles.

Then she began to sing.

Uly was back on that *Auga* barge, quietly sitting in one corner as she mesmerized several thousand pirates.

The Songbird.

Tyberiy played along, chords simply holding a background. A platform from which Nasrin soared.

On the first chorus, many of the Ononguli and Khet in the audience quietly joined in, each no doubt humming under their breath, but combined up into a rising tide of sound under her feet, lifting the Mazhin woman higher.

Utterly magical. And he'd been there the first time.

Back then, Nasrin had been uncertain of the response she would get. Today, she had matured—and Uly had to remember how young she really was—taking everyone in her hands and simply commanding them.

He glanced over at Dan's rapt face. And Suka Kuri's knowing nod.

It had been her idea, and he'd gone along because she was Suka Kuri. Now, Uly could see just how perfect her thinking had been.

Then he leaned back and let the music wash over him.

52

TWELVE

Uly smiled wryly, wishing to tease his friend but unwilling to put him on the spot. He was in his office. Maks was on the comm from his own office aboard *Treta Envoy*.

"You'll do fine, Maks," Uly assured him.

"I know," Maks replied. "Just wish I could go with you."

"Next time, maybe," Uly nodded. "Or should I sell you one of those captured pirate ships as a personal yacht?"

"Ick, no," Maks laughed. "I'd feel safer in just about anything. More likely, I'll haul *Treta Envoy* home in another three or four months and buy something good for cruising. Assuming that the war hasn't started with the *Auga*."

"That front should be quieter now," Uly nodded. "After we hit *Nyri Station Prime*, I disappeared, having made my point. At least as far as various spies should see it. And the *Auga* would have to build up a major effort to chase us all the way out here. I'd like to think that we'd have heard something from someone if they did."

"Losing the new base they were building at Ixtin no doubt hurt," Maks replied. "Nyri and everything you did there likely means they spend years even understanding what went wrong, who was responsible, and how to fix it. And only then doing something."

"Exactly my point, Maks," Uly said. "That bought me time to do this. It bought Anna time to start organizing at her end, which is why Lukyan isn't around here. When you return home, I would expect her to put you in command of a small warship and set you up to cause the *Auga* trouble."

"Here's hoping," Maks sighed. "Really just want to go have adventures with you folks."

"Your time will come, Governor," Uly said simply, watching the impact of that word on Maks Sobol.

Nothing at all like his cousin Adrian. Calm, collected, rational, sneaky. As opposed to the bull in the china shop breaking things.

"How soon until I should worry about you?" Maks asked. "At what point does this job either become permanent, or I have to ask Anna what the hell I'm doing next?"

Uly paused his jocularity and considered that. *Wren* was parked close by the station, providing supplies as Uly bought and stored them from other ships, and would not accompany them on this run.

"I have supplies for a month, Maks," Uly replied. "At that point, either I'll have found someone to trade with, or need to return here. If I'm not back in two months, send Anna a message. If I'm not back in six, something has gone terribly wrong, and I'd appreciate you bringing a force of ships to rescue me. Or avenge me."

"We're nothing without you, Uly," Maks reminded him. "All of this was because you made it happen. I don't think it can hold out for that many years without you at the center."

"Oh, I plan to be careful," Uly replied. "Trust me on that one. But I have to do this, in order to know that what I'm doing here will be safe. That it can survive later without some horde of crazed berserkers coming over the hill suddenly."

"Already got those here," Maks laughed.

"I do, but you've done pretty good," Uly said. "And you will continue to."

"Thank you, Uly," Maks said.

"Thank you for understanding everything I'm trying to accomplish, Maks."

He cut the line and drew in a breath.

Time for another adventure. The next step in the evolution of whatever this thing was he was attempting to build?

Something.

Uly rose and made his way to the bridge.

He had the first team today. His oldest friends, plus a full ring of observers and backups around the outside of the space. Dan sat next to Nasrin on one side, with Suka Kuri on the other, and all of the team along the wall, ready and watching.

Drew and Sterling down front. Pilot and Gunner. And so much more. Haydar, Ethir, Rabiu, and Piruz, affectionately teased as The Legal Department, but his experts on business and capitalism, which still seemed an insane way to construct a civilization.

However, it mostly worked.

His chair was empty. Waiting for him to fill it, as perhaps only he could.

Hadn't that been Maks' opinion? And he wasn't wrong, which was itself wrong.

Uly needed to build a place that would run without him. Either because he was off fighting his war against the *Auga*, or because he'd long since died and left behind a thing that would live.

Lacium was thriving, but that was all the private venture companies hired to crush piracy in the region, slowly moving outwards as the corridor from Z'Gosza to Taeli became safe. The Khet of Z'Gosza were growing even wealthier, and happy to keep things cleaned up over there.

At least for today.

It was still a cloak that they might slip off if the price was right, rather than a way of life. Of business.

Uly took his station and smiled at all the faces smiling back.

He'd gone aboard *King Hewitt II* with four other people. And accumulated an entire civilization since then, regardless of how small it was.

It was still powerful and growing, because he had a dream.

Uly found the intercom and opened the shipwide.

"All hands, this is Uly," he said simply. "We are about to sail into the darkness, to see who is out there that we might make into new friends. Thank you for what you've done for me so far, and I'm looking forward to what we might find. Mr. Roscoe, begin acceleration and stand by to engage the Variable Pulse Spatial Generator."

He closed the line and sighed.

"Course laid in and standing by, sir," Drew replied.

"Take us out, Drew."

ISANN

THIRTEEN

Suka Kuri had spent enough time with the Isann now to understand them. Literally as well as figuratively.

They spoke a new language in private, but she had begun to pick up snatches of it, listening to various people translate things when she spoke to Chief Aibek Sulaymanov, the conductor of the ship Uly still referred to as Number Two. It had a name as well, translated into Standard as *Moonlight*, but everyone spoke of it in the past tense, including the former Isann crew.

They all understood that they had gotten away far luckier than they had any right to expect.

Coupled with a musical concert put on for their benefit, Sulaymanov and his people had grown friendly.

Once they got over their terror at meeting an Emro. Three of them, that first time, with Yanouk and Anari along to make an intimidating point.

Aibek and two others had been asked to accompany her to a small conference room. Neither of them ever spoke, but having friends along helped Aibek relax.

They had even learned to enjoy her tea. And watch in rapt awe as she made it for them after they arrived, setting the pot to steep to one side.

"I understand from the Corsac Fox that we will be in your home system soon," Suka Kuri offered, watching that tidbit worm its way into their minds.

These three spoke Standard well enough to chat, while less than half of the others did.

Remote and isolated, but generally good people. Adventurers intent on learning about this new thing that had impinged on the edges of their explored region.

This Corsac Fox.

All lived in dread of Uly, even as she began to see the signs of respect.

He could have killed every one of them. Most had expected it. Uly had even hinted to her privately that he'd considered it himself.

"What will the Corsac Fox do with us then?" Aibek asked.

"We presume that you are criminals, Aibek," she reminded him. "Thus, he will turn you over to the Chief of Chiefs for punishment."

"That one will see us as fools," Aibek replied sourly.

"For losing to Uly?" Suka Kuri couldn't help but laugh. "Aibek, that Human has declared war on the entire *Auga Empire*. On a place with tens of thousands of star systems. And he intends to defeat them."

It was rude, playing Uly up as a demigod, given the rather primitive state of Isann culture, but it also fit Uly into their knowledge matrix easily.

And wasn't necessarily wrong, but she didn't say that to anyone else.

They didn't need to know. Any of them.

Aibek nodded, but didn't really understand.

"Let me tell you about his attack at Nyri," Suka Kuri began, then walked these three through the entire operation.

Uly had accused her of planning to create a new Emro School.

Something to form a triad with Moss School and Sabre School. Moss was for artists. Sabre taught its students combat, but limited it to the personal. Even in space, Emro Sabre Disciples flew tiny warships.

Until Uly had suggested it aloud, Suka Kuri had not given serious thought to naval maneuvering and combat as a worthy Emro school.

Starfare. It had a nice ring to it. And Uly would need to teach many conductors, captains, and even chiefs like Aibek Sulaymanov how to fly and fight as a combined force. As he did it.

Too many pirates flew every fool for themselves, which allowed the *Auga* to conquer worlds and Uly to take a small warship like *Corsac Fox* and do impossible things with it.

She finished and the three were utterly rapt.

One of the previously silent ones muttered something under his breath, then flushed green when she looked at him, embarrassed.

"He speaks of Zamir Aytiev," Aibek explained. "Great hero from the distant past. His story is part of the *Karaŋgılıkka*."

Suka Kuri nodded him to continue.

She had heard bits of this cultural tale. A foundational epic that framed the Isann as a people in many ways. It probably existed in the records Uly and his people had accumulated from *Moonlight* and the other three, but not written in a character set she had ever encountered.

Which offended her even worse than merely not knowing the story itself.

It was his turn, so Aibek shrugged and told her of a great hero who had set out on a journey of exploration, and then been twenty or more years returning home and being taken as a stranger when he did.

Uly and Dan had spoken in small terms of Odysseus, but didn't have a copy of the tale she could read. Yet another reason to visit a Human colony at some point.

And such things spanned many cultures. Near as she could tell, only the *Auga* lacked such a thing, but they would look on someone sailing past the horizon alone as a fool of fools.

The *Auga* and their Empire were never impulsive. Never lost and wandering.

Not like Humans. Not like Emro. Not like Mazhin.

Or Isann.

Aibek finished his brief tale. They drank tea in companionable silence.

"Will Uly conquer Isann?" Jyrgal spoke up.

Suka Kuri wasn't sure she'd ever heard his voice this loud before now.

"Uly doesn't conquer," she replied. "If threatened, he will use violence, but his preference is trade. Communication. He withheld the blade at *Bastion*. I think he would like to talk to your Chief of Chiefs and establish ties. Assuming they don't attack him on sight."

"Fools might," Jyrgal chuckled darkly. "Once."

Suka Kuri agreed. Dan had mentioned that their ships were primitive. Hardly armed or protected.

And Uly would make a point if someone attacked him as a stranger without provocation.

"When we arrive, perhaps you could help speak for Uly?" she asked, watching all three flinch in surprise.

"We are criminals," Aibek said. "Pirates."

"Uly likes to believe that even fools can learn, Aibek," she reminded him. "That a dead person cannot become better, but a live one, however misguided, might change for the better."

"Us?" he gasped.

Suka Kuri shrugged.

"Who you will become is up to you," she said simply, quoting one of those aphorisms taught to young students just setting out onto one of the Schools of Emro thought.

They were all stunned into silence, but that was acceptable.

She rose, towering over the men.

"Come," Suka Kuri said. "Let us get you back to your crews, that you can meditate on that future as you will shape it."

They followed like ducklings, but that was also acceptable. She had shaken them to their cores.

Such a thing was necessary, if one was to become someone new.

FOURTEEN

Dan listened to Suka Kuri's tale and shook her head in wonder.

"What?" Suka Kuri asked, mischief in her eyes.

"They will have no idea what you've done to them until much later, will they?" Dan asked.

Suka Kuri laughed.

"Probably not," she agreed. "But it opens minds, as yet another way to open doors."

"Long haul from Bastion to Isann," Dan pointed out.

"No greater than Z'Gosza to Taeli, as I understand it," Suka Kuri pointed out.

Dan leaned back and did the math. No, probably about the same, but with far fewer inhabited systems along that corridor where you might stop and trade.

At least today.

"Tell me about *Karaŋgılıkka*," Dan said.

"A man builds a starship and flies into the darkness," Suka Kuri said. "Exploring for trade, and he means to come home, but something prevents him. Each time, some new trouble arises and he must set it to right before he can turn his mind back to the homeland he left. A generation passes before he finally makes it, and the man ends up returning as a stranger. But also, a great hero. Reminds me of someone I know."

Dan shook her head some more.

"I'm not sure Uly is ever going home," she pointed out. "Nor the rest of us, at least as you might consider the planets on which we were born. Or ships in the Mazhin case."

"Humans will come out eventually," Suka Kuri pointed out. "But for that war in a sandbox between *Batyr* and *Danumash*, I might have expected it to have happened before now."

"And the specist, racist, and whatever else shits in *Danumash* hate anything but pink-skinned Humans, so they keep everyone at bay, except to trade for old ships and old tech. Why haven't any of the folks from the interior come out to say hello?"

"They've probably heard that you're like the *Auga*, only crazier," Suka Kuri grinned. "What fool would want that on their decks?"

"Okay, point," Dan chuckled. "Are we about to unleash a terminal culture shock on the Isann? And whoever else might be living or hiding out here?"

"That's why I love you so much, Dan," Suka Kuri noted. "You and Uly both worry about those sorts of things, when everybody else is at the bottom of the Great Hierarchy of Needs dealing with survival and comfort. Starships mean that folks can travel great distances if they wish. That nobody has come into or out of the Spinward Reaches, I think, means that there are few folks around, and most of them either too primitive or to insular to worry about the wider galaxy."

"The *Auga* will come eventually," Dan noted.

"But not for centuries," Suka Kuri replied. "Millennia, this far away from Ajorn. It becomes a question of ants and grasshoppers. Uly works today to prepare. The others will suddenly face the end of summer and panic. It is a story more ancient than any civilization you might mention."

"And all of this will occur well after Uly and I are dead," Dan agreed. "But it is a thing worth doing today, because in those centuries, something like Yarikh might arise that is powerful enough to thwart *Auga*'s Imperial Dreams."

"Yes," Suka Kuri said. "And they will carry Uly's legend as a banner, even as Aibek and his kinfolk would rally to the stories of Zamir Aytiev."

"Are we dreaming too big?" Dan asked.

She wasn't prepared for Suka Kuri to throw her head back and laugh uproariously.

Dan waited. Suka Kuri wound down eventually.

"Better?" Dan asked.

"Honestly, I don't think Uly is dreaming big enough, but I'm not sure how to get him the tools he might need to stop the *Auga* in his lifetime," she said. "That would require a gathering of all the species, like some vast Mazhin Convocation, but even Uly would be hard-pressed to convince that many people. At least today. Still, the things he has put in motion will move empires, possibly in his lifetime."

Dan nodded.

"So what do we need to know or do about the Isann?" she asked.

"I think I have Aibek ready to speak to them on a level they will respect and understand," Suka Kuri replied. "They have overcome many things and framed Uly as some manner of demigod in training, and will respect that."

"Will he have a series of impossible quests to complete to gain them as allies?" Dan asked.

The old woman turned sober. Quiet. Deadly, but you had to see it in her eyes in that blink before it was gone.

Suka Kuri had mentioned that she chose Moss School because it was easier on the knees, but that she could have just as easily been Sabre.

Dan understood that, in that moment.

"Yes," Suka Kuri said. "They will task him. But they will make one fundamental mistake."

"That being?"

"They will forget that Uly has friends who are just as committed and willing," Suka Kuri nodded. "That the combined family that is the Corsac Fox will be able to move entire civilizations, because you already have."

Dan was aghast, but the woman wasn't wrong.

Human. Mazhin. Emro. Thogin. Ononguli. Khet. Guezal. Who else might join this cause?

She nodded. It was a secret they shared.

Uly would need that, when the moment came.

FIFTEEN

Uly studied the plot, looking over Sterling's shoulder.

"You're certain?" he asked, mostly to confirm things.

Sterling Huff was one of the best stellar cartographers Uly had ever known. And he had developed that skill even more, studying the various recesses of the Spinward Reaches for this entire project, and not just this mission.

At nineteen, he was turning into the kind of officer Uly wanted. Demanded.

Respected.

"Certain, sir," Sterling replied with a crisp nod. "They used an entirely different basis system for everything, but I was able to reverse engineer a location conversion matrix with Mr. Ramezani to import all of their records into our astrogation system, then verify it. That's the Isann homeworld."

Uly nodded and looked up at the main screen. It showed a brighter star than any other in the distance, but they'd dropped out of warp well outside of where there should be any defensive watchers.

"What are you expecting?" Uly asked, looking down at Sterling's screen.

"Two stations, neither in geo-synch orbit," Huff replied. "One more of a shipyard than anything, with the other mostly a factory conversion station, taking in raw materials from around the system or nearby places and refining them into bar and sheet stock for manufacturing in orbit. Nowhere close to anything as sophisticated as I'd expect above any Human world, *Batyr* or *Danumash*."

Uly nodded. Two radically different cultures, almost top to bottom, but both interstellar in scope.

This place felt barely past the stellar stage, looking at how Sterling had it laid out. Including a vast number of Sloops, small ships that didn't have any FTL capability, or if they did, it was so slow as to limit them to only one solar system anyway.

Suka Kuri had warned him that they were only a few generations removed from the surface of their world. Uly simply hadn't grasped what that would look like. He couldn't remember a world with so few ships in orbit, to say nothing of stations.

Even *Bastion Station* had dozens of freighters and armed vessels present at any given moment.

This was, as he had to remind himself, the middle of nowhere. In more ways than one.

Uly nodded.

"Excellent work, Sterling," he said, returning to his chair and settling in. He keyed the intercom. "All hands, stand by for us to sail into the Isann system. I have no idea what our reception will be like, so be prepared for combat operations until told otherwise. Wardroom, that includes you serving folks at stations."

Uly cut the line and looked around at Dan and the team. Everyone who had been there for that momentous departure from Bastion. Many who had been there from day one on *King Hewitt II*.

Aibek Sulaymanov had even joined them today, quiet and

nervous, but unarmed and not the least bit a threat. Not with Dan next to him.

Time to make history.

"Drew, take us in on the course Sterling has laid out," Uly ordered.

Corsac Fox bubbled up and blinked quickly across the gap, Isann's star growing from a dot to a disk quickly before the ship dropped out.

And then they were there.

Uly turned to Haydar.

"What's the communications network like?" he asked.

"Civilian," Haydar muttered darkly, which was about as damning an insult as the man knew.

Haydar expected you to encrypt things at least to some level.

To make him have to actually work at cracking it and breaking in.

That didn't look like today.

Uly nodded.

"Anybody reacting to our light-speed wave?" he asked.

"In about ten seconds, I expect it," Drew replied. "We're high and out a safe enough distance for now, in case they shot first and didn't ask questions later."

"Mr. Huff?"

"All gun teams are prepared, sir," Sterling said. "Defensive fire until you or I order otherwise."

Uly found that good. Let the locals absorb a stranger in their midst. Worse, a ship twice the size of the next largest vessel those captured records suggested might be here.

He doubted that anyone was a threat.

It was the *everyone combined* that made him careful.

"There we go," Haydar announced after a bit. "I have significant red shift on several vessels. Hauling ass, I believe you would say, as they flee."

Uly chuckled. Haydar had learned some interesting idioms from those fools in *Danumash*.

"Open me a general hailing channel," Uly ordered.

"Ready," Haydar nodded without looking up from his screens.

"Isann System, this is the Corsac Fox," Uly announced. "I come to speak with your Chief of Chiefs. The time has come for you to join the greater galaxy and learn who your neighbors are. We welcome you for trade and exploration at our side."

He cut the line and hoped that didn't sound too entirely pompous. Especially from a single ship that had just dropped out of warp.

Certainly, more ships were running. Small ones. Presumably they saw *Corsac Fox* as a pirate come to do to them what they had intended to do to him.

Wrong, but they needed to talk to learn that. Them opening fire right now would mean that he needed to teach them some lessons in behavior and manners.

Uly would prefer not to. He was still prepared.

"Chief Sulaymanov," Uly said, gesturing the man to his feet. "Come, add your voice to mine, that they might listen."

Again, stilted and formal, but it made him speak slowly, and in a manner that Aibek Sulaymanov could understand.

The Isann conductor would need time to be fully fluent in Standard.

The chief moved to stand next to Uly, compressed like he expected a blow, but not as twitchy as he had been that first day he became a prisoner.

"Haydar, open the line," Uly said, waiting for the nod and nodding to Aibek in turn.

"Isann, this is Aibek Sulaymanov," the man said simply. "I fly with the Corsac Fox. He brings news."

Aibek looked over expectantly and Uly nodded.

Silence fell.

Aibek muttered something under his breath, then flinched when Suka Kuri replied in that same tongue.

Then the man chuckled quietly.

Uly looked over at Suka Kuri for an explanation.

"*Thus do heroes return as strangers,*" she quoted. "From the *Karaŋgılıkka.*"

Uly caught Aibek's eye.

"That tale ended well, eventually," he reminded the chief.

Aibek shrugged, then made his way back to his seat. Uly watched him move, noting that the Isann was growing more comfortable. More relaxed.

"Corsac Fox, what are your intentions?" a male voice suddenly spoke. Haydar playing it for everyone.

Uly caught his nod to speak.

"To talk," Uly said. "Perhaps peel open the darkness and let light fall on Isann, that you might emerge into the greater galaxy."

Again, words Suka Kuri had prepared for him, drawing on that cultural epic, the *Karaŋgılıkka.*

"Chief Sulaymanov accompanies you?" the man spoke up after a lag for light to get to the planet and a signal to return. "What of the others?"

"Chief Ruslan Myrzaev of the vessel *Skylark,*" Uly replied. "Ninety-five others, from the squadron that attacked my world. They are my prisoners as pirates. I bring them to you for justice. And to see who Isann was and if you remember the *Karaŋgılıkka.*"

Honestly, it was all a script. Almost as bad as the one Ethir had produced for him to talk capitalism with the Trade Factors of Z'Gosza.

"What are your demands, Corsac Fox?" he asked.

"To meet on your larger station, Isann," Uly replied. "To sit and talk, while boasting of our journeys across the darkness. To know who this Chief of Chiefs is."

Uly wondered if it might be a trap, but Aibek had assured them that the Isann were an honorable people, piracy notwithstanding, and even then had acted better than Uly had been expecting.

He had hopes, but he wasn't a fool.

"It is well," the voice said, which Aibek had said many times, according to Suka Kuri when he was serious. "We will transmit arrangements soon."

"Line's dead, Uly," Haydar spoke up. "They said what they wanted to and were done."

"And I have what I need," Uly said, turning to Dan. "Dan, this is now your show. Aibek, you will let your folk know that we're here and that I intend to put them all aboard the larger shuttle and carry them to the station when we go, so they should start packing immediately."

Isann were like Humans, in that moment when his mouth simply fell open and his eyes got big, but he didn't suppose that Aibek had believed him. Or Suka Kuri.

Uly couldn't help fools.

"Just like that?" Aibek asked.

"Yes," Uly nodded. "Just like that."

SIXTEEN

Dan caught that moment of hesitation in Yeong-Suk's eyes as the Guezal woman approached at the arms locker.

"You'll do fine," Dan assured her, thinking back to the raid at Nyri where Dan and her teams had rescued Yeong-Suk and her friends, all petty criminals doing community service as punishment.

The *Auga Empire*, though, had to be shits about it. You got shipped halfway across the empire to do your time, and when you were done, they didn't pay to ship you home. Instead, you were simply shoved out the front hatch on whatever world was closest, and expected to make your own way or start a new life.

Dan wasn't sure she could think of a better way to ensure recidivism if she'd sat down and worked at it.

Slippery slope is what it was. Ethir and his Thogin cousins talked about how important it had been for them to keep on the move, because once you got arrested that first time on any world, the authorities would be looking for you with any excuse to lock you up and put you to work.

Same with Yeong-Suk.

"I know," Yeong-Suk nodded, drawing an Exoripper carbine and checking the charge automatically. "This is just the first time I've walked into a potentially hostile situation armed and expected to deliver violence."

"If Suka Kuri hadn't thought you could manage it, she'd have never said anything to me," Dan reminded her. "If I hadn't seen what I wanted in your training and attitude, you'd have washed out a long time ago. You're here because you can stand on the dojo floor with the rest of us. If you don't have the years of close combat training some of us do, you've got the brains for it. And the temperament. You'll do fine."

"Thank you, Dan," Yeong-Suk nodded, stepping back and off to one side.

Nasrin had been right behind the Guezal woman, listening from the way her tentacles flowed. She stepped up and Dan handed the woman her favorite Omnibow, plus a bandoleer heavy on Painspheres. Exactly how Nasrin liked to step into combat.

Dan looked at her team. Because this was a diplomatic situation, none of the men were accompanying them, though she had Emil and Gennady on standby to lead all of her other troopers into storming the place if they had to.

After more than a year, Dan had the assault force to the size and training she wanted them. Not as big as the one that had taken Lacium, but the hundred and fifty she did have available were the cream of that crop, or trained to it.

This station wouldn't stand a chance if they tried anything. And that was before Sterling and Drew decided to get involved. Or Haydar.

"We're Uly's bodyguards," she reminded them. "And half of the advisors he turns to when he has questions. Remember that. These folks are barbarians, but they've also behaved themselves, so they know how. And they didn't bring any women with them on this raid, because we're icky."

That got a laugh, but these women were the best. She'd assembled them with Suka Kuri's help, then turned them into the sort of thing that would live forever with Uly's legend.

The species didn't age at the same rate, but Dan was the oldest, in relative terms, with Yeong-Suk and Katya not that far behind her, then a whole step down to Anari. Ciah, Yanouk, and Nasrin were the young ones, all barely relatively adults, for all they were combat veterans and killers.

"Let's go," she said, touching her holstered Heavy Exoripper pistol once for luck and crossing through a pair of hatches to the boarding area, where Emil nodded to her.

"All loaded, accounted for, and behaving," he said crisply.

Man had brains. Just no interest whatsoever in ever being an officer. Had threatened to retire and buy a bar if she tried to make him one.

"And Lieutenant Wyndham?" she asked.

"Aboard and in charge of the prisoners, sir," Emil said.

Uly arrived at that moment, so Dan nodded to Emil and turned.

Uly and Suka Kuri, plus Rabiu, Ethir, and Piruz, with Haydar volunteering to remain in command here.

Because he honestly didn't like people that much, and had to be prodded at times, not that Dan blamed him. Her job required it. Haydar's didn't .

"We ready?" Uly asked, stepping right up to her and smiling.

Her operation. Her orders.

Every day, he looked better and better, compared to that punk Lieutenant Michel Dupuis, back on *Marshall Castillon*.

"Just waiting for you," Dan said, matching Uly's smile.

"Following you," he said, gesturing.

Dan nodded and Ciah led, mostly because she was so short that everyone else could fire over her headcrest if they needed to. And Ciah got way low when punching.

Solomon Wyndham met them aboard when they exited the airlock. Seats had been deployed and filled. More of Dan's troopers were around the outside of the room, watchful but apparently sharing dirty jokes with the prisoners, from the way folks were laughing in one corner.

And Blair Mitchell was standing next to Solomon. If Wyndham was big, tough, and turning into the kind of giant that she'd have enjoyed on her old *Batyr* boarding teams, Blair was almost his complete opposite.

A civilian medical technician, he'd originally been hired by the Mistress of *King Hewitt II* as a nurse, when the Mazhin slaves had come with their own medical staff, all of whom hadn't been able to escape the *Auga* with Uly's jailbreak.

"Surprised to see you here, Blair," Dan said as she walked up to the man. Everyone else was in the new *Corsac Fox* uniform of blue with scarlet and mint trim, but Blair had stuck with bright blue and yellow checks.

Civilian.

Blair Mitchell marched to his own drummer.

"At present, I am the most highly cross-trained xenobiologist in the galaxy, boss," he grinned up at her. "Figured I should add these folks to the list. Plus, the locals probably need to be prepared, in case we brought anything with us. Whole hell of a lot of ways things can jump species, even if we've got so many different biologies going. Or because of it."

"Any trouble with the prisoners?" Uly asked.

"Usual sniffles and coughs," Blair said. "Oh, and I speak pretty good Isann these days, after talking to them all pretty much constantly since we picked them up."

Dan nodded. Made sense. Blair handled all of Uly's various people now, but did so in that most lowkey manner that was his signature. Quiet. Competent.

And always there with a smiling face.

She caught Chief Aibek's bewildered look, so Dan walked over and squatted down next to him.

"Yes, you are going home," she answered his unasked question.

"But we're pirates," he replied, still shocked.

"Yesterday," she said, using the language Suka Kuri had prepped her for. "What will you be tomorrow?"

He looked around, gestured, because his hands were free even if he was strapped into the chair until Solomon let him out.

"I still find it hard to believe so many alien species exist," Aibek said. "And you are all one people."

"And that is what Uly offers the Isann, Aibek," she nodded. "You came from ignorance, but now you have seen what there is beyond the darkness. And yes, you will be strangers because your friends and kin have not seen what's out there, so you will be tested. Challenged. You will rise to it."

He shook his head, but it was disbelief, rather than negation. The Isann around him weren't any better, but Blair started walking among them, offering encouragement and asking questions, so Dan rose and moved to the forward lounge where Uly and his negotiating team would be.

Then she changed her mind and signaled the ladies to shift to the front bulkhead, where the Isann could all see them easily. Her men slid to the sides silently. Automatically. Professionally.

Dan smiled. The muttering stilled, then built up again with a different tone. Wonder, this time.

They had seen beyond the darkness, and discovered Uly.

She needed to remind them.

SEVENTEEN

Suka Kuri found it hilarious that she had become Uly's magical soothsayer, like out of so many primitive legends. But she supposed that an Exemplar of the Arts of the Moss School had to do that, more often than they talked about.

Uly was Uly. A hero. He had Ethir, Piruz, and Rabiu to advise on the business and political side, plus Dan and her team.

Suka Kuri was the ancient sage bringing wisdom to the table.

Obviously, she'd be needing to puncture that balloon of ego and pomposity at some point, but only after she came to understand the Chief of Chiefs of the Isann.

To *know* the descendants of Zamir Aytiev.

After Nasrin had charmed them, the sailors had grown more comfortable telling her those tales, but she had the impression that a printed edition would be as thick as her hand was wide. And she would need to acquire and translate such a thing. Or perhaps assign that task to Yanouk, who had the gift for languages. Maybe Anari, who needed the practice.

So much to do, and the learning never ceased.

Right now, they had docked. According to Haydar, the station was hardly better armed than the ships that had assailed them at *Bastion*, so *Corsac Fox* could utterly annihilate this place if necessary. And Dan had her entire team on alert to storm it.

Overkill, in Suka Kuri's opinion, but she supposed that it established up front that Uly's people weren't messing around.

Uly's job, then, was to charm them. As was hers.

Everyone rose. She followed Uly to the hatch opening onto the larger bay where the Isann travelers had been. Dan had remained aft. They were watching now as Solomon Wyndham marched those hundred men out of the airlock and onto the station, following himself before any of his own troopers.

Another one who had learned Uly's important lessons about when to lead. Suka Kuri again blessed whatever deities had chosen to make her life this interesting, that she could see these things.

Dan followed Solomon's men and women. Uly led her after that, until Suka Kuri was almost the last person to board the station. Just as well, as they were a medium-sized species and didn't understand how to have taller doors, but she got a good deal of practice for that on *Corsac Fox*.

One Isann male, surrounded by half a dozen others, all armed and nervous. Aibek and Ruslan remained, as she would expect of ship chiefs, while the sailors had all gone on through a hatch on the far side. Solomon's people lined the walls on both sides, with Dan and her ladies lined up across the middle of the room.

Uly walked through the gap between Dan and Nasrin to stand before the Chief of Chiefs.

Isann tended to be shorter and broader than Humans.

"Chief of Chiefs Usupov, I am the Corsac Fox, Chief of Chiefs Uly Fortier," Uly introduced himself. "My Second-in-Command Dan Chastain. My advisor Suka Kuri, Exemplar of the Arts of the Moss School. Thank you for meeting with us."

He spoke slowly. Clearly. Suka Kuri resisted translating on the fly, as they might understand everything and not realize that she could. At least until Aibek spoke up.

Usupov was shorter than Uly. Possibly massed twice as much, but he had bulky shoulders migrating to his waist as many men did in middle age. And Uly continued to be a bean pole.

The Chief of Chiefs had to tilt his head back to look her in the face. And Anari and Yanouk were even taller. She smiled reassuringly, then nodded slightly.

Dan and her ladies were as keyed up for sudden violence as Suka Kuri could remember.

"You come from distant shores, Corsac Fox," Usupov replied slowly.

Suka Kuri nodded. A traditional greeting for strangers, according to Aibek.

"We seek that which is beyond the darkness, Chief Usupov," Uly replied formulaically.

She watched the guards relax a notch, though not without surprise that an outsider knew such things.

Yet another way to frame Uly as a visiting demigod, at least until they learned the truth.

If that was any different. She had her doubts, living through a history that would be told like those ancient tales someday.

Usupov turned to Aibek and scoffed.

"You failed," he growled at the man.

Aibek surprised everyone—including her—by laughing.

"The Corsac Fox showed mercy," he replied. "Else we would have all died. His power is great and terrible. That one ship broke our squadron in a matter of moments."

Usupov turned back to look at Uly and his silver skin had turned a little gray in places, and green in others.

"Truly?" he asked.

The guards were even more nervous now.

"There are vast wars out there, Chief of Chiefs," Uly nodded. "My warship is twice the size of anything here, and yet it is less than a sixth of the size of the largest vessels I have known. We come seeking trade and friends, rather than to conquer. Until we met

Aibek Sulaymanov, I did not know the Isann existed. We came across the darkness to meet you personally."

Suka Kuri approved. Uly, being Uly. That is to say, charming and forthright in ways that the Mazhin spoke about in awed whispers, because they could taste your lies even before you spoke them.

"Come, Corsac Fox," Usupov said, formal and careful now in ways that made his accent even thicker. "Let us sit down and speak as friends."

Suka Kuri watched him turn to lead his troupe out of the chamber.

"Guard detachment, stand down and return to barracks," Solomon announced in a voice that caused all the Isann to jump, because they'd forgotten the dozen armed men and women around the room, so focused on Uly and Dan.

And her, she supposed, though Suka Kuri still saw herself as nothing but a witness to history.

Not a maker.

Not like Uly and Dan.

EIGHTEEN

Uly let Dan's team circle him and lead him deeper into the station. At least Chief of Chiefs Usupov hadn't gone in for that throne room scene where he expected visitors to prostrate themselves upon entry.

Better, if they thought of travelers as people to talk to, rather than someone to impose upon.

The parade ended in a room big enough for planning meetings. Lots of chairs, but none that would fit an Emro or a Thogin. Ethir solved his issue by climbing up and leaning on the table like a bar. Suka Kuri knelt like she frequently did on the dojo floor, putting her eyes close to his level.

Chief of Chiefs Usupov was still shellshocked. His guards moved to the corners. Dan sat at the table next to Uly on the opposite side from Suka Kuri, while the other women were all directly behind him.

Where they distracted the hell out of the Isann.

He was certain that was entirely accidental on their part. Truly.

Usupov had an advisor on each side, but they paled in comparison to the strength of character etched on the Chief's face. Aibek and the other chief sat off to one side. Not quite ostracized, but not trusted. Isann guards across the back wall watched them as much as him.

Uly watched the Isann study all the alien women, including Dan, eyes filled with wonder more than rage. That was good. It suggested that they were explorers, rather than raiders, at least in the current culture.

Tomorrow might change. And it might not.

"What is out there?" Usupov asked quietly. "We have heard tales, but nothing..."

His voice trailed off, possibly mesmerized by Nasrin's tentacles tasting the air. She was like that.

"Many species, Chief of Chiefs," Uly assured him. "Many peoples. My birthworld is nearly a thousand times as far as we traveled here from Bastion to meet you. And my crew only represents a fraction of the species I have heard about from others, because Humans, like Isann, have lived sheltered in darkness for so long."

Usupov studied Uly's face. And Dan's. Possibly the closest to Isann physically.

And yet.

"What trade do you bring?" he finally asked.

"Tales of distant travelers," Suka Kuri interjected before Uly could do more than draw a breath. "Inspiration to draw your chiefs out to explore that which is. This is a dark sector of the galaxy, hardly inhabited in the current era, but once, it sang with the lights and songs of many worlds. So the *Karaŋgılıkka* tells us."

Uly nodded, not quite certain what she'd said, but it certainly hit them like a magical incantation. Or smack upside the head.

"Thus are our tales," he nodded, then turned to Aibek. "What did you see?"

Uly listened to Aibek give a pretty good rundown of the sail in, the time spent scouting the moorage, looking for a target they could cut out and flee with, filled to the gills with valuable supplies.

Uly was sorry that Haydar missed this part of the story, because

Aibek and his friends had thought that they had secured their communications safely before attacking. Maybe they had, for the Isann.

Nobody had warned them about grumbly Mazhin pirate scientists.

"At that moment, I was the only ship not tumbling through space and bleeding atmosphere, Chief of Chiefs," Aibek continued. "We surrendered and were taken prisoner by Commander Chastain and her team, then transported to the ship. Then here."

Uly noted that he hadn't said home. Fellow wasn't certain if he'd returned a stranger. And they had that cultural note fused deep into their psyche.

"Why did you bring them home, Corsac Fox?" Usupov asked.

"I wanted to talk to you, Chief of Chiefs," Uly replied. "To do that, I needed you to listen. Bringing you a gift of these sailors was the beginning, because it caused you to talk instead of fight. I could have annihilated this station and conquered this system without much effort, but why?"

The fellow blinked. Aibek simply nodded knowingly, but Suka Kuri had explained that he was the Isann furthest along the path of understanding. The others would get there, given time.

"What will you do?" Usupov asked, a hint of nervousness in his voice.

"Invite your ships to come to Bastion to trade, Chief of Chiefs," Uly smiled. "Suka Kuri seeks a physical copy of the *Karaŋgılıkka* that she might translate into our tongue, that all sailors might come to know Zamir Aytiev and his descendants. Once we have become friends, I intend to sail deeper into the darkness behind you to see who else might yet lurk in those shadows."

Uly wasn't prepared for the way all of the Isann flinched when he said that. Like maybe there was a dragon in there, and these folks didn't want it awakened?

He watched them as they grew restless. Even Aibek had flinched.

"Chief of Chiefs, Uly seeks answers to the Yarikh," Suka Kuri spoke up now. "This was their realm, long before the *Karaŋgılıkka* spoke of Zamir Aytiev."

Their muttering took on religious tones now. *Batyr* didn't worship any false gods, seeking to create a New Humanity that grew more advanced with every generation, but *Danumash* was often god-bothered by ancient pantheons worshiped by farmers and shepherds.

This had that look.

"Who is out there?" Uly asked pointedly, ignoring the Chief of Chiefs to focus on Aibek Sulaymanov.

Aibek licked his lips like any answer might get him tortured. It was almost a different person sitting there in the last thirty seconds.

He muttered something that Uly didn't understand. Suka Kuri did, because she answered him, causing the other Isann to flinch even worse.

A conversation ensued, entirely in Isann. And a good one, from the way Aibek grew heated and Suka Kuri disdainful, if anything. The rest of the room were reduced to spectators.

Finally, Aibek hung his head.

"You are correct, Elder," he said, switching back to Standard. "We are superstitious fools. In our defense, the *Karaŋgılıkka* makes that easy. And the most adventurous of us went to Bastion and got crushed by a true monster."

Uly watched the man smile wryly, looking back.

Uly didn't think of himself as a monster, but he supposed he'd been having a bad day that morning, and they'd decided to try his patience.

"The *Karaŋgılıkka* talks of systems and planets guarded by terrible beasts, Uly," Suka Kuri explained. "Most of the systems in the darkness coreward show ruins, but no people, and there are tales of them being haunted by the ancestors who once lived there."

"Is Bastion on a safe corridor?" he asked, turning to the woman who knelt next to him.

"You establishing Bastion might actually fit into their legends as the hero who quests to slay such things," she said with a deadly seriousness that was rare from the woman.

He considered her worlds. And the implications. Suka Kuri had told him bits and pieces of the things she'd gotten from Aibek and the others, but obviously not as much as she'd learned herself.

Then he circled long ways back in his mind, focusing instead on Chief Usupov.

"Where did the Yarikh live?" he asked simply, ignoring everyone else in the room.

Usupov was not immune to dread or superstition. He chewed his lips as he considered his answer.

"You come from the south, as it might be mapped," Usupov finally replied. "According to legends, the Yarikh lived in the north. Deeper into the darkness, as you have described it, coming from a land of lights. Ships that have explored that direction either found nothing at all or they never returned with their tales."

"Suggesting monsters," Suka Kuri offered. "Or others even less interested in trade and communications with outsiders."

Uly nodded. He turned to Aibek and speared that one with a look.

"Have you explored any in that direction, Chief Sulaymanov?" Uly asked.

"Some," Aibek admitted. "As Suka Kuri said, many worlds harbor nothing but ruins. And possibly ghosts."

"Could I convince you to travel with us while we go investigate them?" Uly asked, turning the conversation on its head.

"What would you expect to find?" Aibek replied.

"Monsters, maybe," Uly nodded. "Or strangers. Your ships are small and primitive compared to mine. Perhaps we will be strong enough to see them off."

"Just like that?" Aibek asked, nervous.

"I want to know," Uly said. "The others chose me to *Speak* for them, so they will follow where I lead. Will you?"

He paused, waiting and watching as all the Isann went back and forth in their heads. Superstitious, as Suka Kuri had said, but also bound by the cultural demands that being the descendants of Zamir Aytiev placed on them.

He was a hero who had sailed into darkness. The others would have to match that legend or admit defeat. Admit cowardice.

Uly simply wanted to know. Wanted to understand if there was some terrible dragon or quiet empire hiding back there, where they might trap Bastion between them and the eventual arrival of the *Auga*.

Aibek turned to Usupov, and some unspoken conversation flowed between them.

"I will go," Aibek nodded. "If the Chief of Chiefs will allow it. I will remind you that I am a pirate and a prisoner at present."

And smiling as he said such things, but they had long moved past simply locking these sailors up for their crimes.

"Yet you would have him?" Usupov asked. "Trust him?"

"You are the sons of Zamir Aytiev, Chief of Chiefs," Uly nodded. "I welcome him and whoever else might wish to challenge that darkness at my side."

VATAZHKO

NINETEEN

Maks was enjoying being the governor of Bastion, but still wished that Uly would get home soon. Every day, he made decisions that were tiny in stature and implications, but would be adding up to something eventually.

Hopefully, something Uly would approve of, but it was kinda going to be out of his hands by then.

Maks would have to own everything on that day.

And Uly had taken all of his people with him, so the folks making decisions were almost all Ononguli. One of them rapped on his office hatch, then slipped in.

Maks slid his tablet to one side and looked at the man who was his principle aide. Taras Bondarenko. Possibly the most important spy reporting to someone else, but likely that was Chervonya or Anna, so either Maks was relatively safe, or utterly screwed.

At least he had developed a much finer appreciation of Lukyan and his Tuesday superstitions.

"Got a moment?" Taras asked.

Maks pointed him to the open chair across the desk. He'd moved into the space that should have been Uly's. Or somebody's.

Conductor of the station, and thus Governor of the system. More or less.

"What's up?" Maks asked.

"Chervonya Borisov asked if she could steal a half hour of your time this afternoon," Taras nodded, horns waving. "You've got space now, but I wanted to check before opening the hatch and admitting her."

Maks considered his day. Not a Tuesday. At least as far as he knew.

"Sure, Taras," Maks replied. "Anything that can't be pushed out to tomorrow if necessary?"

"Couple of supply ships are due shortly," Taras said. "You'll want to touch their manifests as soon as I get them, because we're running low on a few things and will need to send a courier or something if they don't have it."

"Understood," Maks said. "She outside waiting?"

"She is," Taras stood. "I'll send her in."

"Send some coffee with her," Maks said. "Feels like that kind of afternoon."

"You got it, boss."

Maks watched the hatch close and drew a heavy breath, wondering what Chervonya might be up to that she needed a sudden meeting.

He doubted that she'd decided to pop in and say hello. Not that he'd mind, because she was a beautiful woman who was smarter than he was and an interesting conversationalist.

She was still Anna's niece, and probably almost as dangerous.

The flirting was only flirting because he wasn't gruff or solemn around her, not because he had anything behind it.

didn't want to get punched in the mouth. And then knocked down and kicked.

The hatch opened and she was framed by the lights in the outer chamber. And smiling, so hopefully something good.

And had a travel mug in each hand, one of which she handed to him as she sat.

"Thank you," he nodded, watching her.

She had a secret smile that he couldn't parse, but there were a lot of things about the woman he didn't understand.

Worse, they were kinda on opposite sides these days, since Uly still hadn't signed any formal treaties with the Horde. All of this was more of a personal agreement between Uly and Anna, with both nations roped in as observers.

"How can I make your day better?" Maks asked, mostly because it caused her eyes to cross a little.

She shook her head a bit and focused on him.

"What?" Maks asked as she watched.

"I'd say you wouldn't get it, but you might," she replied.

"Try me," Maks said, unprepared for the hungry look he saw in her eyes for a moment.

Then it was gone.

"I come in here, and have to remember that you're more like Uly than the people I'm used to dealing with," she offered instead.

"That good or bad?" he fired back.

"Good," she answered. "You act like him in many ways. I'm so used to the Ononguli way of doing things, and you throw me off."

"How so?" Maks asked, already confused, but that was normal with her.

Maks had long since realized that he was about as deep and complicated as a mud puddle, compared to her or her aunt. Fortunately, both of them seemed to like him.

"You really don't get it, do you, Maks?" she countered.

Maks shrugged. Kinda an understatement around here. Especially with her.

"Maks, but for the horns and the rest, you come across more Human than anybody I know who isn't," Chervonya stated.

He paused and considered that. Maybe.

"I'm trying to think like Uly," he replied. "Do things like he would, so that when he gets back, everything is as close to the way he'd have done it as I can get."

"And you don't understand how different that makes you from every other Ononguli—male or female—that I know?"

Maybe. Good or bad? Had Tuesday snuck up on him when he wasn't looking? Lukyan would get it. And laugh himself silly.

"Probably not," he admitted. "Doing a job here."

"And doing it well," she nodded. "Honestly, it's almost like dealing with Uly. Good and bad, but predictable, if nothing else."

"Then I'm succeeding at my job," he sighed inside. "Always gotta wonder."

She stopped and studied him closer.

"What would you do if he didn't come back?" she asked.

"Ask Anna at what point she wants to abandon this place and sell it to the locals, or colonize it as part of the Ononguli Sphere, however distantly displaced it was. The Horde keeps getting pushed back by the *Auga*, and don't really have space to expand many directions without having to absorb worlds filled with aliens, but we could limit immigration here early."

"Why would she want that?" Chervonya asked. "Or the Horde?"

"Because Uly's planning for centuries, in order to build up the sort of power in this corner that could stop the *Auga Empire* cold in ways that the Horde has never managed," Maks said, turning serious and hearing Uly's words come out of his mouth almost verbatim. "Might not work without Uly, but we could create something over here that might. Maybe a whole second Ononguli Sphere."

Her mouth fell open, then she closed it by force of will, eyes going large, then slitting in concentration as she studied him.

"I'm looking forward to that conversation," she said.

"Which one?" Maks asked, confused again.

"With Anna," Chervonya expanded. "Laying it out for her, because she hasn't really seen it take that form before now."

"And you know this how?" Maks pressed.

"Because I'm her Ambassador to Bastion, Maks," Chervonya reminded cheerfully. "And I've been sending notes back and forth with her on a variety of topics so that she is prepared when she gets here. Except that she was expecting Uly and will be meeting with you instead."

"Oh?" Maks asked, frantically trying to remember what day of the week it was. "When's she due?"

Chervonya smiled. She had perfect, comic timing, but he knew that.

"Oh, she'll be here sometime in the next eighteen hours, according to the most recent messages I have," she replied. "I wanted to give you a little extra warning, because neither you nor Uly will be entirely ready for this."

Maks nodded.

He was a business partner of the *Vatazhko*, twice over. And some sort of aide or advisor, to have been sent out here to help supervise the construction of *Watchtower Bastion*, as well as manage the all-Ononguli crew.

And she'd be here by tomorrow?

"Thank you," he told her. "That helps me plan."

"And that, Maks Sobol, is why I like you," she said, standing and exiting as he tried to find his jaw to reattach it so he could close his mouth from where it had fallen open.

Huh?

TWENTY

Chervonya made it back to her quarters on the ship then settled in. She enjoyed leaving Maks off-kilter. Not badly, but it helped balance the scales for what he often did to her.

Maks Sobol was simply unlike any Ononguli male she had ever met. Anywhere. And she'd read the extensive files on him when Anna had first brought him on, so she could compare that to where he was today.

And blame the Corsac Fox for all of it. Not even Lukyan Chayka got that much credit, other than he'd turned Maks into a calm First Officer and prepped him to step up when Uly had first captured *Scavenger Angel*, then decided to make an offering to the Horde that had somehow managed to push all of the positive buttons without triggering any of the negative ones.

Once upon a time, she'd have thought that was impossible for most Ononguli, let alone an outsider.

A year of knowing Uly had caused her to amend that belief. She could draw a line from who Maks had been a decade ago, to where he was today, to the Corsac Fox.

And Anna had hinted at certain things even she wasn't willing to commit to written records, but she'd been expecting to find Uly here when she arrived.

Would she chase him into the interior for answers? Wait for a while and hope he returned on schedule? Return home to Rayzian without accomplishing whatever it was that had brought the *Vatazhko* this far from home?

The only word Chervonya could think of was *momentous*. Nothing less could cause the Lord of the Endless Plains herself to travel to Bastion.

And she would be here shortly.

Chervonya figured that she owed Maks at least that much warning, based on messages that one of Anna's other agents had carried to her.

Maks would be put on the spot, but she figured that he could handle himself. It would likely delay any negotiations, because Chervonya understood that there would be hard limits to what Maks was willing to sign or accept without Uly agreeing.

At the same time, *Watchtower Bastion* would be done sooner than originally planned. Anna might be able to see it formally inaugurated, if she could stay for a month, so far ahead of schedule the construction crew had gotten.

But Anna had paid well, with bonuses included for meeting delivery dates, so those men and women would be making exceptional money.

Chervonya wasn't looking forward to explaining to her aunt how many of those folks might be planning to stay here. This was not Horde space. Not part of the Ononguli Sphere.

And yet, Uly's charm and charisma had worked wonders on everyone. Many were likely to petition to remain behind. Or return with families to start whatever colony Uly built.

And not a purely Ononguli one.

She looked out the porthole from her quarters and watched ships moving slowly in the distance. The *Watchtower* itself was on the opposite flank, but she didn't feel like crossing over to the lounge with a good view and a coffee shop.

She wanted to watch the darkness instead, broken up by all these ships. Ononguli were the majority, or perhaps only a plurality at this point, with a number of Khet traders making that same long run from the other direction. Zuath and Ugotha from the unclaimed regions between. Other travelers from near or far. Even the occasional Mazhin explorer.

What did it mean, that so many folks had stepped outside of the usual species boundaries and moved here?

Chervonya had spent six months exploring that question, and still had no answers.

What she had were more questions, including what she was going to do about Maks Sobol when this was all done.

She couldn't deny the attraction. He was unlike any Ononguli male she'd ever met. In a good way. Like Uly. Calm, polite, considerate.

Civilized, if she wanted to stretch far enough to compare him to the pirate he had been, and all the other men Chervonya had known.

Was Anna coming here to release her from the box that kept Chervonya from getting more serious with Maks? Did she want that?

Chervonya wasn't sure. She simply watched the stars and the ships go by and contemplated what it all meant.

Nothing in her life had prepared her for this.

TWENTY-ONE

Maks had gone ahead and tossed all the paperwork into a bin in his mind, to get to tomorrow or overmorrow. He had way more important things to fidget about today.

So, he was on the station's bridge. Overseeing the crew of primarily Ononguli and Khet who handled flight control operations, and could warm up all those guns at a moment's notice.

Taras had given him the side-eye at first, until Maks had taken the man aside and quietly told him who was coming. After that, Taras had equally quietly gone off to warn the kitchen. And whoever else might need it.

Thus, Maks was in charge today. Walking the deck instead of available in a nearby office to answer any questions the crew he had inherited didn't feel like tackling themselves.

"I have three ships just out of warp at the outer marker," someone called.

Maks walked over to look through his horns.

"Confirm that ID," he said automatically, looking at the names displayed.

Two big freighters, the ones Taras had been expecting, to fill in some empty shelves at the grocer.

The other was *Fire Diamond*. Maks had unconsciously been expecting *Storm Crow*, Anna's Fast Devastator flagship.

Not that *Fire Diamond* wasn't dangerous. That ship was a Heavy Interceptor on a scale with *Corsac Fox* for firepower.

At least it wasn't Tuesday. If Lukyan was still conductor, he'd have made sure to come in on a safer day.

Maks could start there.

"Ship confirms as *Fire Diamond*, Maks," the man said. "Conductor Chayka in command. Hail coming in. Eight seconds lag at present."

"Greetings, Corsac Fox," the message began. "This is Lukyan Chayka aboard *Fire Diamond*. I'm bringing diplomatic dispatches with a high priority for Uly and Ambassador Borisov. Hoping to dock shortly and maybe schedule a working dinner for the *Spatula* to show off. Reply on this channel, please."

Maks considered things. Just the perfect pitch. Hint of importance, without mentioning that those diplomatic messages might be the *Vatazhko* herself, come to visit. Set up a dinner for key players on short notice, so things could be handled quickly.

Only one problem with everything.

Maks leaned over to record a reply.

"*Fire Diamond*, this is Acting Governor Maks Sobol aboard *Watchtower Bastion*," he said. "*Corsac Fox* is currently away on a mission. You should sail down close and come aboard so we can talk, but I'll be representing Uly until he gets back. Also, please be aware that the station is fully operational from a military standpoint and we are close to finishing all the pretty work to make it livable, but most of the crews are sleeping on *Treta Envoy* at present."

Maks listened to it, liked it, sent it downrange.

He didn't figure that Lukyan was here to attack. Anna would

have brought *Storm Crow* in that case. And even a Fast Devastator would have had problems taking on the *Watchtower* by itself.

Still, best if he let Lukyan know in coded terms that a whole bunch of things had changed that Lukyan might not be prepared for.

Kinda like how Chervonya had given him a subtle warning four hours ago.

Speaking of which...

Maks poked at a few controls until he found the one he wanted.

"Hello?" Chervonya answered the comm.

"It's Maks," he replied. "*Fire Diamond* just dropped in to say hello and will be coming aboard the station in a few hours. I presume you'll want to talk to Anna as soon as possible. Should we schedule a late dinner, or push things off to morning?"

"It's your station, Governor Maks," she replied, a smiling flirt in her voice he found so distracting.

"And your diplomatic mission, Ambassador Chervonya," he fired back at her. "The *Vatazhko* is working on out-of-date plans and assumptions. Why don't you contact her immediately on a secured channel and see how quickly we need to jump, okay?"

"I can do that, Maks," she said, voice still light but a bit surprised.

He cut the line and looked around.

"This is a good time for a drill, in case you bums were getting sloppy," he announced, then reached over and triggered the alert button, sirens winding up fit to wake the dead from their hangover.

Because Lukyan would understand. And if he didn't , didn't that suggest that there might be other problems to deal with?

TWENTY-TWO

Looking around the bridge, Lukyan was just happy to have arrived. The *Vatazhko* had been a model guest. A veteran traveler who didn't need a lot of hand-holding as they'd tried to set a flight-time record between Rayzian and Bastion.

At least she'd paid for a full overhaul of everything before they left, so the entire vessel was tuned. And clean.

Nice lady. Beautiful, but so was a freshly honed razor. About as lethal, too, if you got too close.

He'd kept his distance: physical, intellectual, and emotional. Just the taxi driver hauling the boss to a meeting in the boonies.

That he'd get to see Maks and Uly and the gang would be frosting on top.

Except that Corsac Fox wasn't here, and Uly had likely taken everybody with him on some unexpected mission. And Maks was in charge of a fully operational battlestation.

Thank the Lords of the Endless Plains that it wasn't a Tuesday.

He turned to the *Vatazhko*, standing next to him. *Fire Diamond*'s bridge was way roomier and nicer than *Compass Rose*. Prettier, in all the nice ways.

Lukyan didn't trust it. Or her.

Not bad, just waiting-for-the-other-horn-to-hit kind of thing.

He gave her a look that dumped everything on her horns while he sat off to one side, hopefully safely out of the line of fire.

Taxi driver. Lord of the Endless Plains herself.

"Well, that's interesting," she offered in the most deadpan way Lukyan thought he'd ever heard.

Woman should have gone into stand-up comedy.

Or had the Tuesdays infected her instead of him? Had it mutated into a Thursday when nobody was looking?

The Horde might be doomed in that case.

Lukyan nodded vaguely and pretended to be a cow with a particularly good batch of cud to chew on.

"Can you turn over command to Dmytro so we can have a quick conversation?" she asked.

Lukyan turned to his 2IC.

"Try not to run into the station and scratch the paint," Lukyan ordered. "It's coming out of your pay if you do."

"Just the paint?" Dmytro perked up with a grin.

"And any fines Uly or Maks assign the ship, too," Lukyan added to general laughter, unbuckling and rising.

The *Vatazhko* was a tall woman. Almost exactly his height. Lighter. Leaner. Deadlier in anything except maybe unarmed wrestling, and he wasn't too certain there, either.

Woman excelled at the top of Ononguli politics. And that was sometimes a full contact sport.

She nodded as if reading his mind and stepped back, turning to exit the bridge instead of taking it into his day office right there.

Lukyan followed, staying close enough that he wasn't tempted to watch her bottom as she walked. Nice bottom. None of that bureaucratic sprawl.

They ended up in her office. She sat behind the desk. He took the chair in the corner and thought about his cud.

"He left and put Maks in charge?" she asked.

He was obvious. Shit was like that with Uly around. Everybody else came in second place to Anna and Uly.

Lukyan nodded.

"What does that imply?" she asked.

"He trusts Maks," Lukyan said automatically. "Most decisions and outcomes will be what Uly would have wanted."

"Yes, but why isn't he here?"

Lukyan shrugged and chewed his cud. He'd come in on the same ship she had.

"Something came up that was important enough to take the ship," he replied. "And Uly wanted all his people, so it was either important or dangerous. Or both. *Wren*'s in orbit, along with a handful of other big warehouse ships. The usual assortment of country craft and medium traders. Plus Maks has lots of guns to protect everyone."

He closed his mouth and watched her think. That was when the *Vatazhko* got the most dangerous, because she had more brains than about anybody her knew except Uly and Dan.

"I'll need you to talk to Maks—" she began, but he cut her off.

"Governor Sobol," Lukyan stated bluntly. "Acting Governor of Bastion. Uly put him in charge. Maks might be one of my best friends in the galaxy and my former First Mate, but he's also on the other side of whatever's going on. Anything you were going to negotiate with him can wait for Uly to get back, or Maks speaks. *Speaks*, maybe, however weird that might turn out to be."

"*Speaks*?" she asked, confused.

Lukyan occasionally forgot that the woman hadn't walked the deck of a warship as a pirate in at least a decade and a half. She had half a decade on him, so since about her mid-thirties.

"Uly *Speaks* for the Mazhin Convocation he inherited," Lukyan nodded. "Haydar and Nasrin, plus the others, all of whom came from different ships and different clans. They elected him as their own *Vatazhko*. All the Humans agreed. The Emro and Thogin were all in. The rest have joined as they came along. Maks might be *Speaking* for the Bastion Convocation in Uly's stead. Or whatever the hell you want to call this colony."

Lukyan closed his mouth and went back to his cud.

She stared at him, doing whatever processing she needed, then nodded back at him.

"Acting Governor Sobol," she repeated slowly. "He's still your friend, and will talk to you. I make him nervous."

Lukyan couldn't help the bark of laughter.

"You make *me* nervous, Anna," he said. "And I'm pretty sure I'm on your side."

"Pretty sure?" she asked.

Except that it sounded like a tease the way she did it.

Freshly honed blade...

"I just fly," Lukyan retreated to the safest ground he could find. "You make all the important decisions and my job is to execute them. Occasionally, I might tell you something is stupid. Hopefully before you do it."

And cud...

Anna studied him closely. Like, maybe seeing him differently than she had assumed.

Lukyan would have liked to have said he was the same dumbass pirate he'd always been, but the last two years had fundamentally changed him. And the Horde, though the rest of the Ononguli Sphere maybe didn't see it coming as well as he had.

Uly had dropped out at Lacium and declared war on piracy on a Tuesday. And Lukyan preferred being on the winning side.

Big change. That, and going home for the first time in a decade. Finally sitting down with Bohdan to talk like adults. Realizing that he'd gotten over Nadiya sometime in the last however long.

Knowing that there was nothing on Rayzian to call him back again later.

Liberating. Shame it had taken him those twenty years to finally grow up.

He watched her watch him. Wondered what she saw. Kept his distance and chewed his cud.

"Talk to Maks," she said simply. Wasn't an order, though she could. Polite request. "Find out what he knows. What he's willing to tell you. Whatever it is that I need to be prepared for."

"Can do," Lukyan replied. "What will you be doing?"

"Talking to Chervonya and figuring out the future of the Ononguli Sphere."

Lukyan blinked once, then nodded and rose.

Nothing small there. Just the future of the species.

And he knew that Uly would be intimately tied up in it, may the Lords of the Endless Plains have mercy on all their souls.

TWENTY-THREE

Anna Shevchenko had worked her ass off to be where she was. *Vatazhko*. Lord of the Endless Plains herself, the single most powerful Ononguli in the Sphere.

And then Ulysses Fortier had come along.

The Corsac Fox.

She still marveled at how one Human, from so far away that most maps didn't even show that distance, could have had such an impact on so many cultures.

But she'd met the Human. Taken his measure. Sent Maks and Chervonya both out here to keep watch on what he was doing, because too many of her fellows on the Council rightfully worried about what one Human was doing out here by himself.

Except that they all kept forgetting the most important thing about Uly.

He wasn't alone. He had Dan Chastain as his right hand. Advisors that were Mazhin, Emro, Thogin, Khet, and who knew what else?

Plus *Acting Governor Maks Sobol*. So there was at least one Ononguli that Uly trusted at the highest levels.

And here she was, all set to significantly upset the apple cart. Hopefully in a good way, but these weren't conversations she could have with a mere *Acting Governor*.

Well, she could, but nothing could come of them. Maks was smart enough to immediately step back and refuse to even discuss the topic until Uly rescued him.

As he should.

She'd come all this way and might not even cover the actual reason for her trip.

Anna laughed in the privacy of her office, after Lukyan returned to his bridge, possibly like she was chasing him with a whip.

Chayka didn't fear her. Healthy respect. And a calmness out of place with an Ononguli pirate conductor, where so many of them ended up more like Adrian Sobol.

Anna still wasn't sure she wanted Maks's cousin back, at the end of the day. Loose cannon, in all the bad ways, now that Uly had infected the galaxy with a new kind of thinking.

She only had to look at Lukyan Chayka to see the effects. Or Maks Sobol.

Her comm chirped. Anna checked the time and nodded.

"Yes?" she asked.

"Transmitting an updated package for your encryption software," Chervonya replied. "Install it first, then open video."

Anna was intrigued. Her security was as good as the Horde could make it. Chervonya suggesting that it still wasn't enough?

Still, she got the file, and let it unpack itself as she watched. The screen blinked three times and took on a red band all the way around that was a new thing. Obviously a visual cue from an alien species. Mazhin?

"Okay," Anna replied.

Chervonya appeared on the screen. There was something about her niece that took Anna a moment to place.

Smiling. Honest smiles. Relaxed and confident, when her niece had always had something of a chip on her shoulder before. Like any young woman in the Horde, when so many of the old goats forgot how many women usually went to war.

It was the piracy that caused them to step back and take up normal lives.

"You look good," Anna told her.

"Thank you," Chervonya replied. "I feel like this has been a good mission for me. I've learned a lot."

"The security?" Anna asked.

"Uly's Mazhin scientist, Haydar Ramezani, delights in explaining that the Humans and the Mazhin both seem to have forgotten more about information security than most species ever learned," her niece explained. "He routinely rolls out improvements. This is one he distributed before he left. Claims that it will secure against anything he's seen yet."

"Is he afraid of something?" Anna asked, intrigued.

"I think at this point it is more of a compulsion on his part," Chervonya replied. "Pushing the envelope harder and further. Forever inventing new things, which he has apparently been doing since before he met Uly."

Anna nodded. Her files suggested the direction, if not the scope.

"You mentioned that he left," Anna said. "Where?"

"A new species appeared," Chervonya replied. "Pirates from the interior to the north and slightly west of us here I think. Uly captured them, took them with him, and went looking for their homeworld. I'm transmitting a full report for you to read later."

Anna nodded. She'd had Lukyan explain Tuesdays to her. Even let him arrive on a Thursday.

Hadn't apparently mattered.

"How soon is he due home?" Anna asked, wondering if this whole trip was about to be for nothing.

"Current schedule is two more weeks gone," Chervonya replied. "But he also told Maks that he might stay out longer and not to worry for another month after that. Oh, and they finished the combat part of the station before Uly left, though there is a long checklist of little things to be fully complete."

At least Uly had secured his base, much like Anna had charged Harald and Stefaniya with keeping the fire breathers in line while she was gone.

Uly's single raid on Nyri had caused a ripple to spasm brutally through the entire near frontier of *Auga* Space, according to her spies. Word had apparently reached the Emperor himself of the attack, which had then triggered all the recriminations and investigations to find fault.

Anna didn't think they would actually learn, but they would spend perhaps as long as a decade reinforcing that frontier against similar incursions.

Uly had done it to buy favor with the Horde. And to strike a lasting blow on the *Auga*.

Then he'd gone off and built this place. And whatever else he was up to, back in the hinterlands.

Anna nodded.

"What else?" she asked, almost worried about Thursday sneaking up and biting her on the ass like Lukyan feared his Tuesdays.

"Maks has some interesting ideas about what he might have to do if Uly doesn't come back for some reason," Chervonya answered. "Those can wait until we talk in person but before you meet him. He asked me to see if we should arrange a meeting as soon as you could dock, or push it out until station morning. We're late in the planetary afternoon, as they measure it at Bastion. Dinner, breakfast, or something later?"

Anna considered.

She'd been intending to start as soon as she could get Uly in a room, because the negotiations would take time and possibly cause a lot of personal friction before they were done.

Without Uly, there was simply no way in hell that Maks would consider the topic. Nor could she rush anything, because she needed Uly.

That was the part that galled Anna the worst. The more she thought about it, the more she realized that she needed Uly. That the Horde needed this Human as a bound ally. Possibly a warlord of some sort, if he kept growing into the person she'd seen flashes of, back on Rayzian.

And what did she do if he didn't come back?

Hopefully, Maks would have some ideas she could use.

"Let's take this slow," Anna decided. "Some of it will be things that need Uly to decide, even if Maks is acting in his place, so we have time do things until then. Let's aim for dinner tomorrow, and you can come aboard first thing in the morning, after I've stayed up late reading your reports."

"Understood, *Vatazhko*," Chervonya replied. "See you then."

Anna cut the line and blew out a heavy breath.

Even she had come to realize how much she relied on one alien with the potential to change the galaxy.

Would it be enough?

TWENTY-FOUR

Maks was at lunch. Down in a commissary that was a kitchen and a vast warehouse that would eventually turn into a dining hall and an entire hotel of smaller meeting and entertainment rooms at some point. Maybe last, because the kitchen worked and there were a bunch of trestle tables and benches welded down that were good enough for most folks these days.

Nothing fancy. Just like back home. Almost like *Compass Rose* had been, back in the good old days.

Good? Maybe. Old galaxy. Before Uly. Maybe the best way to organize his life.

Dumbass kid. Dumbass pirate. Uly. Whatever the hell he was today.

Everybody's spy, ambassador, First Mate, and whatever else.

Cargo ships had arrived with lots of foodstuffs from home, so the kitchen had started emptying older stocks of stuff that was getting close to end-of-life dates on cans.

Taste of home for the Ononguli, and the Khet didn't complain too much about things being overly spicy anymore.

Like maybe they'd adapted to eating Ononguli cuisine.

Weirder things had happened.

Then Lukyan walked in. Just him. No goons, no bodyguards, no crew.

Just Lukyan.

Maks nodded as Lukyan went to get food from the line. Ate slower.

Dawdled.

Lukyan obviously had something to say. And mostly in public if he'd hunted Maks down at lunch.

Hopefully something good.

Lukyan slid a tray in across from him. Place was huge, and folks tended to spread out in here, because you worked around the same dozen folks constantly.

Meals were private time.

Most days.

Acting Governor Sobol found that he was on duty a lot more than he'd expected.

Maybe more than he wanted.

Lukyan held up a glass in toast. Maks touched his to it silently.

"Who'd have figured?" Lukyan asked.

"Uly, probably," Maks replied, almost automatically.

Lukyan nodded.

"Am I in trouble?" Maks asked after a beat.

"Not as far as I know," Lukyan replied. "Anna ordered me to talk to you, but nothing more than that."

"If I have any secrets from her niece, I'd be surprised," Maks laughed around a bite of muffin.

"So, what happened?" Lukyan asked.

Maks ended up giving him the same speech he'd given anybody who asked. Usually conductors new in system surprised not to find Uly or *Corsac Fox* around.

Same one he'd give Anna in a few hours, more than likely.

"Then you came out of warp," Maks concluded. "Bringing the boss. And here we are."

"And here we are," Lukyan agreed. "Like what you've done to the place."

Maks snorted.

"Got enough twelves to splatter any dumbshit pirate getting frisky," he said. "Uly required that before he went off to investigate the Isann. Past that, I'm literally holding the fort until he gets back."

"What if Anna orders you otherwise?" Lukyan asked.

"She can't," Maks decided. "I don't work for her right now. Uly had me sign some temporary work contracts drawn up by Ethir and Rabiu. Technically, I'm not even Ononguli according to the language involved, but an honorary Human exercising the Corsac Fox's plenipotentiary powers in this system. It gets complicated, but Anna can't order anything right now. Best she can do is blackball me later. Doubt that means I'm out of work, but she might evict me from the partnerships I signed with her before. Like it matters."

"Does it?" Lukyan asked. "Matter?"

"Make sure you're in the room when I explain it to Anna later," Maks nodded. "Not sure I wanna go over it twice today, and it can get messy."

"You doing okay, Maks?" his old boss asked.

"Stretched too thin, but that's me trying to fill Uly's boots," he replied with a sigh. "All I can do to keep the ship running. You and her showing up can't be anything but more chaos at this end, but I think we've got it mostly under control."

"Chervonya driving you crazy?" Lukyan grinned.

"Almost as smart as her aunt," Maks replied. "Still a little young and rough around the edges but she'll be *Vatazhko* one of these days if she wants it."

Lukyan nodded.

"Spent the whole trip out here dealing with Anna on a

personal basis," he said. "Mostly to keep her from bugging Dmytro and the rest. She's a handful."

Maks laughed. Only other woman he knew in that league was Mom. And Mom had connections to Anna that she still refused to talk about. Scary connections.

"We in over our head?" Maks asked.

"Figured that out as soon as *Corsac Fox* dropped out of warp at Lacium," Lukyan laughed. "Been running for all I was worth every day since then."

"Same," Maks agreed. "At the same time, I think I'm doing pretty good here."

"I got that impression from Chervonya when she came aboard *Fire Diamond* this morning," Lukyan confirmed. "She had good things to say, for the bits I heard before she and Anna locked themselves in Anna's quarters to talk. Got a question for you, kid."

Kid? But it was Lukyan. He could get away with that kind of language, having known Maks for over a decade now. And one of his true friends.

At least among the Ononguli. What did it say that most of his friends were aliens?

What did it say about the Horde, come to think of it?

Maks nodded.

"When the station is done," Lukyan turned serious. "When *Treta Envoy* heads home. Are you likely to be aboard? Or sail to Rayzian just long enough to hitch a ride back?"

"I could buy something outright," Maks said. "Been drawing pay and investment income, and not spending it on anything for a year now. Dunno if Anna would let me buy anything nice or dangerous, but there are always deals to be had if you have cash on the barrelhead. As to when and what, that's out of my hands."

"True, but you gotta have opinions, Maks," Lukyan pressed.

"I like what Uly's doing out here," Maks admitted. "And while I might not pursue turning myself into a merchant, there's going to be a lot of trade coming and going. Might have to turn myself into a Trade Factor like Rabiu is doing."

"There aren't any Ononguli Trade Factors, Maks," Lukyan pointed out.

"No," Maks agreed. "Just a bunch of pirates who are either going to have their reserve commissions activated, or be tossed out on their asses by the Horde when the war gets serious. You taught me a lot about business, Lukyan. Anna and Uly have put me through an advanced degree on the shit."

"Really?" Lukyan asked, suddenly ears and horns pointed inward towards Maks's face. "So I should look at investing with you after this?"

"Go see my Mom when you get back," Maks nodded. "She's got sneaky connections. Dad's good on the investment side, when you have cash you want to turn into passive income. Way better rates than anything I imagined."

"Huh," was all his old conductor had to say, but Maks saw that gleam in Lukyan's eyes. "Trade Factor?"

"I know a few important folks," Maks laughed. "They might even like me. Oughta put that to use."

Lukyan grinned. It was almost like the old days, back on *Compass Rose*. Before Uly, when he'd just been a dumbass pirate.

Trade Factor? It had slipped out, but more and more sounded like something that he could slam his horns into. Might as well get first-mover advantage around here, when he turned into an Ex-Governor.

Or whatever the hell was next.

"And make sure you are in the room tonight," Maks demanded.

"You said that," Lukyan nodded. "Why?"

"I think we're looking at the next chapter of galactic history unfolding, boss," Maks said. "Like, one volume ended yesterday and the next one begins with *Fire Diamond* arriving at Bastion, carrying the Lord of the Endless Plains herself, to talk to the Corsac Fox. Got that feeling to it."

"Should I bring a documentarian?" Lukyan asked.

"If they were here, I'd bring them myself, but they're all busy being rich and famous on Z'Gosza these days," Maks joked.

He watched his friend absorb that tidbit.

And then one particular Tuesday, the Corsac Fox had dropped out of warp at Lacium, *and changed the galaxy.*

TWENTY-FIVE

Hadn't taken much effort to be in the room. Lukyan had opened his mouth to ask Anna and she'd ordered it before he took a breath.

So here he was.

And sitting on Maks's side of the long conference table, or it would probably look too much like a board of inquiry hosting.

Dumb idea. Maks had probably saved all their asses more than even those two ladies understood it.

"Coffee?" he asked Maks as they started to settle.

After all, he owed Maks for it, that one time before the Lords of the Endless Plains.

"Yeah," Maks brightened up. "Add a little honey and some milk, please."

Lukyan nearly stumbled, processing that.

This was not the same Maks who had once described wanting his coffee as dark as his soul.

Unless it was the soul that was different these days.

There was always that.

Lukyan made up two mugs the same, just to see what Maks was up to.

Not bad. Cut the bitterness pretty decently. Smoothed things out.

Lukyan decided that maybe he could drink it this way for a while. Look at who he might become in galactic-history-volume-number-whatever that was about to unfold as he sat across from Anna and handed Maks his coffee.

Certainly, that interlude had broken some element off the rigidity everyone had been holding.

Anna glanced sidelong at Chervonya and the two shared some silent, inside joke about men.

But hey, he was just the taxi driver here. Those two were the power to be feared.

Or at least respected.

"Hello, Maks," Anna said, taking the friendly approach instead of addressing him as Governor Sobol.

Lukyan approved.

"Anna," Maks nodded back.

"Chervonya has briefed me extensively on the latest things," Anna continued. "And Lukyan has added a few observations that I find interesting."

Maks glanced sidelong. Lukyan answered and they had an entire conversation in a few looks and gestures.

Kinda like what the ladies had done.

Huh.

Hadn't ever seen it that way. That was how close those two ladies were. Almost as close as him and Maks. Good to know.

"Some of what I came out here to talk to Uly about will be things I won't bother roping you into, Maks," Anna said. "Partly because you'd listen, throw up your horns, and back away without wanting to get involved, and I appreciate that. But I do have questions about the possible future you mentioned to Chervonya if Uly doesn't return for whatever reason."

"Go ahead," Maks replied calmly. Smoothly.

Coffee-like.

Huh.

"You mentioned that this might turn into an Ononguli system, far from the core of the Horde," Anna noted. "Why is that?"

"Because at least half of the people here right now are Ononguli," Maks replied. "The next largest group are Khet, then Zuath and Ugotha. Plus some others I don't know all that well. With a station, folks are already setting up to mine, process, manufacture, and grow things, so this is going to be a place. Even if something happens to Uly and the Horde doesn't end up claiming it. Dumb idea, but that's also a third- or fourth-level contingency on my part. I'd personally hire someone to go look for Uly, if he ended up being overdue. *Fire Diamond* would be first on my list if Lukyan was available, but Uly confiscated those four pirates and I have them docked and being repaired for sale at some point. Crews wouldn't be a problem."

Lukyan nodded. Kid didn't sound anything like he had. Had grown up and turned into a power player who could fence with Anna on equal-enough terms. Trade Factor in the making?

"This is not Horde space," Anna bristled.

Maks shrugged and Lukyan grinned.

"It could be," Maks countered. "The *Auga* will keep pushing, and at some point the Sphere won't be a sphere anymore. Uly's playing an exceptionally long game here, establishing something in a corner nobody really claims. Without him, the Horde might need to look to where we could flee in another century or six, assuming nothing can stop the *Auga* from taking our worlds away from us."

Man, it was like a stranger had taken over Maks's body. In a good way.

Anna was a bit gobsmacked. Chervonya was grinning and trying to hide it. Lukyan's smile caught Anna's eye. And her attention.

"You agree with him?" she asked in a voice dripping with acid.

"I agree with the logic," Lukyan clarified. "With the understanding that we've stuck our heads in the sand too many times over the last however many centuries, raiding and swarming when the *Auga* do attack, but slowly losing ground anyway. How long until we don't own Sector Twenty-One anymore?"

Oh, that was an interesting look. Freshly honed razor gone a little ragged and rusty, going to tear your skin and poison you as it cut flesh.

"He's right, *Vatazhko*," Chervonya stepped in and rescued them. "This is much longer-term than the Horde generally considers, but it has value."

"We should send other exploration ships out to find places we can hide from the *Auga*?" she growled.

"Unless you plan on recruiting as many outsiders as you can to help break the *Auga* in the near future, while Uly has them distracted and looking over their shoulders," Maks offered. "The *Auga* have a lot of enemies, but nobody is individually strong enough to do anything about them. We should still outnumber them, collectively. That's where Uly is headed. Getting everybody together to stop the *Auga*."

"Can he pull it off?" Lukyan asked, feeling like the straight man in the comedy routine.

Like was apparently the new normal with Maks.

"He thinks so," Maks chuckled. "What was it you said about betting against him?"

"*I'd rather be on the winning side,*" Lukyan quoted.

"*Uly gets shit done,*" Maks quoted back at him.

They sobered. The ladies caught that and let it slide.

New volume of galactic history, possibly starting with this meeting right here.

Weird.

And compelling.

"Should we go looking for Uly?" Lukyan turned and asked Anna.

"We don't know where he is," Maks said. "I mean, I have directions and estimates, but Sterling didn't leave me with all his notes.

By now, he knows everything and has plotted out a whole series of new trade routes for folks. That one gets cartography."

Lukyan nodded. He was using charts that Sterling Huff had updated and improved, even on *Fire Diamond*.

"It feels wasteful, sitting around waiting for Uly to return," Anna groused.

Lukyan had spent enough time around the woman to understand that there wasn't any threat behind it. No anger. Bit of peevish frustration, but she'd worked herself up to spring something big on Uly, and he'd slipped away before she could do it.

Because, Uly.

"I can use the help," Maks spoke up. "*Fire Diamond* is heavier than anything else around here save *Corsac Fox*. You want to go survey a few places we think might be habitable, but empty? Or turn loose some of your crew to help build out facilities here on the station for R&R? *Treta Envoy* has that stuff, so the working crews are entertained, but they'll take the ship home at some point and the station needs a replacement. Either we convert some warehouse space, or we buy an old freighter and turn it into a casino resort. Or build something on the surface, but Uly hasn't identified his future capital city and I don't want to make assumptions there."

Lukyan didn't bother keeping his jaw from dropping open. Anna was the same. Chervonya had seen it coming, but she probably knew this new Maks better than Maks did.

How much better? Not too close. They didn't have that body language communication. didn't touch.

Working comrades, but not anything romantic. Smart move on Maks's part.

Keep to yourself until the woman walks up and grabs you by the horns.

Especially around dangerous women like those two.

Lukyan looked a question at Anna.

He worked for her, after all.

"We have time," she agreed. "Let's see what we can do to improve things before Uly gets back."

Lukyan nodded.

Progress in the right direction.

Because they were following the path Uly had laid out.

And only a fool bet against the Corsac Fox.

KARAŊGILIKKA

TWENTY-SIX

Uly grinned as he saw the sour look on Kadyr Usupov's face on the main screen.

"Damn it, Uly, why couldn't you have come along ten years ago, when I was still young enough to chuck everything and go sailing with you?" the Chief of Chiefs of the Isann demanded with a grin.

Uly and most of the folks on the bridge laughed. The last three weeks had done wonders to bring Kadyr around. Bit of jealousy that Aibek might have all the adventures, but nothing bad.

The Chief of Chiefs was a smart man. Could see which way the hurricane was blowing and adjust to handle it.

But circumstances still bound him to his palace.

"Sorry," Uly replied, still smiling. "Promise that we'll stop here on the way back and let you know what we find, Kadyr. Assuming that there is anything to find."

"Anybody but you, I'd assume hydras would get you, Uly," Kadyr answered. "Or that they'd find absolutely nothing worth the trip. Huff, you've got everything programmed?"

"Aye, Chief of Chiefs," Sterling replied crisply. "Thank you again for letting me mine your nav records."

"Fair trade, young Human," Kadyr said. "We now know that there are many places beyond even Bastion that we could travel to trade. The darkness has been pulled back enough to show other islands."

"There is still one curtain, Kadyr," Uly noted.

"And you're going out to map it, Uly," the Chief nodded. "Discover it. Add it to the modern version of the *Karaŋgılıkka.*"

Uly shrugged. He didn't see himself as another Zamir Aytiev, but Suka Kuri had hinted that the legend of the Corsac Fox was likely to fill a particular niche in modern Isann culture. One that had readily turned them from wary strangers to enthusiastic allies far quicker than he might have originally believed possible. But getting them all in a room to talk had worked wonders, as had Aibek explaining that all the ships currently in harbor might be hard-pressed to successfully attack *Corsac Fox.*

And Uly had come to talk and explore, rather than conquer.

That spoke to the Isann soul.

"We'll be back," Uly promised.

"The lighthouse will be visible," Kadyr Usupov promised soberly, another thing that went to their very soul. "I've sent the freighter *Surly* to Bastion to update them on what's going on. And loaded them with trade goods."

Then the comm went blank and Drew brought up a bow view of nearby space. Orbital space above Isann. Uly hadn't been to the surface, but Dan had taken her team to scout things. Mostly showing off dangerous women, because the Isann tended to be even more chauvinistic than the Khet, separating jobs into things men did, like sailing and fighting, from womanly chores, like running households when the men were away.

Karaŋgılıkka mapped the road they all needed to take.

"Mr. Roscoe, stand by to engage the Variable Pulse Spatial Generators," Uly called.

Then he paused and turned to Aibek Sulaymanov, seated off to one side between Dan and Suka Kuri.

"Aibek, this is properly an Isann mission," Uly said conversationally. "You give the order."

Aibek blinked in surprise and looked at Suka Kuri, who merely smiled and nodded back.

"Steering, take us into warp," Aibek said in a voice that cracked in the middle with emotion, but Uly wasn't surprised, even as the stars blinked out and *Corsac Fox* was in its own pocket universe, moving faster than light could travel as it left Isann and sought out those places where the Yarikh had once lived, so many centuries ago.

He unbuckled and rose, looking proudly around at the bridge and officers he'd assembled. Pure luck, but he'd take that luck. Everyone here had proven themselves in the fire, time and again.

"Drew, you take this watch," Uly ordered. "Sterling, I believe you're next on rotation?"

"Aye, sir," Sterling nodded. "Back to normal?"

"As close to normal as we can manage," Uly said. "I'll see most of you at dinner."

He headed back to his working office, off the bridge. Dan fell in beside him, matching his steps with her long legs as he walked.

He looked over, but she shook her head minutely so he kept going. Eventually, they arrived at his office and she closed the hatch behind herself.

"What can I do for you?" Uly asked, watching her eyes.

Not disturbed, but intent, as only she could do.

"*Karaŋgılıkka*," she said, summing up a tremendous amount of distance in one, simple word.

If you understood that the printed version of the book was a doorstop that weighed six kilograms. And he'd acquired several for Suka Kuri and her students to translate.

"Sailing into Darkness," he replied, roughly translating the name itself.

"The Isann aren't Yarikh, except as intellectual descendants," Dan reminded him. "We still don't know what happened to them."

"We'll find out," Uly reminded her. "Sterling and Haydar have been able to synthesize all of Kadyr's records from their various libraries with older things known to the Emro and the *Auga*. Both of them date back to an era when the Yarikh were still a thing. What's really bothering you?"

It was only evident because he'd spent so much time studying her face. Learning every little thing about her that he could, because Uly knew that he needed her more than anybody else anywhere.

"What happens to a civilization when it collapses?" she asked.

The small group of senior folks had chewed on that topic over dinner several times, but come to no conclusions.

"According to the legends Suka Kuri has heard, the Yarikh slowly pulled back over several generations towards the end," he said. "Presumably emptying some of these worlds of population. Other places like Isann were mostly a single species that stayed put. Or a clan that moved there and claimed it after the Yarikh left. But they fell into a form of barbarism for a long stretch and are only now coming out of it. I suspect without knowing that there might be many such worlds out there ahead of us, where there are people, but they don't have a stardrive until someone comes along and supplies it. Don't know who brought the Isann up, but they've embraced it and will start trading with the Ugotha and Zuath, plus whoever else they might meet at Bastion."

"That's the part that niggles at me, Uly," she said slowly. Deeply. Contemplatively. "That we might find several cultures, currently locked in on one world or one system, that then get unleashed on the wider galaxy as a threat."

"I'm given to understand that Humans are still the most violent species out there, for whatever reason," he nodded. "*Auga* next, but they have raised bureaucracy to a religion. Most of the rest aren't as bad. And if they do wake up to aliens and decide to go off on some terrible crusade, then maybe we'll have to deal with that before we circle back to crush the *Auga*."

"You know how crazy that sounds, right?" she smiled. "Us talking about taking this one ship and destroying an empire with thousands of inhabited systems?"

"We could easily live out our entire lives in comfort, over here in Sector Fourteen," Uly agreed. "Get fabulously rich and live like royalty do back in *Danumash*. And the rest of the galaxy would keep going slowly to the hell of whatever the *Auga* will inflict upon them when it finally arrives, however many generations of our descendants will be there to meet it."

"Our descendants?" she asked with a teasing grin.

"Collectively our," Uly deflected. "This thing we're building."

Much as he might want to reach across that desk and take her hand. Talk about things they'd slid around time and again unsaid.

She nodded, silently acknowledging that today wasn't the day to have that conversation. Not with yet another mission ahead of them.

When would it be? Uly didn't know.

"So we have to stop the *Auga* by ourselves?" she asked, stepping sideways with him.

"And all our friends," he nodded. "Every day, we find more people willing to help. They just need inspiration. The Corsac Fox provides that."

"What about Uly?" she pressed. "What's he think about all this?"

"He sees it as just another grand adventure, doing things he never imagined and meeting folks he couldn't have dreamed existed, back when he was a mere ensign on *Marshall Castillon*," Uly grinned. "Here, he's making a difference."

"He is," she agreed. "What do you think we'll find?"

Uly shrugged and considered it. They'd spent hours on the topic but that was then.

Corsac Fox was in motion today.

Sailing Into Darkness.

"I'm hoping that the Yarikh are out there," he said quietly. "Not their homeworld, which the Isann believe was abandoned long ago, but that place they retreated to, up in the mountains where the cold and winds would protect them. I'd like to know what happened at the end. Who they turned into, once they stepped off that stage, assuming some level of cultural collapse. If nothing else, it gives me an idea of how we might weaken the *Auga* enough that they become just another nation, rather than the grand monolith that will eventually conquer the entire galaxy."

"Will they, though?" she asked. "Suka Kuri mentioned once that they were having fewer children every generation, even as they expanded outwards. That there might be trillions of them today, but because of the way they had engineered themselves as they saw perfection, that they might vanish on their own."

"That just means a civil war at some point," Uly noted, thinking back to his academy days.

"Is that a bad thing?" she asked. "If it stops the *Auga*?"

He had to remember that Dan, as brilliant and sharp as she was, had enlisted and worked her way up from the bottom, without the breadth of education demanded of an officer in *Batyr's* Navy.

"Whole worlds might be bombed out of existence," he said. "There have been records of the *Auga* sitting in orbit and bombarding the surface, when folks resisted being absorbed into the Empire. It will get worse if they want to leave."

"If they didn't want terrible things to happen, maybe they should have been nicer to people along the way?" she asked.

It sounded polite and friendly, but the look on her face was fierce.

And she was right. If the *Auga Empire* hadn't turned out to be more or less just like the *Combined Crowns of Danumash*, he might feel bad.

In *Danumash's* case, an inherited aristocracy of blood that controlled everything and everyone. For the *Auga*, it went another step down the scale, as the elite were all *Auga*, and only *Auga*. At least the *Danumash* middle classes could harbor the fantasy of being lucky enough to marry into one of the ruling clans.

The *Auga* ruled. Everyone else accepted.

Or not.

Exactly the opposite of what he was trying to build here. What he'd asked Dan to create, where everyone was equal.

If the two of them in charge were Human, that had been the luck of the draw, and he still had advisors from every direction that he could listen to. Or even seek out.

What a proper republic was supposed to be, rather than another form of aristocracy.

"Tomorrow's problem," he decided. "Today, we're going to seek the Yarikh, and hope they can teach us things from the far end of history. We're just starting out. Maybe we can make decisions today that stretch that endpoint as far out to the horizon as possible."

"With you all the way," she said quietly.

"That's the only reason I think I can do it," he nodded.

TWENTY-SEVEN

Anari had wanted to be Sabre School. Had studied for it. Trained for it.

Stupid *Auga* had taken her test results and announced that she was too intelligent to be Sabre and had assigned her to become an engineer instead.

Which really, at the end of the day, told you all you needed to know about how they saw learning, but she kept that opinion to herself. Nobody around here liked the *Auga*, but nobody had as much reason to hate them.

Except maybe Ethir and the Cousins. And Yeong-Suk and her clan.

Okay, maybe a lot of folks had been mistreated. All the more reason to help Uly break them.

This morning, she was deep into her project of translating the *Karaŋgılıkka*. Suka Kuri had made electronic copies available, but Anari preferred having that heavy paper edition in her lap as she fought her way through it.

Mechanical translation was dumb. Mechanical. It lost all the nuance of idioms, making the results look like something a child had written. You needed brains and literature and poetry and art to make it prety. And she supposed that she might have been a candidate for Moss School, in a different lifetime.

Good thing she had an Exemplar who told her she could do both, because this paragraph was driving Anari utterly sideways. It didn't make any sense at all. She'd even put it into the computer and asked for that stupid mechanical translation, and it hadn't given her anything better.

Anari closed the book and her tablet, sliding them into a bag as she checked the clock.

Early, but Suka Kuri rose early. Said that it was the time of day most peaceful for contemplating deep and serious things. Or simply enjoying your tea before anyone else rose.

She should be at tea. Anari exited her cabin and headed aft to where she expected to find the Exemplar.

Sure enough, back in a corner of the wardroom, with part of a muffin dismantled on the plate in front of her and an Emro-sized tea pot.

Anari snagged a muffin. Looked like the *Spatula* knew Suka Kuri's schedule, and pulled them exactly as she walked in, since they were still warm. She filled a mug with coffee and approached.

"You look like a woman on a mission," Suka Kuri grinned up at her.

"Confused, elder," Anari replied.

"Sit, and perhaps we can share it," Suka Kuri gestured.

Anari did, taking time to nosh on warm muffin and coffee. Those little things that should be appreciated by both Moss and Sabre.

Warm muffin. Nuff said.

"What troubles you this morning?" Suka Kuri finally asked.

Anari opened her bag and filled the table with book, notebook, and notes. She opened the source to the page driving her to distraction and located the offending paragraph.

"Here's what it says," Anari replied. "And this is the best guess I can translate, but it makes no sense, even poetically."

Suka Kuri studied the page.

"You're farther along than I am," she noted simply, causing Anari to blink.

Was she going too fast?

"No, at the speed you find appropriate," Suka Kuri said, so apparently Anari was muttering this morning.

She bit on the muffin to shut her mouth.

"I see your confusion," Suka Kuri said. "This almost reads as if it came from a third language, and was reproduced almost verbatim here in Isann."

Anari blinked. Cycled back through that chapter of the book.

"Yes," she breathed heavily. "Something older. Something original? The poet who composed this piece? I know it was once passed down orally rather than written. Did someone try to render this directly from Yarikh and had to rely on a machine to do it? And why write it like this?"

Anari had anguished over the paragraph. Directions for sailing, but written as if one were in a boat on the surface of an ocean, rather than in the stars, in spite of this being part of a tale where Zamir Aytiev was out having yet another crazy adventure.

Dan had mentioned a Human legend of a similar hero, undertaking a series of impossible labors because he was busy trying to clear his name from some crime. Or others like Aytiev who got sidetracked on the way home from a war and took decades to make it.

Nowhere else in the *Karaŋgılıkka* did anyone sail on water.

At least so far? Anari hadn't read the rest, merely sat down and began her translation, because Suka Kuri would eventually take several versions and assemble them into a definitive copy that would be transmitted to the Emro. And others.

"Let me challenge you, Young Anari," Suka Kuri said. "Can

you reverse engineer that part, if it was mechanically translated into Isann from something else?"

Anari blinked, wondering what the Exemplar was driving at. If there was anything beyond the student doing better today than they had yesterday.

That was what Sabre School implied. And Moss.

She turned the book back and thought about how it had come across. How dull and confusing the output had been, because Aytiev was sailing on water, when he'd been in a starship the chapter before.

Original poet? Original language.

"He's seeking some prize," Anari said. "The elders have hidden it away from the Isann because the gods decided that the Yarikh weren't worthy."

She paused and read it again, noting that the artificial language went on for several pages when she'd merely stopped here and bashed her skull against this one paragraph again and again.

"Twin lighthouses that mark the safe channel," Anari read, translating as she went. "He emerges on the far side in calm waters, to find a hidden harbor lit by a black moon, which makes no sense. Move on a bit. There, he sees the prize that had drawn him, but he is unable to scale the rocks to reach it, and must ride at anchor at a safe distance, cursing because the greatest prize of all time is just out of his reach. Plus, his superstitious crew refuses to try to shallows, demanding instead that he sail home. They leave, and he is never able to return."

"And what does that suggest to you, were you to sail stars instead of water?" Suka Kuri asked.

"It's a set of sailing instructions," Anari mused. "Two bright stars and a dim one that is dangerous. Oh. OH. What if that black moon was a black hole? That would be a dangerous place to sail and most crews would likely balk. But why was it taken directly from Yarikh into Isann so badly?"

"I suspect that Zamir Aytiev himself wrote those various directions, and told people to keep them exactly as he had put them down," Suka Kuri nodded. "A form of treasure map, if you will, requiring that future generations not lose anything reproducing it."

"How do we translate that into actual sailing instructions?" Anari asked.

"We cheat and ask an expert, Young Seeker," Suka Kuri grinned. "That is one of the most important lessons you will learn, in becoming an Adept yourself, one of these days."

Anari didn't follow, but she watched Suka Kuri look across the room.

"Sterling, may we borrow you for a moment?" she called to Mr. Huff, the astrogator who was *an expert at stellar cartography*. Yes, of course.

Anari watched the Human blink in surprise, a spoon frozen halfway to his mouth and eyes almost as big as Nasrin's.

"Ma'am?" he managed.

"We have a mapping problem, Sterling," Suka Kuri continued. "Or rather, Anari does and I'm merely consulting. She needs you. Anari, go explain it to Sterling and see what he thinks."

Anari jolted in surprise. She'd spoken with the Human, but not really interacted that much. He'd been almost a youngster when she met him, extremely close to Yanouk in relative age.

Anari felt old standing next to him, but she also understood how smart he was.

Smart enough for Moss School. Or Sabre, since she'd seen him take on pirates.

Sabre School Human. Like Dan, but only a Seeker. Like her.

Anari smiled and packed her stuff up, carrying it over to where Sterling was busy shoveling the remains of his porridge into his mouth, then drinking coffee.

She finished off her muffin as she waited, then smiled at the Sabre School Seeker.

"Here's where I'm at," Anari began.

TWENTY-EIGHT

Sterling wondered if he was nuts. No, he knew he was. How nuts?

He stood before Uly's hatch and rapped.

It opened quickly, with Uly standing there.

Still tall and skinny. Twenty-seven these days, even as Sterling would be twenty soon.

"What can I do for you, Lieutenant?" Uly asked, taking in the stack of books Sterling had under one arm.

"Navigational exercise that might have turned into something big, sir," he replied, falling back on the formality of his *Danumash* midshipman days.

Uly didn't act very military these days, but it was one thing the two of them shared that wasn't all that common. Most of the rest were civilians or pirates, honestly.

Or had been. Before the Corsac Fox.

"Come in," Uly said, stepping back.

Sterling followed him into the front room and set his various books down on the side table.

"Get you anything?" Uly asked.

"Already got enough coffee in me that I might not sleep for three days, sir," Sterling acknowledged with a wry grin.

"What can I do for you, then?" Conductor Fortier asked.

Not the Corsac Fox today. Or even Uly, though it was still hard to call him that.

Conductor Fortier. Captain Fortier, had they stayed on *King Hewitt II* for these adventures.

How far they'd come, literally as well as figuratively.

"I'd like permission to haul us off on new mission, sir," Sterling said. "Something came to my attention and I think it warrants investigation. Somewhat off the track we had intended."

"Okay, Sterling," he said. "What do you have?"

Sterling laid out the plot for him. And explained the almost-impossible set of sailing instructions necessary to get there. Maps. Images. Scans. The works.

"Where did you get this?" Uly asked as he finished.

"A poet, sir," Sterling replied. "Well, two, really. Suka Kuri is having Anari Supasei translate the *Karaŋgılıkka* and she came across it. Suka Kuri asked me to work with Anari to take it back into what Anari thinks was originally written, then had me translate that into sailing instructions, based on an assumption that the original words are thousands of years old at this point. And I don't think anybody will be able to find it after this."

"Oh?" Uly asked. "Why not?"

"The two lighthouses are a pair of superbright blue giants in close proximity, sir," Sterling replied. "Or were when this was composed. One of them has already gone supernova at this point, creating a decent-sized nebular cloud. I took the original starting point and those two stars. There should be a black hole at the third point of a gravitationally-stable triangle, through to the back. I don't know what Zamir saw that he couldn't get to, but I'm willing to bet that it sits down in close to that black hole itself, where you need an impossibly good sailing master to get you in and then out again. I'm also willing to bet that Drew is good enough, though I won't know until we're there."

Uly looked at the notes again, and Sterling relaxed when the man smiled.

"This is where I remind you that we were sailing into the darkness, just as Zamir Aytiev did," Uly said. "I don't have any fixed course we had to follow, save what my cartographer finds interesting."

"Permission to come about, sir?" Sterling asked, feeling his grin grow.

"Absolutely, Lieutenant," Uly grinned. "Let's go see what's out there."

Sterling smiled. Honestly, he should have expected that this would be the easy part, but he could still remember watching Dan and Uly coming aboard *King Hewitt II* and taking command.

And all the light-years they'd crossed.

He could do this.

TWENTY-NINE

Drew matched Sterling's notes with the scan ahead. Measure twice, cut once, though he'd probably tweaked the scanner at least a dozen times in the last hour, just getting to this point.

Still, he was pretty certain they'd made it to the place Sterling's poet had marked.

And not just Anari. Whoever that nameless guy had been. Maybe Aytiev himself, but nobody would likely ever know.

Drew keyed a switch.

"This is Uly."

"I think we're there," Drew replied, responding to all the people who had asked him over the last three days if they were there yet.

Not that they deserved to be teased. Much.

"Let Sterling know," Uly said. "I'll grab the rest and we'll join you in a few minutes."

Drew looked around. Smiling faces looked back at him, though he was in his station instead of Uly's even in command.

Easier, because nobody else was going to fly the ship while he was on the bridge.

Able Spacer Delbert Blakeslee had communications and sensors today. They'd been together even before Uly and Dan came along, though he was about the quietest person Drew knew. Not intimidated by all the newcomers, but didn't have much to say, except when he was on duty. Haydar had taken over as his boss, so Del was often aft in one of the other control spaces, in case something happened.

Like the day *King Hewitt II* had taken a wavebolt through the bridge and killed everybody up front.

Weren't many Humans this far from home. Drew still dreamed of sailing into some quiet, distant Human system somewhere and offering all the kids the ride of a lifetime.

Maybe he'd convince Uly one of these days. Or at least Dan. She knew the places to look.

"Del, anything?" Drew asked.

"Static," Delbert replied. "Blue giants are noisy. Plus all the other crap around here. Nothing artificial that I can isolate from the background noise."

Drew nodded.

He opened a line aft.

"Engineering, Roux."

Another one that had come aboard a broken ship and helped reclaim it.

"We're about to thread the needle, Kolya," Drew told him. "Everything balanced and behaving back there?"

"Everything except Marlowe, but he never behaves," Kolya replied.

Drew laughed and cut the line. All the strangers they had picked up along the way to go with two crews of Humans and a load of slaves.

All one family today.

And about to make history.

He dialed Sterling's cabin.

"Huff."

"We're there, Lieutenant," Drew said with a smile as he cut the line.

Nothing more needed to be said. The kid had taken apart five maps and welded them into something entirely new. The most up-to-date atlas of Imperial Sector Fourteen that Drew figured existed anywhere in the galaxy.

Sterling had laid out the breadcrumbs. All Drew had had to do was follow them, a narrow path in dark woods with a ledge nearby.

Quickly, the bridge filled up. Bodies on all sides. All colors. All shapes.

All friends.

"Sterling, you take command," Drew called, looking back over his shoulder at his friend and occasional sidekick.

Sterling gulped once and nodded.

"I am taking command," he said formally.

Uly and Dan were off to one side. Drew motioned Anari to take the Gunner's station. It would give her the second best view of what was coming.

Drew still had the best spot in the universe.

She looked nervous, but Suka Kuri gave her a little shove that got the big, green woman in motion. She settled and moved the chair well back.

"All hands, this is Sterling Huff," the voice echoed out of the speakers. "We are about to thread the needle in search of buried treasure. I thought that all of you should know. Mr. Roscoe, take us in."

Drew nodded and let his fingers dance. He already knew that he'd achieve flowstate with hardly any effort. The day had been like that from the moment he'd opened his eyes.

To starboard, one baleful blue eye scowling at the universe. Down the port side, an expanding cloud of gases still being driven by the initial explosion that had killed the other lighthouse, about four hundred years ago, according to Sterling's calculations.

Drew brought up the Variable Pulse Spatial Generators and the ship slipped into a ball of deformed gravity, rocketing along the edge of the cloud at FTL speeds like a guy on a surfboard racing the curl.

Single best feeling in the galaxy. Even sex only came close to that high from the perfect wave.

Corsac Fox punched through clouds like a shuttle landing on a planet. Up ahead darkness, but Drew wasn't monitoring any visible frequencies.

He was sailing into darkness, like Aytiev had instructed everyone. Had that guy meant for them to specifically come here, and all those folks had misunderstood the reference? According to Anari and Sterling, the *Karaŋgılıkka* had been written and transmitted without any notes about ever finding the treasure hidden under the black moon.

There.

Black, because no light could escape from it.

Fluorescing some from gases pushed off by a nearby supernova as they got pulled in, leaving it a quiet beacon. A candle on a windowsill.

Not enough to navigate by from any distance, but it marked a place where that third star had been hiding. That Black Moon.

"Target identified," Drew remembered to announce to everyone. "Course corrections plotted and adjusting now."

He'd slowed down some. Mostly because everything had been theoretical until this moment.

"Drew, I'm calculating the event horizon," Sterling replied. "Stand by."

Drew nodded and cut speed back some more.

It was a stellar gravity. A huge dimple in space-time that was dark.

In darkness.

The whole thing had collapsed after exploding in some distant past so long ago that the nebula had faded. Or been eaten by those two supergiants.

Hardly kilometers across the event horizon itself. Zamir Aytiev had seen something down in the harbor, which suggested a stable orbit deep enough to be a risk, but not that the ever-expanding black hole would eat it anytime soon. But black holes measured things in millions and billions of years.

"Okay, here's your orbital distance, Drew," Sterling said after a few minutes. "I've left a margin of error that we can refine as we watch, but you should be safe outside that zone."

Drew took it in, nodded, and programmed his systems to automatically keep the ship well outside that. Variable Pulse Spatial Generators didn't work, close to any gravity source. And this one appeared on all sensors like a star by mass that just happened to occupy a small moon by overall volume. Tiny and intense.

Safer over here.

He brought the ship to rest, relative to that black moon. Turned and let his systems plot the course to hold *Corsac Fox* at this distance, tracking sideways as the black hole moved through space.

Safe.

No second chances here.

"Oh, wow," Del said suddenly. "Mr. Ramezani?"

Drew listened, but didn't take his eyes off his controls, in case things were about to get weird.

"I agree, Delbert," Haydar replied. "Oh, wow."

"What are you two talking about?" Uly asked from somewhere in back.

"I think there's a ship down there, sir," Del said.

Drew blinked and looked up, bringing up a secondary screen on his console to see what Del and Haydar were talking about.

Oh. Wow.

THIRTY

Uly had given them a day to research. Better if they had too much information than not enough. Then he'd pulled all the troublemakers into the biggest conference room on the ship, and it was still almost overflowing, because everyone had some facet of the overall puzzle, though not the whole.

Sterling was standing at one end, pointing at various projections and images as he finished up his explanation.

"At that point, we're in something I might call a geosynchronous orbit above it, at least if you could somehow stand on the event horizon and look up," Sterling said. "Scans hardly work with all the energy and radiation floating around, but we've been able to get a pretty good parallax image to scale it."

"How big?" Uly asked, glancing around at all the rapt faces.

Anari caught his glance and blushed, but grinned.

They were here because of her. She needed to understand that this discovery was her glory, first and foremost, with Sterling stepping in for a share by translating things into motions.

"Not as big as most Devastator-class ships, sir," Sterling replied. "Maybe about the same size as *Storm Crow*, that traveling flagship of the *Vatazhko* of the Ononguli. Bigger than any Striker I know, including the one we killed at Nyri."

Uly nodded and leaned back.

Big, at least compared to what bits and pieces he had picked up from various parts of the *Karaŋgılıkka* that others had shared.

He found himself really looking forward to Anari finishing the first translation, to see what other mysteries might have been buried in there for all this time.

"And Zamir Aytiev wailed and gnashed his teeth when his ship proved unable to easily sail down to visit it," Suka Kuri quoted. "Then his crew revolted when confronted with his madness to go anyway."

She paused and looked around.

"Is this a dumb idea?" she asked.

Everybody turned to Drew. Sterling had gotten them this far. He and Haydar had mapped and scanned every frequency they could.

"Here's the thing," Drew interrupted. "There isn't a second gravity field around here, generating LaGrange points to keep it stable."

Uly suddenly saw that and his mouth fell open. A few others did as well, but most were simply confused.

"Are you suggesting what I think you are, Drew?" Sterling gasped from the end of the table.

"Could someone help a poor old woman out?" Suka Kuri asked before Drew could speak.

"If you have two gravity fields interacting, they generate five stable points," Drew replied. "Where something that gets put down, figuratively speaking, stays until you move it. Any planet and moon. Any star and a gas giant big enough. We don't have a second one here to hold that ship stable over time."

"Meaning?" she asked.

"So what's kept it from either being pulled into the black hole, or being tossed sideways by something else coming close?" Drew replied. "Only thing I can think of is that the ship must be somehow actively maintaining itself in orbit."

Uly nodded. The others caught up with him by the way their mouths fell open.

"For how long?" Haydar asked.

The Mazhin were probably the experts on long-term starship travel, since they tended to live their entire lives on ships, given the choice.

"Story's a couple thousand years old," Sterling noted, looking around. "And the evidence suggests a chain of oral transmission prior to that. Suka Kuri, when did the Yarikh finally end?"

"Nobody knows, Sterling," she said. "I've heard legends and rumors that would suggest some three to six thousand years ago, give or take several centuries and probably towards the longer end. Plus, we don't know if the Yarikh left it."

"We'll assume that until proven otherwise," Uly announced. "Timelines matter less than that the ship seems stable. Is it broadcasting any signals?"

"None we've been able to detect, Uly," Haydar said. "I will also admit that I wasn't looking that hard, either, since I presumed it had to be a derelict, after all this time. I'll review those logs and devise some new filters to see if anything stands out against the background radiation."

Uly nodded. He turned to Anari and smiled.

Her smile was at once triumphant and nervous.

"What else did Zamir tell us?" he asked her.

"That it was a treasure of the gods, Uly," she nodded back. "Some of the things I've gone back and retranslated after knowing this place existed suggest that he was working from some older log books or something, that got him here. At the time, their ships were capable of long voyages, but weren't all that powerful. Maybe halfway between Aibek Sulaymanov's *Moonlight* and a comparable Seeker/Probe built today."

Uly considered his options.

Nobody really understood the Yarikh, except through the lens of the *Karaŋgɪlɪkka*, itself written much later by a people striving to live up to those legends themselves, long after the place itself had faded.

"We have time," he announced. "You folks sit down and figure out if we can somehow get down there and then get back out again later. The folks who put it there had a reason, because they could have just as easily crashed it into the black hole, so presume that they wanted it found. Especially if they left notes that got Zamir Aytiev and us here to see it. Do the math and then figure it out. And we can leave and come back later with better tools if we have to. Am I clear?"

He looked around at hopeful faces, all of them balanced against the possibility that they might have to sail away, just as Zamir had, cursing their luck and their failures.

"Sterling, you and Drew come off duty and handle this until you're satisfied," Uly ordered. "I'll happily pull doubles as a working officer instead of a glorified paper-pusher. Rope in whoever you need, remembering that you have Ononguli, Khet, Emro, Thogin, and others who might all have snippets. We've come this far. Can we do it?"

He rose, and the others automatically did as well. Uly smiled as they started breaking into groups to talk.

He'd let them sort it out.

Then see if the gods really did love them.

THIRTY-ONE

Anari had ended up spending a lot of time with Sterling, helping him understand what Zamir Aytiev had written, because she was sure those were his words composing the *Karaŋgılıkka*.

And she'd come to appreciate just how smart the kid was. Kid. She wasn't much older, but he'd really been a kid, and was only now growing into what he'd be as an adult.

That was even scarier, considering where he was.

"No other clues?" he asked her.

They were in an office he'd taken over, filled with all his notes, all her notes, and everything anybody else had been able to think of that might be useful.

All she needed was a ball of yarn to connect various things stuck to walls to look like one of those silly conspiracy vids.

"I've gone back and retranslated this tale from scratch," she told him. "And the next one, just in case, but he was off rescuing a princess from some warlord in that one. He occasionally laments that he didn't have the weapon of the gods by his side, but that's it."

She watched him nod. They'd spent enough time together that

she could see his exhaustion. It was a young face to have that many lines. Or eyes that bloodshot.

"I still feel like I'm missing something," Sterling muttered.

"Angry dragon in their lair, waiting for fools to awaken it?" she joked.

"YES!" he cried. "That's it."

"What is?"

"Drew thinks that the ship is somehow operational," Sterling replied. "That it must be doing something to remain stable in its orbit of the black moon. That suggests that there is someone aboard. Or something."

"People don't live that long," Anari reminded him.

"No, but systems do," he nodded. "There must be a system running. Tracking things. Making adjustments as gravity and nebular density cause the ship's location to fluctuate. And we won't know until we board it, because nobody knows what language it might respond in."

"I presume Dan is planning on taking the team to board it, if you and Drew can get us close," she reminded him. "Would a shuttle work better?"

"No," he said definitively. "The gravity around here is a little hairy, and it couldn't generate the thrust to escape from that deep."

"Can *Corsac*?" she asked.

"Maybe?" he looked up at her. "Hang on."

Anari watched him dial a number. Heard Drew reply with a couple of choice profanities.

"Roscoe. I was asleep."

"It's Sterling. I need your help calculating how close we can get the *Fox*, in order to direct dock with a soft seal on an airlock. I think Anari has solved the rest for me."

She felt a blush take hold. Mostly, he'd asked questions and she'd reviewed Aytiev's descriptions while trying to put them into useful terms for her favorite stellar cartographer.

She caught his smile, and then Sterling blushed as well, so she didn't feel so bad.

"You in your office?" Drew asked.

"We are."

"Lemme grab some coffee and I'll be there in five."

He cut the line and Anari watched Sterling sag in relief.

"You don't have to do it all today, you know," she told him.

"I want you to be able to walk those decks, Anari," he replied with an utter sincerity that took her breath away. "You found this thing. You got us here."

"*You* got us here," she countered.

"I just took your directions and plotted them on a map," he said.

"Which nobody else could have done," she replied.

He started to say something, then caught himself, smiling crookedly at her.

"Yeah, I guess so," he admitted. "We make a pretty good team."

Anari blinked. Considered it.

They did, as weird as that sounded even in her head. Sabre School Emro. Sabre School Human, except that Suka Kuri had mentioned quietly that she was in the process of creating a Starfare School. Uly would be the first Adept, and Sterling a Seeker.

Like her.

"We do," Anari admitted.

They watched each other awkwardly for a long moment, then the hatch opened and the whirlwind that was Drew Roscoe swirled in.

"What have you got for me?" he asked.

THIRTY-TWO

Uly was surprised at how messy the office was. Normally, Sterling kept everything sharp and military at all times, but there were papers piled on every surface. Notes stuck to maps and images printed on walls, and an overall sense of chaos.

Until you looked closer and noted that everything was in piles that seemed related. Specific.

Sterling had asked him to join them for a breakthrough. Uly had found Dan and brought her along, because she was the other half of his brain.

"From there, Drew thinks that we can sail right down to the ship and link airlocks," Sterling finished explaining. "Commander Chastain and her team will board and confirm that the environment is not hostile, then we can see if it's possible to get the other ship clear."

"And you expect hostility?" Uly asked.

"Something's got to be operating, Uly," Drew spoke up. "Otherwise, that thing can't stay here that long. Nine times in ten, it's already fallen into the event horizon."

Uly nodded. He'd studied enough orbital mechanics to under-stand the math. And the probabilities.

"Will it open fire on us as we close?" he asked the group.

Sterling. Drew. Anari. Dan.

"I have no idea, sir," Sterling replied. "We can be prepared, but I'm not entirely sure how accurate a wavebolt will be in this envi-ronment. Never tried it."

"If nothing else, we'll try firing one in a safe direction after we're done, just to record the results scientifically," Uly nodded. "But we can do it?"

"The math works," Anari said. "I've watched them go over it several times. Zamir Aytiev was sitting someplace close to this, doing that same math, and decided that he didn't have the engines capable of escaping again later. And then he never came back with a better ship. Nor did anyone else."

"What's the margin of error?" Uly asked Drew and Sterling.

"Generators are in good shape," Drew replied. "We'll have everything back to the navigation displacer thrusters ready to go to the redline, but the math says we've got about a twenty percent safety factor over that when we get close. I'm confident."

Uly accepted that. Drew Roscoe was still a small, slender man. Even more so than Uly. But he had a top-notch brain. And didn't let his ego get too big for his hands to fly.

He turned to Dan.

"Boarding a potentially hostile alien ship?" he asked.

"Hogan's Alley," she replied, summing up the semi-automated training simulator she and her team used to practice with weapons in a hostile environment.

Like this might be.

And his job was to send her over, then try not to worry too much that she might not make it back.

All part of the legend of the Corsac Fox.

But he'd come this far. And the people he trusted thought that it could be done.

Thus, the next step.

"Everyone, fantastic job and well done," he nodded to them. "Sterling, you look like you need to sleep for a day. We'll aim for thirty-six hours from now, mid-morning, to make our approach."

The smiles warmed him. It would be exceedingly dangerous.

But they could do it.

THIRTY-THREE

Sterling was on Guns. Drew might be flying with his notes, but the ship over there might suddenly wake up angry, and it would be on Sterling and his teams to protect everyone.

Just like that first time, when they'd stolen *Wren* from the *Auga*, then stumbled into an *Auga* patrol ship.

"All teams, check in on status," he said into the private comm he shared with the various turrets.

Green lights all blinked once, but that was him making sure.

They'd only get one chance at this, and any mistakes might mean that they were trapped in here forever, though Drew had drawn up a couple of contingency plans that got progressively crazier as the risks increased.

For now, Drew had every scanner pointed inward and pinging. Nothing had responded to all the noise prior, but that had been at range.

Now, they would be sailing right up to the beast.

And it was huge. *Storm Crow* was about a match for size. *Corsac Fox* would look like a calf nestled up next to a momma cow when they docked.

"You ready?" Drew asked from beside him.

Sterling nodded.

"All hands, stand by to close," Drew announced, then they both looked back over their inner shoulder.

Uly was in command today. As he should be. This might have been a joint effort, with most of the work coming about because of Anari. All he'd done was translate her words into places on a map for Drew.

One hell of a team.

"Mr. Roscoe, as you bear," Uly said quietly.

All of this was quiet. Careful. Subtle.

Drew pressed a button and *Corsac Fox* started down the slide of the gravity well towards the *Black Sword*. That was what he and Anari had taken to calling it, because Aytiev had considered it to be the greatest weapon he'd never been able to reach.

And under a black moon.

Slowly, they closed, Drew marking off the distances.

"Mr. Roscoe, bring us about," Uly ordered.

Sterling kept the turrets counter-rotating to remain locked on the *Black Sword* as *Corsac Fox* turned on a flat plane, the bow now pointed straight up, relative to the black hole below them.

"What's the status of your engines?" Uly asked.

Drew did something and nodded.

"Maintaining our calculated threshold, even as we close, sir," Drew replied.

Meaning, they could light the afterburners and still make it up and out to safety if they had to.

Not be trapped down here forever.

Had that crew ever escaped? Or had they faced eternity at the bottom of this particular well?

Sterling wasn't sure how long he'd last before something cracked, if he'd been down there with no way to ever escape. Might step out an airlock and throw himself at the event horizon, just because it would be over quickly as you started getting close.

What had they done? Were they still there?

How derelict was that ship?

They'd find out soon.

"Backing on thrusters," Drew announced. "Fifteen minutes to docking maneuvers."

Nothing had responded. Reacted. Twitched.

No turrets were visible. Nothing had suddenly opened up a scanner or firing port.

Just a *Black Sword*, sitting here for all eternity.

Or at least until Anari came along.

He glanced over and shared a quick smile with her. Lots of brains inside all that green muscle. And really cute. Nice, too.

Sterling went back to his gunnery boards with a smile and focused on the job at hand.

Uly was counting on him. They all were.

THIRTY-FOUR

Uly watched *Corsac Fox* move close. Monstrous ship. Hopefully, it could still move. Could be removed from this situation to some-place safe.

It had been important enough to draw no less than Zamir Aytiev to the edge of the cliff, where he'd railed at his failure.

Uly wanted to succeed. didn't every kid joining the navy want to go down in history as a hero?

Somewhere, *Batyr* no doubt had him listed as *Missing, Presumed Lost*. Four years was a long time to not check in.

He supposed that he was technically a deserter at this point as well, since there had been any number of opportunities for him to simply go home. Get home.

Be home.

But he was home. And had all these various people counting on him. Every one of them would want to go with him, and only five would be vaguely welcome, were he to sail into a *Batyr* port and identify himself. The others would be *Danumash* sailors to be locked up and traded home. Or ex-slaves. Or unknown alien species.

No.

If Uly had to remain out here for the rest of his life, that might be for the best for everyone.

Today's heroics merely involved topping anything Zamir Aytiev had done in the one place that fellow had ever failed.

"All hands, maneuvering to dock," Drew announced, finally close enough to show details with the naked eye that had only been blurry before.

The hull was a rainbow vortex of metallic hues rather than standard charcoal gray, like a cake that had been dyed, then swirled. Vahid had made something similar for Uly's most recent birthday, showing off. He would appreciate this image.

And the scale. Huge. *Corsac Fox* was a large, fast, heavy Interceptor. This ship was larger than a Striker, what *Batyr* would have called a Forward Cruiser like *Marshall Castillon* or *Vanguard Lesauvage* that he had once served on. A bit smaller than Devastators or Battleships, but still massively impressive.

Dan had gone aft. The Team had gone with her, including Suka Kuri because they had no idea what languages anything might be written in and the Exemplar was far and away the best linguist on the ship.

Uly grinned that the men had been left behind, including him and Solomon Wyndham, who was Chief of Security these days, in spite of being all of eighteen years old.

He'd finally grown into his size. Big. Strong. Tough. Intelligent. Competent.

Another *Danumash* Midshipman that Uly had originally intended to turn into an officer that their next commander would thank him for.

In the *Karaŋgılıkka*, all the men went off and had their adventures, leaving the women behind to run the households.

And the civilization. Fitting that things were a little reversed today.

"Distance stabilized," Drew called, bringing Uly back to the present. "Airlock corridor extending. Contact. Locking in with magnets, but the connection is a bit squirrelly. Stand by for soft seal. Combat Team, you are cleared to approach the other vessel."

Uly held his breath and concentrated on good thoughts.

Dan and her ladies were about to walk into danger.

And history.

THIRTY-FIVE

Dan had put Ciah on point in her boarding armor, like usual. Shortest, in case the rest needed to shoot around and over her. The corridor was wide enough to provide both overhead and sides for people shooting, and the group had trained extensively on how to do it. Ciah would kneel. Dan would step up and slide to her right to fire. Katya to the left. Nasrin with her Omnibow. Two Emro with the ability to fire high.

Adding Suka Kuri just meant that the elder was at the rear today if trouble broke out.

They walked down the telescoped corridor that was the extended airlock. The colors were a welcome surprise when they got to the other airlock, a thing Haydar had identified from pictures, though nobody could be certain it would work.

Still, everyone had faith that the ship was powered and working. Waiting patiently for someone to come rescue it from the black moon.

The hatch felt perfectly normal, which was itself perfectly weird.

Dan was used to their Ononguli ship, where the decks and

hatches tended to be taller and skinnier than a similar Human vessel. Khet were just the opposite, more short and wide than anything she'd grown up with.

Everyone had a peculiarity to their naval architecture.

Next to the hatch, a box of twelve buttons in a format she recognized, three across and four deep, where Humans counted from the top left and had a pair of function buttons bracketing the zero at the bottom center. Nothing she could read.

And nothing jumped out at them as they got close. They were in vacuum, snugged up against the side of the derelict, which also sheltered them from the black hole on the far side.

Dan studied the buttons. Whoever had built this place had been the size and scale of a Human, so they were on the right at stomach level. Perfectly natural.

Looking closer, she could see a clear screen over them. Protecting the buttons from wear?

"Thoughts?" she asked on the team line, everyone shifted about to see.

"Dan, if I may?" Suka Kuri replied.

She slid to the side so the taller woman could step up, then kneel down so she was at a better level to see.

"Ah," Suka Kuri replied. "There."

She pushed on the clear screen itself and it opened by pivoting out and up on a hinge. Inside, Dan could see a series of letters etched into the hull itself. Or numbers in this case. A code.

It matched the numbers on the buttons.

"Should I?" Suka Kuri asked, looking up.

"Go ahead," Dan said. "Everyone spread out a bit."

She stayed put, but the others moved back and away, in case something happened.

What, she had no idea, but best to be prepared.

Suka Kuri moved deliberately, entering the sequence. 1-5-9-3-7-# if this was a Human keyboard. Easy enough to remember. Someone had put it here forever for someone else to find.

What did it do?

A moment later, the hatch lit up all the way around, save for one bulb that had apparently failed on the bottom right. Then the entire thing slid sideways into the hull, revealing a room beyond.

Dan knew that Uly and others were watching over her shoulder from her helmet cam, so she turned and steadied.

"Uly, we appear to have opened the outer airlock hatch," she said. "Ciah and I will make entry at present, then see if we can get the others cycled in as well."

"Understood," he said. "Be careful."

She nodded, knowing he'd see that.

Her mission. She was in charge until she was back aboard the *Fox*.

What she really wanted out of life.

Ciah had already moved in. Dan followed her. Corridor or airlock, more like the latter. Three meters on the square by six deep. Nothing in here, but there were hooks and clamps about shoulder height down both sides, like she might want to store suits in here.

Ciah moved to the far end and located an identical control system.

"Open it?" she asked.

"Go ahead," Dan answered.

Like before, pressure on the clear plate caused it to open, revealing a code beneath the set of keys. 2-5-8-4-6-# this time, so someone was intelligent about it. Obvious, but different.

The outer hatch slid shut exactly how Dan expected. Lights came on a few moments later, but her external sensors didn't read any atmosphere. Possibly those tanks had bled fully dry by now.

However long that had taken.

"Inner door is opening now," Dan announced to everyone listening. "We have lights coming on. They feel comfortable."

"Comfortable?" Uly asked.

"Like I was back on *Marshall Castillon*, Uly," she said.

"Weird," he replied.

And he was right.

Another room beyond. Felt like the mud room where you stored suits. Lockers and hooks around walls. Same rainbow metal for the walls and ceiling. Deck was a raised grate design like a standard diamond, done in a brown that wouldn't show dirt. Good traction, because there was gravity in here.

Power, like the ship was still alive.

Dan reached down and dialed the magnets in her boots to a lower setting. Not off, just in case, but easier to walk with only a little stickiness. Ciah did the same.

"Nasrin, your turn to cycle the lock, as we're in the chamber beyond," Dan said, gesturing Ciah to keep watch on the only hatch, opposite the airlock.

Right where she'd have put it for efficiency.

Even *Corsac Fox* had been built a little weird that way, but she knew enough Ononguli these days to understand that it felt perfectly normal to them, and a Human ship would have thrown them off instead.

The airlock hatch flashed several times then began to close. Presumably, atmosphere would have revealed an alarm hooting as well.

Like she'd have done it.

Dan waited. A few minutes later, the inner hatch slid open, revealing the rest of her team. Nasrin. Yanouk. Katya. Anari. Yeong-Suk. And Suka Kuri.

The ceilings were high enough for the three Emro women. The hatches would be a closer fit, but more manageable than the *Fox*.

"Uly, we're inside," Dan announced. "No atmosphere, but gravity is working. Feels almost human standard. Lights are mostly working, with about one in twenty failed as I look around. No indications of life or movement. What can you see?"

"Stand by," he said. "No changes on sensors as we approached. No movement from the ship at all. Outwardly, it remains a derelict. What are your next steps?"

"Wide end still feels like Engineering and thrusters," she replied. "Going to head forward and maybe up a bit to see if we can locate the bridge and discover what we might learn."

"Understood," he said. "We'll be monitoring your progress, but your signal isn't even as degraded as it would be aboard *Marshall Castillon*."

Dan nodded.

Every ship was a Faraday cage, insulated on a variety of wavelengths to protect the crew from harmful radiation. That usually included simple radio propagation, but not today. Not this hull.

At the same time, none of her sensors were indicating any dangerous levels of radiation to worry about.

If there was air and heat, she could walk around in her usual uniform.

"Dan, take a look at this," Nasrin called.

Dan followed over to where Nasrin and Ciah had the inner hatch. Same control next to it, but only one button, with a small fisheye lens below it, like you might hold out a hand to be scanned.

None of them would be in whatever databanks still worked, but something was alive around them. Or at least working.

"Try the button," Dan said.

Ciah did. Nasrin had a Firesphere loaded, pointed at the hatch as it opened smoothly.

No monsters emerged.

Ciah leaned out and looked both ways.

"Corridor," she said simply. "Feels like the main port corridor. Nobody visible."

And no atmosphere present. Temperature was a shade above open space, but their suits were designed to protect them in this sort of environment for several days.

"We're about midship from the bow," Dan reminded the Khet woman. "Turn left and start counting steps. Katya, you have the rear behind Yanouk."

That put Nasrin, Anari, and Suka Kuri in the middle, where

the Mazhin woman had her Omnibow and the Exemplar was protected. Anari deserved to be up where she could see what her efforts had yielded.

And it was only going to get better.

They walked deeper into the semi-derelict.

THIRTY-SIX

Nasrin would have liked to have her helmet off. Or at least her louvers open. She was half-blind, stuck inside her boarding armor. Almost as bad as everyone else, save that she could at least listen to their breathing with her tentacles and track their physical and emotional status as they traversed the alien vessel.

The natives were Human-sized. Mazhin were generally skinny like Ononguli. Khet tended to be broader, and shorter. Even the big ones. Emro were Emro.

This corridor was three Humans comfortably walking side-by-side wide. Tall enough for an Emro with some room to spare, but the lights were recessed, so the only time Yanouk and Anari had to duck was at the frame hatches, all of which had worked thus far.

Colors were pretty in here. Someone with an acute visual sense had taken pains to align hull metal into one long mural of abstract art that was incredibly soothing to watch.

Most ships were gray. Even *Corsac Fox* was only a little better, generally done in whole-wall tones of colors that Omid had approved before they were painted on.

This was the metal itself. Nasrin couldn't wait until they had enough atmosphere that she could lean into one of the walls and let her tentacles taste it.

She was willing to bet it tasted as pretty as it looked to her eyes.

A hand on her elbow caused Nasrin to pause.

"Hold here," Nasrin said quietly, looking back to see what Suka Kuri had seen.

The Elder had dropped to one knee, studying the wall intently. They had opened a few hatches along this long corridor, but those had been offices or cabins. Nothing important, save that they'd all been in decent shape.

No organic remains anywhere to be seen. That was good. Probably.

Suka Kuri studied a hatch controller. Nasrin had the center, so she watched while both flanks covered.

"I believe this is a stairwell," the Elder announced. Then pushed the button and revealed that she was right. She stood and Nasrin could hear the smile in her voice. "The language is not all that far removed from Isann. More complex, as if our friends took to using fewer letters and spelling certain words more phonetically."

"Can you read that?" Dan asked.

"I have made a few breakthroughs," Suka Kuri replied. "Translating the *Karaŋgılıkka* has helped. Yanouk and Anari, the words are longer, possibly more descriptive, but still with a similar meaning."

Nasrin nodded. She hadn't bothered learning it, since the book was going to be available soon, but maybe she'd need to learn Yarikh?

Especially if Uly was somehow successful in retrieving this ship from its eternal tomb.

"Dan?" she asked.

Ciah and Dan slipped around and started up the stairs. This felt like the bottom deck, though the way the external hull rounded, there might be one more below them that only ran down the middle, instead of the full width of the ship.

"Dan, how many decks are we ascending?" Ciah asked as they got to the first switchback.

"Three," came the reply. "I'm working on my old ship for scale, and things feel like that. The bow section slopes down some from the shoulders, so the bridge might look forward from the flat hillside of the hull."

Nasrin paused to visualize what Dan had seen. The front was an arrowhead, separated from the middle with something like a neck. And slightly lower, as if shoulders. The bridge as eyes?

Or a type of land lizard that was wider than it was tall. The big, meat-eating predators like Dan had once described an alligator. Tailless in this case, with big engines aft where it flared out again.

They climbed. Things were a bit heavier than she was used to.

"Dan, how close to Human standard gravity is this?" she asked, knowing that Uly kept *Corsac Fox* lighter for all the other species.

"Just about exact," Dan replied. "Two percent heavier than normal for a *Batyr* ship."

Nasrin nodded.

She didn't think Humans had been out in the galaxy that long ago, but nobody really knew. Even Dan and Uly had admitted that the Human homeworld had been lost to history at some point.

Presumably somewhere over in Sector Seventeen.

Right?

Or were they from Fourteen, and all those folks were more colonists that had somehow gotten all the way over there and never encountered the *Auga* or anyone else?

So much they didn't know. And Nasrin had smelled Uly to understand that he didn't , and was occasionally angered that he didn't .

Third deck up, they exited the stairwell, though it kept going up at least two more.

Big ship. Empty as a looted tomb. Quiet.

Nasrin kept a Firesphere loaded and followed Ciah deeper.

THIRTY-SEVEN

Suka Kuri once again blessed whichever gods might listen that she'd been alive in a time to know Uly and Dan. There was simply no other way to handle it, if one ascribed chaos as the only backing feature of Creation.

They were walking on a ship that was a Yarikh relic. Left here by someone so long ago that Zamir Aytiev had followed a trail of clues, given up, and conveyed the *Karaŋgılıkka* to eternity, that someone might return later and succeed.

Of course it would be Uly.

She paid attention to the hull and corridors, noting that Dan considered this to be a close match in dimensions to her original vessel, one *Marshall Castillon* in *Batyr* service. That suggested that the largely unknown Yarikh were similar in size and shape to Humans, themselves a bit of an anomaly that way. Not Khet. Not Mazhin or Ononguli.

"What do you think?" Ciah Dambe asked on the general frequency.

Suka Kuri perked up. They had approached another hatch, but one that felt much heavier, looking closely.

Six meters wide, with a smaller hatch set into it, matching this particular corridor. The first one had been smaller. Dan had mentioned that this one felt like the main spinal corridor, running the length of the vessel once they had ascended to this deck and made their way inward.

"Nasrin, how close are we to the slope of the forward hull?" Dan asked.

"Another fifteen or twenty meters, Dan," the Mazhin woman replied.

Suka Kuri visualized it as Dan had explained. The entire bow section, sloping gently down from the neck like an amphitheater, providing an exceptional view forward. Except that in space, things would normally be so incredibly distant as to largely be nothing more than brighter stars against the background.

But the Isann were sailors. And descendant from sailors, it seemed. Would they want a proper cockpit bridge, from which they could watch the stars as they traveled?

That sounded correct to Suka Kuri.

"This might be the dead end, then," Dan announced. "Everybody stand by. I'm about to open the smaller hatch."

Suka Kuri didn't have anything to do except stand by and enjoy herself, surrounded by Dan's Combat Team, all heavily armed, well trained, and eager.

The hatch opened as the others had, by sliding into the wall as a single unit, revealing a chamber beyond from Suka Kuri's vantage.

"Making entry," Ciah told everyone as she stepped through.

Suka Kuri wasn't last, but only because Katya waited.

Inside, it was a small auditorium. That was the thought that immediately crossed her mind.

The group stood on something of a balcony, with ramps down both sides of a V-shaped room that narrowed as it went forward. Everyone else had split, so Suka Kuri walked up and stood next to Dan looking down.

One station at the center, in front of doors back into the wall beneath her feet. Possibly a toilet and a storage closet. Or a day office like Uly had.

Four stations in a straight line in front of the commander, all facing forward. More stations around the walls of the balcony and inset on little platforms raised from the ramp.

The forward view was utterly stunning. A single window that followed the slope of the hillside, perhaps twenty meters from front to back and more than ten wide at the bottom.

From up here, Suka Kuri could see the entire bow of the vessel laid out like a field of flowers.

It was a pity that this was nothing more than a museum.

At least today.

Looking down, Suka Kuri could see all five of the workstations with lights on. Something was working here.

"It appears to be the bridge," Dan announced unnecessarily, but Suka Kuri presumed that she was talking for Uly's benefit. And everyone else back on *Corsac Fox*.

"Things working?" Uly asked.

"I see consoles operational," Dan replied, even as Suka Kuri moved to take the closer ramp.

She wanted to see things up close.

Some of the side stations were intended for someone to stand at, while others had chairs.

Odd chairs, too. Too wide for Ononguli. Too tall for Khet.

Human-sized? Or at least Yarikh who were a close match physically?

Yes, that fit her sensibilities.

"Suka Kuri is investigating," Dan announced. "Her camera is on channel twenty-nine."

It was? Oh, how delightful. Everyone could follow along, though she supposed that she'd have to watch her language when talking to herself.

didn't need those sailors suddenly discovering that she wasn't a quaint, old woman. They might grow embarrassed at having to learn new profanities.

She suppressed a mad giggle and got down to the commander's level. That was how she saw it. One person overseeing four others, though she wasn't entirely sure what those four would do. Corsac Fox had Drew as a Pilot and Sterling as a Gunner, with the other stations around the outside of an oval space.

But then, it would make perfect sense to the Yarikh, whatever it was. And the *Karaŋgılıkka* would possibly provide clues.

"Anari, I have four stations," Suka Kuri announced, glancing around.

Anari and Dan had joined her below, with the others up on that balcony, presumably on guard against whatever.

"Who would the Isann station here?" Suka Kuri asked, knowing that Anari Supasei had gone the furthest in translation, apparently a natural in ways that had surprised the young woman.

But then, she'd wanted to be Sabre School and the *Auga* had recognized her brains, but not her artistic abilities.

Fools.

"Astrogator, Sensor, Archer, and Speaker, Elder," Anari replied.

Suka Kuri nodded. That made the most sense. Pilot, Sensors, Weapons, and Communications, all where the conductor had them immediately handy and supervising things.

Life support and Engineering could be monitored from here, but they would be handled aft, where their systems were located. Or all over the place, for the actual air blowers that kept people alive.

"And the handedness of the Yarikh?" Suka Kuri asked.

There was a pause. Always good to have your students learn new ways to think. New details that might be important.

"The Isann are primarily left-handed," Anari replied slowly. "Ninety percent, as a rough standard. But the Yarikh were right-handed."

Suka Kuri nodded. She made her way to the right-most station, facing forward.

Without touching anything, she knelt down and studied the controls. Three screens in something of a circle, with a variety of controls and gauges, plus a keyboard far more complicated than anything she'd ever seen. Some two hundred letters, numbers, and perhaps functions.

The screens were all dark, though there were lights that blinked randomly around the outside. Presumably a code that would inform someone of various statuses on the fly, without needing to bring up anything and study it.

Suka Kuri looked up as Dan approached.

"Thoughts?" Dan asked.

"I was about to consider touching this wider bar," Suka Kuri nodded. "On our systems, that's functionally a space bar, and it is an ancient design. Having gone to all this effort, I feel like they wanted someone to find this ship and rescue it, so things should be easier than if it was entirely dead in space."

"I've had that same feeling," Dan replied. "Go ahead. Uly, we're going to try to bring these systems live."

"Understood," Uly said on the line.

Suka Kuri took a deep breath, considering the vast age represented here. A possible Yarikh vessel, so ancient that nobody could even begin to guess.

And she got to do this.

She tapped the bar once. All three screens flickered, then stabilized, showing words, images, and colors.

A little giggle of excitement snuck out, which was better than a profanity, given the probable size of her audience today.

She studied the letters and combinations, comparing them to written Isann. Yes, this was probably Yarikh.

How utterly wonderful.

"Can you read it?" Dan asked.

"Partially," Suka Kuri replied. "Anari and Yanouk have a head start, but we can begin language lessons for folks. I will need to make a complete survey of just this screen before I'm willing to touch anything."

"Ma'am." Sterling Huff was there. "I've captured the image on your screen and can print it out for you here. Can you move to the open square on the bottom right below the keys and touch it with one finger?"

She did, unsure of what she was doing, but trusting Sterling. Anari had mentioned how smart the young man was.

On the central screen, a small cursor blinked, then moved as she shifted.

Oh! Delightful!

"Sterling, are you seeing this?" she asked.

"I am," he replied. "Looks like primary control systems are working. Ship is running reasonably well, but I see a lot of controls indicating standby status, if I'm interpreting this right, which I probably am wrong about."

"No, I agree," Dan said. "Someone left the console unlocked, and set up for the next person who came along to be able to quickly assess status."

Suka Kuri turned enough to look up and back at Dan. She was willing to admit that she had never served in any formal navy, nor had she flown a starship.

The Moss School generally took one's life in different directions.

Look at this silly old woman, for instance.

Suka Kuri wondered if her cheeks would hurt from all the grinning.

"Now what?" she asked Dan.

"Now, we need to look at Engineering," Dan replied. "Uly, I have Anari, but a fully trained engineer would be helpful."

"I'll get someone to the airlock shortly for you to pick up," Uly said.

Suka Kuri rose and studied the room one more time.
Today was turning into a wonderful adventure.

193

THIRTY-EIGHT

Sadeq Akhtar figured this was payback. He'd managed to win the draw twice, back in Engineering, so that Marlowe was the Chief Engineer these days and Kolya his First Assistant.

Second Assistant Engineer didn't have nearly the responsibilities on a daily basis, leaving him a lot more time to tinker in the machine shop.

Marlowe had grinned in that most evil way the man did when Uly had called for an expert to go assist the ladies.

The man might also be a little sore at losing so much money in the most recent poker game, but what fool played cards for money with the Mazhin?

So, he was here. Walking down the airlock corridor towards Katya Zehlennko, the Ononguli who had been about as trained in engineering tasks as Anari. Both had happily transferred to Dan's combat team, not that Sadeq could fault them.

Generators were messy, balky, greasy beasts when they were working correctly. Part of the reason Sadeq spent so much time building gizmos for Roshan and Haydar.

Like the bad old days, when the *Danumash* had been in charge, may the Creator of All piss on their heads with great vigor and an endless bladder.

"We good?" he asked as they got close.

"Dan wants somebody else getting dirty," she laughed.

Sadeq nodded. He'd presumed as much, since she had folks with engineering training. Not experts, granted, but not newbies, either.

And it got him the day off, more or less.

"Following you," he replied.

Ship was in pretty good shape, just eyeballing things. A few dead overhead lights, but way fewer than the supposed age would have predicted.

Not quite as bad as a *Danumash* vessel in service, but Sadeq was willing to admit that he had a low opinion of them on all matters. He'd have said all Humans at one point, but then Uly and Dan came along to rescue them.

Ta-da.

Inside was oppressive. Low ceilings, for as far away as the walls were. Someone had said something about being closer to Human standards, but honestly he'd been soldering and ignoring folks as he worked. And he had the Combat Team handy if it turned out to be dangerous.

Sadeq was happy to bet on them.

Right turn and back. Couple of sliding hatches that felt balky, though there was no atmosphere to transmit the squeaky grinds of a dirty rail. He could still see it. Might jar loose with motion along, if the lubricant had gotten gummy. Or he might figure out who was on report for whatever shenanigans this week and assign them a spray bottle and a checklist.

Second Assistant Engineer still meant that the shit got to roll downhill. Assuming Marlowe wasn't frosty about anything.

Up some stairs and aft. Bigger corridor. Like, huge. Six meters or so across. Four tall. End to end, he was willing to bet, interrupted with all the usual frame bulkheads you built into something like this when you were serious.

Those moved easier, but Dan and the ladies had already been this way, so they might have broken things loose.

Then he was at the big hatch. And smiled.

Somebody wasn't screwing around. Katya led him into an armored airlock that looked good enough to survive the entire aft quarter of the ship exploding, when you vented crap sideways.

Everybody in Engineering would be vaporized, but that was the daily risk when playing with big, powerful toys like that. Rest of the ship ought to survive a detonation aft.

Corsac Fox was built the same way. The smart way.

The warship way.

He'd been on too many civilian boats in his time.

Inner airlock hatch cycled and Sadeq tried not to drool. Managed to get his mouth shut in time.

He might be in love.

Or a good, solid gear lust. Hard to tell them apart some days.

Generators were generators. Only so many ways to build them. The first really important choice in your design aesthetic was building them big, or having a whole bunch of little ones.

The Yarikh had apparently been inspired by a bee hive. Open vault in front of him spanning several decks. A catwalk structure down both sides with four rows of small generators, stacked like eggs in the tray.

Four ENORMOUS engine systems across the back. Like HUGE!

More drool. Acceptable. Marlowe would have demanded it of him, looking at all this.

He followed Katya aft to where the Team was standing in a loose circle in front of a standing console not all that different from the one on *Corsac Fox*, save that it didn't look like it moved up and down for various species on duty.

All Human-sized crew, and all that. More efficient. Less elegant.

Dan turned and sized him up. didn't catch him drooling. Today.

"We have a working theory that the last crew members left everything for whoever next came aboard," she said, gesturing at the screen on the console.

Automatically, Sadeq measured the status of both generator walls and studied things, working his way through the various read-outs visible. Only a handful running, but only six of the batch reported failures sufficient to keep them off-line. Engines were in standby and had all four tested good recently.

"You understand all this?" she asked.

Sadeq paused and realized that he'd stepped right by her to the station, then started running a finger over all the readings without touching anything. *Corsac Fox* had touch-sensitive screens, so you developed the habit early.

"Uh, yeah?" he said, stepping back and licking his lips. "Got four generators out on that side. Two over there."

Good, her mouth had fallen open. Looked like shock instead of lust, but at least he wasn't alone in having that kind of day.

"Can you read the language, Sadeq?" Suka Kuri asked, suddenly looming over him in a way that brought back uncomfortable memories of Mom and a cookie jar.

He turned back and studied it.

"Nope," he decided. "No clue what the words are telling me. I'm reading these sets of symbols and comparing them to the lights blinking on the fronts of the generators themselves when I walked in. Seems reasonably standard."

"Sadeq, we don't even know what species built this ship," she said sternly.

"Well, yeah," he agreed, wishing that he wasn't rubbing his tentacles on the inside of the helmet as he did, but words were such a limited way to communicate. "But I've seen systems like this. Not

Danumash or *Auga*, but others. Only so many ways a visually driven species can do this, you know?"

"No, I didn't," she replied.

He shrugged. Maybe you had to be a little crazy? It certainly helped. He was the wrong person to ask what normal was. Even on *Corsac Fox*.

"How are the engines?" Dan asked in a smaller, quieter voice.

Sadeq turned and studied things. No clue what the letters were, let alone the words, but someone had left the standby, self-test mode active, and it looked to be robust enough to handle things.

Roshan and Haydar would probably have snide things to say, but *nobody* programmed systems to their standards. You only had to get either of them a little wound up and sit back to listen to the ranting about amateur script kittens.

"Uhm," Sadeq muttered.

Hands found the touch pad and he moved a few things around before he caught himself and realized what he'd done. And how.

Automatic.

Heh.

Three screens to work with, instead of the one big one he had on *Corsac Fox,* so he slid panels off to the sides and looked for options as icons.

There.

"That doesn't make any sense at all," he muttered.

"What doesn't?" Anari replied, also looming, but not as scary about it.

He pointed.

"Fuel tanks read ninety percent full," Sadeq said. "How old is this thing?"

"Millennia," Suka Kuri told him.

Sadeq muttered a profanity, then hoped it was quiet enough that he didn't need to get his tentacles washed out with soap for it.

"Even Mazhin ships break down and get scrapped after several centuries," he reminded the galaxy at large.

"Sadeq, that word might mean fuel siphon," Anari said, leaning over and pointing. "They drawing hydrogen off the gases being pulled into the black moon by gravity?"

He shrugged. Felt like the right kind of crazy answer, and nothing else would explain fuel tanks full for the generators and the engines.

Not after this long.

"Maybe," he said. "Engines all report a firing in the recent past, but I can't translate that clock into anything useful to tell you how long ago."

"Four somethings," Dan offered helpfully.

Sadeq turned completely around to look at her. didn't bother closing his mouth. She could deal with drool.

"How?" he stuttered.

"Ten key touchpads on the outer airlock," she nodded.

Right, he'd seen that. Same as on his keyboard in front of him.

"Yeah, four somethings," he agreed, if that symbol meant that you counted the top row of keys from the left. "Months? Years? Decades? No clue here."

"But the engines work?" she asked.

He touched a couple more icons and squinted at the screens that opened. Then he found the schematics folder he was looking for and suddenly had an engine projected as a hologram in the air above the console.

Hands went in and moved things around.

"Stop," Marlowe ordered over the comm line. "Shift back fifteen degrees and pitch up twenty."

Sadeq did, uncertain what the Chief Engineer had seen, but willing to trust the man. Marlowe Michaels only got up in your shit when you were screwing up. If you were paying attention and following the book, he'd sit back and watch like a raptor instead.

"Sonofabitch," Marlowe muttered, so he was the one getting the soap first. "Uly, that's not all that far from the standard *Auga* design that *Wren* uses. Might even use some of the same parts, looking at that feed line array leading into the combustion chamber."

"We could repair it easily?" Uly asked.

Sadeq kept his mouth shut and his hands out of the projection. Big bosses talking politics at this point.

"Piece of cake, Uly," Marlowe said. "If so, the generators might be a fairly standard design as well. All the galaxy trades. And has for a long time. Looks like everybody uses a lot of the same kit, including lost civilizations, apparently."

Sadeq nodded. Then went utterly, stupendously cold.

Marlowe wouldn't, would he? Was he still that pissed about the poker game?

"Sadeq, you've just been promoted to Chief Engineer of the derelict," Marlowe confirmed. "We'll sort out how many crew members I can transfer over, once Dan is confident in the rest of the ship, and you'll be in charge of repairing everything that needs it."

Sonofabitch.

THIRTY-NINE

Uly looked at the empty mug of tea. He already knew that the pot was empty, because he'd emptied it, listening to Dan and Suka Kuri give him an executive summary of what they'd found on the ship.

No crew. No remains. Nothing personal at all, anywhere aboard, though granted they'd only done a random sample of exploration.

Enough that anything they did eventually find would be exotic.

"I need more tea," he announced. "And a walk, because I've been sitting too much."

The two ladies nodded and followed him into the corridor and aft. The ship was abuzz with the news, rumors flying every which way, but only Dan and Suka Kuri had all the pieces at present.

"We could fly it away?" he asked as they sauntered.

"I got that impression, Uly," Suka Kuri replied. "I will need some time to begin rough translations, but both Drew and Sadeq thought that there were sufficient systems operational that the ship could at least be flown to safety."

Uly grunted.

For a moment, he wondered if it was his life's karma to keep stealing alien starships, having barely enough crew to operate them, and then figuring out how to make it all work.

Iron Wasp that was now *Corsac Fox. Wren. Scavenger Angel.* The *Workshop.* The *Watchtower.*

And now Zamir Aytiev's *Black Sword.*

He looked up at Suka Kuri.

"We know they were Yarikh?" he asked.

"We presume," she corrected him carefully. "Reading Isann, I can sound out many of these words and make a good guess on translating. I'll need Yanouk and Anari to really make progress. But yes, it reads like the parent language of Isann."

Uly nodded.

He turned to Dan and smiled.

"So, Commander Chastain, are you ready for your first independent command as a conductor?"

It wasn't often that he could surprise the hell out of her. She was at least as smart as him. And more cunning, a lot of the time.

Got her good this time, though, as she stopped walking entirely, mouth hanging open and eyes like a Mazhin.

"That was rude," Suka Kuri chuckled. "Appropriate, but rude."

"Agreed," he laughed as Dan finally started walking again.

"I'm not ready for that," she started to say, and he cut her off.

"You are," Uly said. "And you'll have Drew and Sadeq. They know what to do. All you have to do is aim them. That's a good portion of my success. Smart people."

"And later?" she asked. "If this works, and we have a Devastator-class ship?"

"Oh, I'll probably transfer my command at that point," he nodded. "Might even promote Sterling to Commander and leave him aboard *Corsac Fox,* so that you can remain as my Chief of Staff and everything else you do."

"Then why not start now?" she asked.

"Because I need you setting the precedent, Dan," he said

soberly. "That you are my right hand in *everything*. The other half that makes what we're doing work, because there's no way in hell I could do this without you beside me. Simple as that, really."

Her mouth fell open again. Hopefully, it wouldn't become a habit.

Uly turned to Suka Kuri to give Dan a moment to recover.

"I think we need to start a formal training program for naval officers," he said to her. "Your Starfare School. I'd like to be one of your first students, with Sterling second and Dan auditing as many classes as she wishes."

He wasn't prepared for her howls of laughter.

"Uly, I expect you to be teaching many of the classes," she said when she finally wound down. "I have a framework and a vocabulary for the Schools. You are the expert on starship command. You and Haydar, though I need to talk to Nasrin about appropriate blackmail to get that man off his ass."

Okay, maybe she was getting even with him for what he'd just done to Dan.

He nodded and closed his mouth. Rather than speak, Uly simply headed aft some more.

Tea. Maybe Vahid would have something sweet to eat.

He needed to reboot his entire day, it seemed.

Over and above rescuing a forgotten starship.

FORTY

Nasrin scowled at Haydar with all of her tentacles, as well as her face.

"Absolutely not," he grumbled, digging metaphorical heels into the deck like a recalcitrant mule.

Dan had used that term. Nasrin had looked it up.

Had an example across the table from her in the office.

"I will play rough," Nasrin told him.

Something got through because his tentacles got indecisive. Askance. Nervous, even.

"And I can get *mean* if I have to," she continued, hammering the point home.

"But why me?" he whined.

Old wet hen whine.

"Because you are all Uly has right now," Nasrin said flatly. "Sterling is frankly amazing, but he's even younger than I am. You remember Young Gentleman Huff. Drew Roscoe is a concert pianist when he flies, but he is a civilian who got hired by Mistress of Sail Hobbs to learn the trade. He has learned, but he doesn't understand squadron operations. I'm not sure the Ononguli could spell *Combined Forces Operation* if you spotted them half the letters, because they're pirates in the bad way. The Khet are merchants. Even the Isann don't know enough. You do."

"That was a long time ago," he offered, trying to deflect her, but Nasrin wasn't having it.

"So?" she snapped. "I seem to remember you telling me on more than one occasion that you had forgotten more about piracy than *Danumash* had ever learned."

His tentacles grumbled at her, but his mouth wisely stayed shut. Anything but an admission would be a lie right now.

"Fine," he huffed at her. "What is she doing?"

"Suka Kuri is creating an academy for advanced starship command," Nasrin said. "A third School equivalent to Moss and Sabre, as the Emro measure these things. Uly will be head instructor. Sterling, while learning, will teach classes on Gunnery operations. Nobody here has as much experience in squadron operations, except maybe Lukyan Chayka, if we were to head back to the Sphere and recruit him."

"That might be a smart choice on your part," he muttered. "On hers. Somebody's. He ran a small argosy before he met us."

"And the other two fled like mad when *Iron Wasp* showed up and started shooting, if you recall," Nasrin said. "But yes, he's on my list. You're first. And having him doesn't let you off the hook. It merely lets you share the load. We'll need someone to program a whole series of training exercises for students to study and fight."

"Program?" he snapped to. "Why didn't you say so?"

"Because you weren't listening, Haydar," Nasrin let her scowl speak volumes. "Too busy being grumbly. I'm half tempted to let Roshan do the programming instead of you, but Suka Kuri asked me to start here."

"Don't you dare," he hissed, but there was nothing behind it.

Well, maybe professional pride, but Nasrin didn't think he understood how big a soft spot he had around his ego when it came to programming computers.

And as long as she didn't take advantage of it too often, he might never figure it out.

She relented visibly and offered him a neutral smile.

"So I can turn Suka Kuri's notes over to you and let you start translating them into something Uly's students can train on?" she asked.

"Absolutely," he nodded, intent on not letting Roshan score any points.

Those two had been competing as genius inventors for as long as she'd known them. And before *Danumash* had added her to the group as a *Social*. They'd obviously expected her to work as a... prostitute, for lack of any better word. Comfort girl, or something.

Fools didn't know anything at all about how the Mazhin thought. Just as well.

Uly *Spoke* for them today.

"Excellent," Nasrin stated, rising. "I'll have her send it over shortly."

She slipped out before he figured out how badly he'd been swindled. She might have paid attention to all the things Piruz did.

That one deserved his nickname as the Used Camel Dealer.

Nasrin made her way forward and rapped on Suka Kuri's hatch. It opened and she entered to find the woman busy translating at her desk.

"Did he fall for it?" she asked with a grin as Nasrin settled on the chair nearby.

"By this time tomorrow, he might even think it was his idea," Nasrin laughed. "Haydar can be a bit vain."

"Geniuses generally are," Suka Kuri nodded. "Uly is really the only one I know who tempers it with true humility. Sterling is well on that path, but he desires to grow up with Uly as the defining father figure. And that will be an excellent choice on his part."

"Have you ever figured out what makes Uly so special?" Nasrin asked, comparing the two in her mind.

"I would have to meet his parents to be sure," Suka Kuri said.

"Uly hardly ever talks about Anselm Fortier or Tamsin Simon. And his sister Winter is young enough that he might have had to watch over her growing up. But I have no doubt that they framed the young man he was when you first met. Dan has done much to help him flower, as has the responsibility that was originally placed on his shoulders. In many ways, he is still in command of *King Hewitt II* and the crew and passengers he found. Uly takes that seriously."

"Why have he and Dan never...?"

She trailed off there, uncertain which verb might be appropriate.

Suka Kuri paused what she was doing and put her pen down, turning to look up.

"I forget how young you are, most of the time," the Elder said, nodding to herself. "Even younger than Yanouk, relative to maturity and overall lifespan for all you are a seasoned combat veteran and adult. But Omid was the only female of your kind before we picked up the group from Ahmadi, wasn't she?"

"She was."

"And none of the newcomers have caught your eye?" Suka Kuri asked.

Nasrin shrugged, using her shoulders too because.

"None of them measure up to..." she began, and faltered.

"To Uly," Suka Kuri said. "I understand. Dan sees that as well. And Human relationships are different. Plus, both of them are extremely special people. Neither wants to risk fracturing that thing they have by possibly forcing it to change."

"Would it?" Nasrin asked, suddenly aware that there were obviously things that the older men around her had intentionally sheltered her from. As had Omid, come to think of it.

"It might," Suka Kuri said. "And Dan is the only Human female for all the males, but she commands all of them like a goddess. Just as Uly might be the head of that pantheon."

Nasrin leaned back and tried to process that, but understood that there were things she wouldn't grasp until she'd taken that fruitful, final step into adulthood.

Except that none of the Mazhin aboard interested her. Some were uncles and cousins she had inherited, and the strangers were only now learning how to make better gumbo that the brown that had been their lives before Uly.

Before Uly.

It didn't make a lot of sense, but that described a great many of the things she'd seen in her short life.

At least she had a family around her to help sort it out.

She nodded to the Elder and rose.

"You'll do fine, Nasrin," Suka Kuri told her.

Nasrin hoped as she exited that the woman was correct.

FORTY-ONE

In the end, he supposed that there were only so many ways to design a control system for an erect biped with two hands and ten fingers.

Drew studied the console. And the list of terms he'd learned, taped just above the keyboard so he could quickly scan it when something new came up.

Everyone assumed that the ship was Yarikh. And ancient. But the *Auga* were equally ancient, and still around. And everyone pretty much used the same designs for things, with most of the differences really in the execution of your construction tools.

Even the pad under his butt felt comfortable, for all it was designed for an alien's bottom.

Dan had said that everything felt Human in scale, and Drew had to agree. *King Hewitt II* was the only Human vessel he'd trained on, having been hired young by Hilda because she'd seen something in him he hadn't even known was there at the time.

Today, he was walking the system, learning what all the screens and buttons did. Where to find various commands and screens by icon.

And a lot of them were what he was already used to from *Corsac Fox*.

"Engineering, this is the bridge," he said, keying the line open. "I'm about to test fire that thruster pod. As a reminder, the plan is to adjust the ship just the slightest amount, so that we can confirm that everything is working and responding to commands."

"Understood, Drew," Sadeq replied. "Got a team ready to cut the fuel line manually if something goes wrong."

Drew nodded. Even one pod couldn't drop them into the event horizon, but it might introduce a flat spin that made recovery a pain in the ass later.

He looked over his shoulder to where Dan was seated in the command station instead of Uly. Felt odd, but also felt natural. And Uly had taken him aside to let him know that Drew should fill in the details as he went, then let her know later so she could learn starship command.

He still remembered her coming aboard *King Hewitt II*. Big and mean. Angry as shit. Ready to chew nails.

Dumbass Thorley Eldridge hadn't been able to keep his mouth shut about the color of her skin, and Uly had kicked his ass right there on the deck. Making the galaxy a better place.

He caught her eye now and nodded.

"Engage thrusters," Dan said.

Simple as that. Let him do the details. Just like Uly would have done it, instead of Captain Winter, who'd had opinions on everything that he expected were more important than mere facts.

Drew nodded and tapped the key on the keyboard once. Watched the feed sensor. Watched the thrust indicator. Watched the relative orientation of the derelict above the event horizon.

One thruster wasn't going to do much to move two docked ships, but that wasn't the point. Suka Kuri had translated things with Anari and Yanouk, but until somebody had actually done the work, it was all theoretical.

"Thruster pod engaged and pushing," he said to everyone

listening. "Fuel lines look good. Developing basic pressure everywhere."

Drew waited a ten-count, marking them by his heartbeat, then tapped the key again.

"Shutting down thruster now," he told Engineering. "Confirm status."

"We're quiet here," Sadeq replied. "Fuel feed looks good, but I'll need to have tentacles into the space to confirm that we didn't jar anything loose. It's standard enough, so I'm not that worried. We ought to be able to roll forward with other tests in a day, unless you're in a hurry?"

Drew looked back at Dan to answer that one.

She shook her head.

"It's been here a long time, Sadeq," she called loud enough for the pickup to hear it. "Won't be going anywhere just yet."

Drew nodded.

A day to check things and review logs, to make sure everyone and everything was working like it was supposed to. Then a round of tests on all the other thrusters, even as every engineer available had been busy inspecting, maintaining, and repairing various systems with spare parts or fabricating new ones.

Then, he could light the big engines, and see if they could rescue this beauty.

FORTY-TWO

Dan was in her new quarters. She'd moved enough clothes and personal gear over to live here, but had only taken the First Officer's space, according to translations of the ship's map.

Uly would have the commander's actual space when he transferred over, and she didn't feel like moving twice. Wouldn't have even moved once, but he had insisted.

And he'd been right. Worse, her Team had sided with him over her.

Commander Sheridan Chastain, Commanding Officer of this vessel. Whatever name it had.

She supposed that Uly would ask her to name it. Might even be saving that surprise for her for later, after they ran it through all the tests they could.

Ready to sail it again.

A hand rapped her hatch. Dan put down the latest reports and rose to open it.

Suka Kuri stood there, grinning even worse than usual. She had Anari with her, somewhat apprehensive.

Dan stepped to one side and gestured both women in. She

returned to the table where she'd been working and got them seated on a couch that could just barely hold both sets of shoulders and hips.

"There's news," Suka Kuri began.

Dan already didn't like it, just from the way the woman was smiling. She looked at Anari and got a nod.

"Anari was translating records and looking for various things," Suka Kuri continued. "We've gotten a solid start on the engineering and technical aspects of the ship. And how much like *Auga* technology it is, but I'm told that physics is physics and there are only so many ways to solve certain problems."

Dan nodded. Even *Batyr* used this same technology, but it had been acquired at least fifth-hand.

"I asked her to go spelunking," Suka Kuri said, nodding to Anari. "And she found the most delightful thing."

And the woman stopped talking there. Dan waited, then turned to Anari.

"I found the original conductor's logs, sir," Anari said, getting formal like she did when she was nervous.

Must be good.

"Most of the stuff was technical," Anari continued. "Sailing here in argosy with a smaller vessel. Plotting the orbit and standards necessary to remain functionally forever. Or at least as long as the ship continued to work, with most of the systems shut down or in maintenance mode."

Dan nodded to prompt her, unwilling to derail *whatever* until Anari got past her introduction.

"I found the conductor's personal logs, too," Anari said. "And her video logs she kept. Not just written or oral."

Dan perked up. Visual meant that they could confirm if this was the Yarikh. Or somebody else, since nobody was really certain what the Yarikh had looked like.

Anari pulled out a small tablet. Well, standard sized. It just looked small in Anari's hands.

She activated it and turned it around.

Dan's breath caught with a hard gasp. She looked at Anari and got a nod. Same from Suka Kuri.

"She's beautiful," Dan whispered.

"She could be your cousin, Dan," Suka Kuri pointed out.

Dan nodded.

Same broad, flat face with eyes that came to points on the outer edges. Same flat nose. Same curly hair, though this woman's was white on the sides and only black on top. Longer than Dan ever kept hers, too.

Dark eyes that conveyed intelligence and humor. Full lips. Age in the lines, but firmness and conviction. That rich depth of brown in the skin.

"Is she Human?" Dan asked quietly.

"I don't think so," Suka Kuri replied. "At the same time, you've said that nobody knows where the original Human homeworld is. The bones in her face are ever so slightly off, but that could still be within normal biology for Humans. She is speaking and writing in the language that we have taken to calling Yarikh, so that's the culture. The parent of the Isann and whoever else. But yes, she looks Human. At least, the shade of Human you represent, understanding that Humans had a wider range of skin tone and hair color than just about any other species I've encountered or heard about in my time."

Anari handed her the tablet and Dan took a moment to study the woman.

An aunt, perhaps. Left her home on Aurtan a generation before Dan had, and drifted all the way across the galaxy somehow. Except that she'd presumably been dead for thousands of years.

"Are there other crew records?" Dan asked.

Anari nodded and smiled.

"I went looking before I talked to Suka Kuri," she replied. "All of them fall into a fairly narrow range visually, both female as well as male."

Dan nodded. Contemplated what that meant.

Were the Yarikh Human? Or did this represent another aspect of the convergent evolution that had shaped so many erect bipeds in a similar manner? Number of fingers and toes varied. Size varied. But tool-use imposed certain tendencies.

And the Yarikh just might be her ancestors somehow.

"I thought that you should know immediately," Suka Kuri said, rising now. "I've tasked Anari with translating her more recent logs both for the technical information, as well as to understand who she was as a person."

"What was her name?" Dan asked.

"Selene Praxis," Anari replied. "Her first name meant something like Moon and her last name was another word for beauty, as near as I can tell right now."

"Selene Praxis," Dan echoed. "Good to know. Thank you."

"And with that, we'll leave you," Suka Kuri replied.

Dan saw both women out, then studied the image of Conductor Praxis. Captain Praxis, perhaps.

She wore dark clothing. Not black but maybe a close gray, trimmed at the seams and around the placard in a dark blue. Gold or brass icon on both sides of her turtleneck collar presumably indicating rank, but Dan had no idea what they might be.

The woman spoke to her on a level Dan found oddly comforting. Perhaps because they might be cousins, however far removed. Certainly, not Isann, with their silver skin and straight hair.

Anari had translated some of the personal logs, when Dan spent a few minutes poking. Listening to her speak while reading a translation. Mundane things that Selene hadn't added to the official log. Memories. Tidbits. Details of a life long since ended and forgotten, save that her ship had been found.

Might be rescued, if Drew was correct in his assumptions.

She considered naming the ship *Yarikh*, after the civilization and the people but decided against that. It might confuse people.

Instead, she considered her own history. Her tribe, back on

Aurtan, as it were. What they'd been through, being so different from the folks that generally made up *Batyr*, where they tended to look more like Uly than anything. *Danumash* were pale, with lighter hair, like Kolya.

Only Dan looked like this.

And her people had legends from the primitive days. Or the lost past.

Could Selene Praxis be an ancestor in blood, and not just spirit?

She would honor the woman.

Dan moved to the comm and opened a private line.

"This is Uly."

His face appeared on the screen, breaking into a smile when he saw her. It warmed her soul.

Dan held up the tablet for him to see.

"Who's she?" he asked.

"The last conductor of this vessel before me," Dan said. "Anari and Suka Kuri think that this is what the Yarikh looked like. Look like, if we find any today."

"She's almost as beautiful as you," he said.

Dan blushed.

"I'd like to name the ship in her honor," Dan said. "Her people, and mine, because they might be one and the same."

"You are in command, Dan," he said firmly. "That is your decision. What will it be?"

Just like that. Every day, in every little thing, he reminded her of how different he was from every other *Batyr* officer she'd known. He saw her dark brown skin and nodded, instead of assuming she was lesser. Dumber.

Inferior.

"*Nubia*," Dan replied. "That was the name of a tribe that supposedly migrated from somewhere in the distant past, and turned into my people today."

"Beautiful," he nodded. "Congratulations, Commander Chastain, Conductor of *Nubia*."

It hit her like a punch in the gut, but Dan didn't let any of it into her eyes.

Conductor, because Uly trusted her. Believed in her, even on days she might not.

Dan could do anything, as long as Uly believed in her.

"Thank you," she said.

"No, Dan," he replied. "Thank you."

He cut the line and she nodded, needing time to process her new responsibilities. Her new role.

Her new life.

FORTY-THREE

Dan sat in the command chair and considered the folks in front of her.

Drew flying, because he wasn't about to let anyone else do it. Similarly, Haydar had taken the role of both Sensor and Speaker, handling all of the scanner suite and communications to *Corsac Fox*. Yuriy Kovalchuk and Tyberiy Petrenko handling various engineering and life support duties.

Not that there was much crew aboard. A team in engineering, monitoring things and available for repair on the fly. Everyone else was aboard *Corsac Fox*, itself backed off a safe distance while they waited to see if *Nubia* could be rescued.

"Drew, what's the status on engines?" she asked, knowing that she'd asked him several times, but he nodded as if he understood that to be her nervous tic in command.

"Everything green, Commander," he said without looking back.

Whether or not he was rolling his eyes while facing forward, Dan didn't care.

Her first independent starship command. She'd led assaults. Captured stations.

Never sat here in the big chair and issued those orders herself.

However, Uly and Suka Kuri had both insisted. And they were probably right.

Dan went down the checklist in her head and nodded. She opened the intercom to talk to empty chambers and any ghosts that might have remained behind hidden when the Humans boarded.

"All hands, stand by for maneuvering as we break free of the black moon's gravity hold," she announced. "Mr. Roscoe, all ahead."

She didn't say how much. Drew knew what he was doing better than she did. And could have taken command and done this himself, same as Sterling could have.

Uly wanted a precedent to remind everyone that she was his *Second-in-Command*.

"Engines coming up to pressure," Drew called calmly, like he'd done this a million times before.

Dan listened for any sounds indicating a change. A groan. A thump.

Anything.

Nubia continued to purr as life support put out clean air.

Even those settings had been remarkably close to *Batyr* standard. Dan really wanted to find the Yarikh homeworld—or their final resting place—to see how alike the two were.

"Engines one and four stable," Drew continued, following the process he and others had laid out for this. "Two and three coming up now. All stable at one-quarter power."

"Movement is subtle but detectable," Haydar said. "We are lifting to a higher orbit, but have not achieved escape velocity."

That magic number. According to what they'd said, it wasn't a stable number, but would slowly grow over time as the black hole absorbed more mass and theoretically got more powerful, even though the actual event horizon wouldn't change.

Supposedly. Even Roshan admitted that the math got tangled as only a Mazhin's tentacles could truly manage.

Dan just needed *enough* today. *Nubia* needed to be free.

"Engine three is showing signs of overheating," Yuriy called. "Engineering, what's happening back there?"

"Stand by," Sadeq replied. "Coolant issues. We're going to try something."

No, that didn't sound ominous at all, but she trusted Sadeq. Just as she'd had to step up and take command, he'd had to become the formal Chief Engineer, a role he hadn't played since early on with *Corsac Fox*.

"Bringing engines one and four up," Drew replied. "Fifty percent thrust achieved. Two and three remain lower. Haydar?"

"Better," Haydar replied. "We're walking away slowly, but it will take a while to get anywhere at this speed."

And they might run out of fuel for now. Or insert into a higher orbit and have to try something else.

There was so much Dan didn't know about this business. Occasionally, she wondered if she should join the Starfare School, but that was a lower priority. She had to invent a new form of government for the Corsac Fox and all of his followers first. One that would outlive them by perhaps as long as the Yarikh had survived.

Long enough to thwart the *Auga*.

"Bridge, this is Sadeq, try the middle two."

Dan watched Drew's hands move over the keys like a pianist, tapping and typing with the same ease that he flew *Corsac Fox*. Practice, both on this vessel as well as a lifetime on the other ships.

"Two and three coming up to fifty percent now," Drew said. "Sensors, what's the deflection?"

"We are drifting a shade to starboard, Drew," Haydar replied. "Beginning to slowly accelerate up and away."

"Commander, permission to push?" Drew asked, looking back at her.

It took Dan a moment. They were making progress. Would eventually get fully clear, though it might take hours or even days.

Drew wanted to try something.

"Go ahead," she said.

That had been Uly's best lesson. Let the experts define the parameters, then pull back on the chain when you needed to. Otherwise, let them run.

Drew nodded. She caught the edge of a mad smile as he turned back to the forward porthole and started typing.

"Engines coming up to seventy-five percent," he called. "Eighty. Eight-five. Ninety. Engineering, how's she holding?"

"Couple of vibrations," Sadeq replied. "Things we'll need to tighten down later, but coolant and fuel flows remain stable. Number three had a coolant valve stuck partially closed. We thumped it open and it's flowing now."

"Coming up to ninety-five," Drew continued. "Engineering, stand by for a push to redline. I want to see how things hold and now is a good time to do it."

"Watching my boards, Drew," Sadeq replied. "Everything good enough for your concerns. I've got a list of things to adjust and replace later."

Dan nodded. Experts experting. Things holding. Things powered up more fully than they probably had since Selene Praxis had sat in this chair.

Had she thought these same thoughts?

That brought Dan clarity. And resolve.

"Haydar, how soon until escape velocity?" she asked.

Dan liked that little flinch of surprise in his tentacles. Like he'd been expecting her to simply remain quiet and possibly passive while they worked.

No.

Commander Chastain.

Conductor, *Nubia*.

Hers.

"About eight minutes at current acceleration, sir," he replied after a moment. "Conductor Praxis put the ship relatively deep. Safer there, but it will take some time to extract us. And this is why Zamir Aytiev failed. His ships were closer to Isann standard today, in spite of the gap. Or maybe they've only just gotten back up to that level."

"Correct, Mr. Ramezani," Dan said. "They fell, just like the Yarikh did before them. Zamir Aytiev was on the way down, not the way up."

He nodded and concentrated on his boards, but she saw a couple of tentacles pointed back towards her now. Maybe permanently.

Dan smiled and turned to watch Drew work.

They would be free. It would take patience, but Dan was composed of the kinds of granite necessary.

Just like Selene Praxis had been.

FORTY-FOUR
CHAPTER

Uly smiled as he approached that line in the deck where the floor changed colors. Textures. Vessels.

Civilizations.

Dan stood on the far side of it, smiling back.

"Permission to come aboard, Conductor?" he asked brightly.

"Permission granted," she grinned.

Uly stepped across the line and aboard the starship *Nubia*.

Dan looked exhausted up close.

"You doing okay?" he asked.

She shrugged.

He wanted to simply grab her into a hug. It looked like she needed it. Instead, he held out a hand that she took. He gave it a squeeze.

She smiled.

He understood that stress. She was learning how heavy command really was.

"So, show me your ship," he said, watching her face race through almost the complete catalog of emotions before she finally settled on a tight smile that slowly relaxed.

And she didn't let go of his hand, so Uly let himself be drawn along by her side, walking closer than normal.

Partners.

Corsac Fox had had a full crew when they'd arrived. Smaller than when it had been *Iron Wasp*, but that was Dan only wanting one hundred and fifty troopers instead of the four hundred or so that Adrian Sobol had routinely carried for his pirate raids.

The corridors weren't filled with people, but Uly saw folks moving around.

Omid had put her foot down and taken charge of what cleaning was initially necessary over here. Probably wouldn't need to paint these walls, as colorful as things already were, but that would be Dan's responsibility.

At least for now.

They emerged in Engineering. Uly understood a lot of the equipment at first glance. Reasonably standard, at least by how this galaxy worked.

Only so many ways to build a generator or engines.

"Sadeq, how are we doing?" Dan asked as they got close to a cluster of folks covered in dirt and grease.

"Rebuilding most of the coolant lines to engine three, now that we're a safe distance off," the Mazhin replied. "Don't like the way it heated up or cooled down compared to the rest, so better safe, when I've got the time. How much time do I have?"

"How much do you need?" she asked, rather than turning to Uly.

Her ship. Her decisions.

"Two days if you are in a hurry," Sadeq said. "Four if you aren't."

"We going anywhere?" Dan did turn to ask him now.

"Not that I'm aware of," Uly replied with a nod.

"Take your time, Sadeq," Dan ordered. "I'd rather it be right the first time."

He nodded and turned back to his group. Uly let Dan lead him around them and through the vast space, then up and forward.

The ship felt empty without a full crew, but Uly suspected that it might need at least a thousand people to begin to fill it properly. He'd have to do more recruiting when he got back. Or when he got to Isann.

Those folks would probably jump at the chance to sail into darkness on the ship Zamir Aytiev hadn't been able to save. That would call to them at a deep, cultural level.

The bridge looked better in person than it had on the camera. A fully functional life support system rendered the colors softer. Warmer. And things really did feel like they fit Humans.

Sterling was working with Bello Temitope and Tyberiy Petrenko when they arrived. The young man stood and nodded.

"What is the armaments status, Mr. Huff?" Dan asked, sounding just like a *Batyr* officer when she did.

As she should.

"We classed the ship as a Fast Devastator when we first spotted it, sir," Sterling replied. "Somewhere bigger than a Heavy Striker, but smaller than a full Devastator. Maybe a Battlecruiser back home."

"And?"

"And that's a generally safe bet, with a few clarifications," Sterling said. "For instance, looks like we've got the speed of a Striker, yes. And the firepower of a Devastator, but it appears that we might also have the durability of the big ships as well. I've been working with folks to test the hull alloy and it's something new. Tougher than what the *Auga* or Ononguli use. Hopefully, we've got the formula somewhere to fabricate more of it, so that we don't end up having to make weaker patches."

"As durable as a Devastator?" Uly asked.

"Aye, sir," Sterling said. "Battleship and possibly tougher, in spite of the size. Maybe better, because packed tighter, like a cruiser."

"What are the guns?" Dan asked.

Sterling's face scrunched a little sideways.

"They didn't use a standard we recognize," he finally replied. "Three turrets of what measure out to about fourteen and a half decimeters. Triples in each turret, with six tubes forward and three aft. Plus a bunch of what are close enough to 6dm and 2dm that feel like defensive batteries."

"Fourteens?" Uly pressed.

"Technically, you could round them up to fifteens, sir," Sterling replied sheepishly. "Fourteen point seven and a little change."

"Wow," Uly said, then turned to Dan. She was lost. "You didn't follow that, did you?"

"Nope."

"*Batyr* battleships mount twelves," Uly said. "Most of the ships that size that I'm aware of do the same. As do stations. Fourteens theoretically have a greater offensive range, if you wanted to stand off and bombard someone from outside the range that they could shoot back."

"So more dangerous," she said with a nod.

"I'm not entirely sure if anybody builds anything comparable," Uly nodded.

"*Auga* Star Controllers, sir," Sterling interjected.

"Not a class I'm that familiar with," Uly admitted.

But he trusted his Gunner to have done the research.

"They look kind of like a horseshoe crab from above," Sterling nodded. "Rounded bow, flat vertically, broad through the shoulders then tapering to the waist. And they mount something roughly comparable to a fourteen. Not many of them, from what I've been able to research. Maybe one per Imperial Sector as something of a flagship. Enormous, but they are also transporting significant numbers of ground troops and smaller craft designed to let them exercise complete authority in orbital space, wherever they go. Something like our Heavy Carriers back home, with the addition of a couple of battleships for firepower and about ten thousand ground troops."

Uly whistled. Sounded like something as wide as *Nubia* was long. Enormous. Monstrous.

He'd have to be sure to stay well away from such a beast in the future. Even as dangerous as *Nubia* might be.

"Good work, Sterling," Uly said. "Remember that you have officially moved up to First Officer aboard the *Fox*, so don't spend all your time over here playing."

He liked the blush that filled Sterling's face. Nineteen and enthusiastic.

And coming along as an officer, but he needed to get into the habit of handling all the paperwork on a daily basis, because that was frequently what the job entailed. Filter out things that could be handled by the Lieutenants and just needed review. Identify those things that he could handle. Escalate the key things to Uly.

"Will do, sir," Sterling said.

Uly still had Dan's hand, so he pulled her aft to her new office and installed her behind the desk while he sat up front.

And the chairs were more comfortable than his on the *Fox*. He'd never appreciated how little things like that could add up.

"You're scowling," she pointed out after a second.

"I need to hire someone to make new chairs," Uly said. "Or find a way to steal some of these and take them home with me, because the one I have isn't as comfortable."

"I noticed that," she agreed. "Everything on this ship feels like it was designed for me. For us."

"Any luck on identifying if they really were Humans, that long ago?" he asked.

"None, but Anari is almost conversational in the language now, and digging deep," Dan nodded. "I'm getting there."

"Are you?" Uly perked up.

"All Selene's video and audio logs," she answered. "Also transcribed, and now slowly being translated. Makes good practice."

Uly grinned.

"What?" she teased.

"Yet another way to draw the Isann into our orbit," he told her. "Over and above having this ship. Being able to read and speak the ancient tongue. That's imprinted deep on their culture. And their psyche."

"We still planning to sail it back to Isann first?" Dan asked.

"We'll need to resupply," Uly explained. "And I honestly think that they should be given the first chance to volunteer, since we'll be needing more crew for both ships."

"How big will Uly's nation-state be?" she asked.

"How big should it be?" he countered. "Already, we have places like Lacium and *Taeli Station*, however remote. They aren't formal members, but perhaps part of a larger trade network that just grew significantly to the northwest."

"On paper, you might claim the entire Spinward Reaches, oh dread warlord," she laughed.

He laughed with her.

"And we've just doubled the size of our fleet," he reminded her. "No easy way to protect all that. Or enforce my will. That's why I need friends. Allies. Trade partners."

"Isann will join," she nodded. "Especially now, when they look at this vessel and reread that chapter of the *Karaŋgılıkka*. We'll find ways to bring others along."

"And Bastion will need people," he agreed. "More people. Folks from all corners of the galaxy, eventually. Hell, even *Auga*, if they promise to behave."

"Because the Empire is coming eventually," she said.

"Yes."

Uly could build any number of things. Governments. Networks. Even warships.

But the *Auga Empire* was coming for them eventually.

They planned to consume the entire galaxy at some point into a single polity.

And it might not even be that bad, except that only *Auga* were allowed to rule. All of the elites were *Auga*. And only *Auga*.

It was *Danumash* times a thousand, without even the chance of marrying your children into the upper class.

"What does this ship do to change the balance of power with the Horde?" she asked.

Uly considered.

"On the surface, not much," he replied. "It's probably a good match for *Storm Crow* or any of Anna's biggest vessels, but it's still one ship. Politically, it becomes a symbol of the Spinward Reaches and all the folks that have been ignored or overlooked, back here in this corner."

"What's beyond it?" she asked.

It took him a moment to process that.

Uly was used to thinking of things east and southwest of him, seen on a map. The Ononguli Sphere and Khet space. All the smaller regions between them, slowly building up their Silk Roads as trade got safer between two anchors.

More Spinward and more Coreward?

"I have no idea," he finally admitted. "Presumably, the descendants of the Yarikh, somewhere. And maybe more people. When we get a little more stabilized at Bastion, remind me to charter a couple of Probes to head that direction with maps assembled by Sterling."

She nodded. Then keyed the comm.

"Bridge. Huff."

"Sterling, this is Dan," she said. "When you get back to *Corsac Fox*, I want you to initiate a long-term project, possibly with Anari."

"Sir?"

"I want you to pull in all of the maps we have currently, then add everything from *Nubia*'s records that you can find," Dan described. "Target is the world where the Yarikh retreated to after they left the ship here, but I also want to know what's beyond the Spinward Reaches if we kept going."

"Beyond the…" he mused, voice trailing off. Then it came back enthusiastic. "Aye, sir. I'll get right on it."

"After your other duties are done, Mr. Huff," she reminded him and Uly nearly laughed out loud.

"Aye, sir," he said sheepishly.

She cut the line and Uly loved that dazzle of excitement he saw in her eyes.

"You need the entire galaxy on your side, Uly," she reminded him.

And he did.

NUBIA

FORTY-FIVE

Sterling was still getting used to his promotion. To being First Officer of the *Corsac Fox* itself, with Commander Chastain taking *Nubia* for the time being.

Deep in his heart, he knew that Uly would transfer over at some point, and most likely Lieutenant Huff would become Commander Huff, Conductor of *Corsac Fox*.

That thought thrilled him only slightly more than it terrified him.

Mapping things in his spare time kept him sane. Mostly.

He looked up in surprise as Anari entered his office, sliding into the chair across from him with a grin.

That smile alone took at least half the weight off his shoulders.

"Whatchadoin'?" she asked simply, gesturing to the screen he'd been working on.

"Data," he said. "Maps, using at least five different reference points, separated by several thousand years in their source points. Kinda a mess."

She nodded.

"Hit save and come with me," she told him in no uncertain terms.

Sterling made a sound that was kinda like *huh?* but did as she said. Wasn't like he'd made much progress in the last…

Crap, he'd been at this for three hours?

"Good," she said, reaching across the table and pulling him to his feet, then drawing him after her to the hatch. "Come with me."

He did.

They headed aft.

Sterling smelled the muffins before he even got to the wardroom, and found that his stomach was rumbling loudly in anticipation. Or hunger.

Late in his personal day. He should have been in bed at least an hour ago.

He started to speak and got shushed, so Sterling followed along as she moved to a table and sat.

Vahid appeared with two muffins on a tray, still steaming slightly, and a trough of butter. Near-butter. Close enough in taste and texture. Pink was just a bonus.

Tea also got delivered. Hot and freshly steeped.

"Eat," Anari instructed him, so Sterling obeyed.

Fresh muffins from Vahid. Only a fool or a dedicated carnivore turned those down.

It vanished too quickly, even as she laughed and ate hers more delicately. Tea washed it all down. Hopefully decaffeinated.

"Better?" she asked.

"Better," he agreed. "I might have gotten a little too wound in on myself."

"Agreed," she grinned. "You've doubled your workload as if you won't burn yourself out doing it. Suka Kuri puts extremely sharp limits on how many hours per day I can spend on each of my tasks, from translation to close combat training. You need something similar."

Sterling opened his mouth to say something and a big, green finger touched his lips.

Silence sounded good.

"We'll get there," she reminded him. "The ship has been waiting for a long time. Everyone else has been waiting for a long time. Even Uly doesn't need to do it all today."

"But I'm so close!" he moaned through gritted teeth.

"To?" she asked, watching him.

Sterling sipped some tea and let the warmth start melting the knot that he hadn't realized sat between his shoulder blades.

"Finding the Yarikh," he said. "With your notes, I have it down to a handful of stars, deep spinward from here and a little closer to the core. At the same time, those aren't the Yarikh homeworld."

"How can you be so sure?" she asked.

"Because I have references to places much closer to the rim," he said. "And so much more detailed that mere astronomical records. Like they came from there."

"Where?" she asked, suddenly leaning forward in quiet excitement.

"Deep into Imperial Sector Forty-One," he told her. "Most of the sector away from Z'Gosza, beyond a pretty deep rift. Lots and lots of stars with a tremendous amount of data, the kind that you only get from needing to navigate them."

"Maybe you can convince Uly to send you exploring them, sometime," she offered.

Sterling let himself fall into that sort of daydream for a moment. He was good as a Gunner, but that was *Danumash* demanding that all young officer candidates master those things if they wished to ever get their commission.

That, and Uly had needed him to step up and handle it. Time and again.

But to take a ship and sail into darkness?

His own, personal *Karaŋgılıkka*?

Sterling might give his left arm for that.

She was smiling at him when he came back to himself. Sterling forgot how cute she was sometimes. Not now.

"I'd like that," he said simply. "Would you come?"

She started to say something herself, then paused and blinked. Sterling realized what he'd said to her and blushed himself.

He started to stammer an apology when her hand came out and stopped him. Fell onto his hand and he gripped it.

"Yes," she said simply. "I would."

Sterling smiled and nodded.

Maybe that darkness wouldn't be as deep.

FORTY-SIX

Dan had the afternoon off to burn some energy, so she'd gone to the training floor to work out.

She had just enough crew to sail the mighty ship, as long as nothing happened. The engines and Variable Pulse Spatial Generators were in good enough shape to keep up with *Corsac Fox*. They'd be faster once they got the ship back to *Bastion Watchtower* and had a chance to pull a full overhaul.

She found herself looking forward to that for a variety of reasons, not the least of which was that Uly would transfer his flag over after Isann and she could go back to her real job.

Dan wasn't about to say she hadn't enjoyed command, but starships weren't her strength. She was better in close.

Sabre School, rather than Starfare. And, she supposed, a mid-ranking Adept at it, but she also had decades in front of her to keep practicing. Keep learning.

Getting better.

Suka Kuri even reminded her occasionally that she might make Exemplar someday. Certainly the first Human to ever achieve it.

One of the few aliens, because the Schools tended to be Emro things most of the time.

Except when the species lines blurred.

Primary class had ended, and most of the students had gone back their usual chores. All of the Combat Team was aboard *Nubia* with her, plus Suka Kuri, because that put the three Emro translators here where they could make the most progress.

The black belts had all left, save Anari, but she'd needed the time to simply work through movements, so the two of them were at opposite ends, Anari working on variants of Sunflower Fist while Dan tested elements of Terrible Gaff to see how they could be used against Ononguli. Not that she expected to fight one in hand-to-hand, but those gill strikes could be adapted to grapple a horn and twist it pretty easily.

Dan finished and moved to watch Anari.

Anari's form was off today. It happened. Dan's wasn't much better, but it was exhaustion in her case.

"You seem distracted," Dan pointed out.

Anari sighed and came to rest. Nodded.

"Something you want to talk about?" Dan pressed.

All of them were a team. This woman had helped her storm two different stations and capture them, Human audacity coupled with Emro size and skill.

Anari sighed again. Came to rest and turned to Dan.

"Sabre School has its limits," Anari said with all the gravity that only a young adult can manage.

Not that Dan was much older, but she was a lot closer to middle age than the others on her team.

"Oh?"

"The combat forms bring me relaxation and comfort," Anari nodded. "They do not bring solace today."

"What would?" Dan asked her, falling into the role of Adept to a Seeker.

Elder to Student.

Anari looked at her blankly for a moment.

Dan gestured the young woman to follow her to the benches along one wall, various sizes that had been brought over from *Corsac Fox*. They sat.

Dan had to remember that while Anari was the third oldest, behind only her and Yeong-Suk, they'd been sheltered years in Anari's case. Sabre School when young, then a square peg forced into a round hole when the *Auga* decided that she should be an engineer instead.

But for being assigned to the crew to maintain the captured *Iron Wasp* for later resale, and being able to convince Suka Kuri to take her with them, Anari Supasei might have lived an entire life of wasted potential and unhappiness.

Today was merely grumpy.

"What's distracting you?" Dan asked, point blank.

"Sterling might have a map," Anari replied. "He was working on it before we finished splitting up the crews to travel back to Isann, so I don't know if he's figured out the final pieces yet."

Dan studied the woman closely. Elder, Student. Adept, Seeker.

Some of what she saw surprised her. And didn't .

"Tell me about the map," she prompted, mostly to watch where Anari's face and emotions went as she thought and spoke.

"He might have found evidence that the Yarikh traveled to this sector from someplace on the far side of Forty-One, well beyond Fifteen and Z'Gosza," Anari began in a slow, quiet voice. "And he'd gotten it down to a handful of systems where they might have finally consolidated after they parked *Nubia*, but we can't know which was the final one until someone visits them to see."

"And you'd like to go," Dan pointed out, watching Anari's face light up with excitement, blush with embarrassment, then compress into neutrality.

"Sterling would," she mumbled just loudly enough for Dan to hear.

"And you'd like to go with him to help," Dan filled in.

Again, that surge in the eyes that just as quickly got crushed under the weight of *duty*.

It was a thing Dan knew well.

"To see," Anari corrected. "To know."

"Tell me about Sterling Huff," Dan prompted in the sort of voice that students learned to obey.

"He's smart," she said immediately. "And curious. And nice. If he was Emro—"

"Ignore the Human part for now," Dan interrupted. "If he was Emro?"

"The sort of person I'd pursue more seriously," Anari said, her face flushing almost brown with blood.

"How does he feel about you?" Dan probed.

Nothing she'd seen from day one had registered bad about Sterling Huff. And Suka Kuri spoke most highly of him, which was a significant bar for *anyone* to clear.

"I think he likes me," Anari said, voice back down to barely a whisper.

"Think?" Dan pressed.

"I believe he has feelings for me as well," Anari said, eyes coming back up to lock on Dan's. "And neither of us know what to say or do about it."

"Is he an interesting *person*?" Dan asked.

"Very," Anari lit up now. "We can sit and talk, or just be in the same room enjoying the warmth. It's just that he's Human, and that—"

"Means nothing at all," Dan interrupted again before the words were spoken. "I want you to listen, and pay extremely close attention. Okay?"

"Yes, Adept," Anari said, going all formal, but that meant that she understood the gravity.

Dan nodded and marshaled her words.

"We're going to build a new place, Uly and I," she reminded Anari. "Uly has tasked me with designing the government structure, but that has to be built on a social and cultural foundation. With me so far?"

"The various history books you've been reading," Anari nodded.

So, she'd been paying attention to that. Possibly not understanding the depth of questions Dan had been asking, but noticing.

"Those," Dan agreed. "Most civilizations out in the wider galaxy tend to be composed of a single species. The *Auga* are something of an exception, but they still dominate the Empire and rule all the subject species with an iron fist and a watchful third eye. But at the end of the day, the Khet of Z'Gosza aren't that different from the Ononguli Horde, when you look closely. Uly demands something different."

"Different?" Anari sobered, eyes narrowing as she focused on Dan about as closely as when they were doing touch-hands drills to develop speed and sensitivity.

"Different," Dan nodded. "Part of that is the understanding that all species will be welcome to participate, as long as they agree to play by the rules Uly *and I* will establish. Rules that enforce a level playing field with a big, fucking hammer. Everyone. That means that no single species should ever come to dominate things. If that happens, something has gone desperately wrong and folks probably need to step back and throw a small revolution anyway."

"Revolution?" Anari gasped.

"Nothing we're building today can possibly hope to answer every question asked two hundred or five hundred years from now," Dan described. "Culture and society will evolve. Should evolve, in order to stay relevant. Future folks will need to change things to stay ahead."

"Okay," Anari breathed quietly. "What does this have to do with me? Or Sterling?"

"If everyone is welcome, and everyone is equal, then sometimes you'll have people decide to make a life together where it's not possible to have children," Dan replied. "Across species, perhaps. One of the things we intend to institute is a fosterage program."

"Fosterage?" Anari asked, her eyes crossing a little.

"Folks send their kids to be raised by other families," Dan nodded. "Khet sending promising guppies to be raised by an Emro family, for instance, to give them exposure to a wider range of thought and understanding."

"Because you'd learn to see everyone as people instead of species," Anari nodded, eyes huge as the implications settled in. "Adoptions?"

"Exactly the same," Dan nodded. "Take them in and raise them as your own. Inheritance will look to those relationships and weigh them equally with blood. Heavier, in many cases, because adopted children grown up should have better rights than distant cousins by vague relationship. Marriage, such as it will be, must take those concepts into account."

"Will more Humans come?" Anari asked.

"Eventually," Dan decided, musing internally. "Uly might send a ship home with messages. Others might decide to explore to the far end of Sector Seventeen and meet them. Or maybe those folks just sail into darkness themselves and stumble across the rest of the galaxy. Don't know today. They would be just as welcome as Zuath or Ugotha when they do show up. If they behave. I might need to send home for more Humans, simply because I'm the only female around here, and the men shouldn't have to give up any chance of having kids, though none want to go home at this point. And I've asked several times."

Anari leaned back and her eyes took on a thousand light-year stare.

Dan fell silent and let the young woman process. She had seen the first elements of a romance budding there, but doubted that either Anari or Sterling had been able to get over the difference in size and skin tone to see how well they did mesh as a couple.

And Dan also felt a little mercenary, setting them up like this.

Wouldn't have moved yet, if Anari hadn't seemed open to the concept.

She'd have to talk to Uly at the next stop. There would be one more before the argosy sailed into Isann, and all that such an arrival entailed.

"That's a lot to think about," Anari finally managed, eyes still a little glossy.

"And nothing you need to do anything about today," Dan reminded her.

"No, but I need to talk to Sterling," Anari said. "See how he feels about it. We've danced carefully around the topic, but it feels like big and important things are lurking just beyond the next corner, you know?"

Dan nodded.

Nubia was a significant change that would impact this whole corner of the galaxy.

For good or ill.

FORTY-SEVEN

Uly enjoyed the bridge of *Corsac Fox* as they sailed that last bit into the harbor at Isann.

Dan had gotten a little upset that he'd more or less forced her to remain in command of *Nubia*, but she'd been focused on today, rather than the historic repercussions that the ship would garner tomorrow.

And her commander, once the Isann learned that Dan was extremely close to what the Yarikh themselves looked like, given that all Isann records were largely lost in the era of darkness after Yarikh had finally vanished from this neighborhood.

Plus, Uly remaining here freed up Sterling to spend more time digging into the ancient records that they had recovered from *Nubia* and started translating. Sterling was even getting pretty good at the language. They all were. Necessity inherent in the promise of the vessel itself.

And the Yarikh, wherever it was they had finally vanished to.

Uly wanted to know, but he had more important matters to attend to today, like an even greater disruption of Isann culture than *Corsac Fox* had been.

Changes were coming. Looking around, Bello was flying today, with Sterling understanding that much of Uly's original team would eventually transfer to *Nubia* with him. Bello, Yuriy, and Vitali were all up for promotion to Lieutenant, shortly after Sterling made Commander.

It didn't make sense today to fill out eight ranks of officers when he barely had that many true military types to begin with. Commander (O-6) was good enough, at least until Uly took up a proper flag rank as Echelon (F-1) or something.

And maybe the Starfare School would transmit *Batyr* naval ranks and concepts to the wider galaxy. That was Suka Kuri's responsibility, until she insisted that he make a decision.

"Bello, time to arrival?" Uly called to the Khet sitting next to Sterling for one last mission.

"Four minutes, Conductor," Bello replied, his headcrest flaring up and down once for emphasis. "*Nubia* is right behind us going in, but we've timed it to let us talk to the locals without them freaking entirely out."

Uly chuckled with the others.

Corsac Fox had been a monster, sailing into their orbit. *Nubia* was a revolution.

"Dropping us close to the station?" Uly confirmed.

"Expecting about a one-second lag," Bello nodded. "They might jump a little, but they know who we are."

"Excellent work, Bello," Uly said. "All of you."

He let his voice expand to include the rest of the bridge crew. And the rest of the ship.

Shortly, he'd be transferring his flag to *Nubia*. Presumably, they would need to have a ceremony to rename this vessel, since the cases of mistaken identity would only get worse once THE Corsac Fox wasn't always flying aboard *Corsac Fox*.

Tomorrow's issues.

They dropped out of warp and Uly was surprised by the image.

"Blakeslee, what's going on?" Uly demanded.

Instead of orbit being filled with ships, things were clustered tightly around the two stations, with only a few ships any significant distance away.

A voice suddenly rang over the speakers in Isann.

"Corsac Fox, beware of pirate vessels in orbit," it said. "They have been attacking and stripping shipping and there is almost nothing we can do to stop them."

In many ways, that was truth. Isann vessels were even more primitive than *Batyr* would field, themselves a distance behind the rest of the galaxy.

Uly was in a modern warship.

He keyed the intercom ship-wide.

"All hands to action stations."

FORTY-EIGHT

Sterling had approached today as something of a graduation. A new era dawning shortly, where the legendary Corsac Fox would become an even more powerful Warlord of the Spinward Reaches.

Some things, it seemed, never changed.

He felt the surge of adrenaline root him to the seat as he brought all his systems live. Gun crews would have been sitting around talking and maybe having a snack. After all, Isann was a friendly port. Why would you need the guns?

Because pirates.

Sterling took Del's feed and began rotating the Twin Six forward to a larger vessel not all that far away. Two ships, docked together, outside any gun range. Normally, you did that to transfer cargo without having to pay a deck fee on a station. Or in deep space, like they'd done moving some stuff over to *Nubia*.

"Del, I need a hard scan of every ship in orbit," Sterling called, falling into his role as Gunner when the ship was sailing into harm's way. "Some of them will run. None of them will escape me."

Part of him was aghast at how cruel and ugly that sounded,

even in his own ears, but the Corsac Fox needed to make a point to the folks around here.

You behaved, or somebody would make you.

Like him.

"Bello, slide me around to port and accelerate," Sterling continued. "I need to pounce on this one here."

He marked the target with a reticle on his screen and sent it to his Pilot. If Bello Temitope wasn't as good as Drew, he was still pretty good to be flying the ship today.

And Drew was bringing the big hammer in a few minutes.

"Sir, do we charge?" Sterling asked, glancing back over his shoulder at Uly.

Sterling wasn't sure he'd ever seen the captain so mad. Not even when the subject of Thorley came up.

"Foxes in the henhouse, Mr. Huff," Conductor Fortier snarled. "Rout them."

"Aye, sir," Sterling nodded.

He had the bow where he wanted it, so Sterling put a 6dm downrange at the first target, a cutter partially converted to haul cargo that his systems identified because it had been in harbor at Bastion not all that long ago.

Where they had, no doubt, heard about a new system they could attack. One not sophisticated enough to handle a modern warship like a cutter.

Cutters that were half the size of a heavy Interceptor like *Corsac Fox*.

"Gun crews, signal me green when you are fully operational," Sterling ordered his people.

Mostly Khet that had been with him since Lacium, he'd weeded out a few and then trained the remainder to the sorts of standards that Uly demanded of everyone.

Meanwhile, he put the other 6dm into a ship that had already started to red-shift.

Runner.

Another one that his systems knew from Bastion.

Somebody was getting smashed when he got home.

Home?

Yes, home. Bastion was where Uly was putting his new capital. And Sterling would be there to defend it from people like this.

Predators that didn't understand anything except force.

Today, he had a hammer. And shortly, a maul.

FORTY-NINE

Dan had settled herself into the command seat, prepared to deal with the shock and surprise she was bringing to Isann.

They dropped out and the bridge was suddenly filled with Sterling's voice.

"*Nubia*, this is *Corsac Fox*," he was saying. "Isann is under siege by a pirate argosy. I've started desrtroying them, but one of them has already run. Looks like the ringleader, listening to traffic being decrypted. Pursue and destroy."

"*Fox*, this is *Nubia*," Haydar replied sharply. "Confirm those orders."

"Uly wants an example made of them, *Fox*," Sterling said. "I want the fear of God Herself haunting them in hell."

Dan blinked at the raw vehemence in the young man's voice. And noted at least two ships badly damaged and leaking atmosphere, possibly from 6dm hits on bare metal.

However, she also understood making the bad guys afraid. The only thing that changed was the scale of going up from a bar fight to a squadron action.

Was that the key? Treat a fleet battle like her and the team in a bar with drunk and rowdy sailors?

Dan had a LOT of experience at that sort of thing.

"Drew, do you have their course?" she asked in a hard voice.

"Aye, sir," Roscoe replied. "Bello sent it."

"Engage and pursue," she ordered. "Bring them down."

She turned to Yaqub Zobo, with a purple stripe across his shoulders in case you didn't know who he was from behind.

"Yaqub, since we don't have full gun crews, I'll be relying on you to handle them," Dan said. "Order three teams of engineers to take over the turrets and damage control operations until otherwise notified."

"Three?" he squeaked, turning enough to bring a big eye onto her.

"The Corsac Fox wants them destroyed," she replied. "Maybe we'll take prisoners, but I don't have my combat companies with me today, and don't feel like taking the Ladies to capture an enemy vessel by ourselves unless I have to."

His gills flared twice, then settled.

"Engineering, this is the bridge," he said into his line. "I need folks manning the big turrets first, plus the Neutron Omnipulsars for defense. Whoever you have available."

"Roger that, Bridge," Sadeq replied. "Coming up."

Dan sat back in her chair and watched. She didn't have Sterling on Guns, but she had Drew chasing them. They would not escape her. And Yaqub was pretty good as a gunner.

Good enough to earn his rating under Sterling Huff's supervision, which she supposed was about as sharp as hers, when it had come time to add Ciah or Yeong-Suk to her personal combat team.

And that covered it.

Nubia leapt back up into warp.

FIFTY

Drew had their scent.

Variable Pulse Spatial Generators left a trail in the aether when a ship moved at FTL. Faster ships could sniff it like bloodhounds and chase.

Like today.

One track. Messy, because they hadn't tuned their systems in a while, so it was almost like following someone holding a flashlight in a dark park.

Not moving all that fast either. Probably figured that Sterling and the *Fox* would pounce on everyone there and capture them, letting the boss get away.

Drew smiled cruelly.

He didn't go in for all that military stuff. Had been a civilian at every stage of this, though he supposed that at some point he should let Uly hang more rank on his collar than Pilot.

Not that anything else in the galaxy mattered.

Fools had gone straight out on the solar ecliptic. Reciprocal course to Bastion, more or less.

Why do that?

Because they knew they'd been made, and were running to where they could load up on supplies before they disappeared forever.

Because they had to know that the *Corsac Fox* was coming for their souls.

Just didn't understand how quickly.

Yaqub was manning the big triple turrets today, with whoever might be available to handle issues with reloads. They'd fired each of them once during cleanup, just to make sure they all worked, but things happened in service.

Lines kinked, like the coolant system on engine three. Magnetic bottles for the wavebolt generators broke.

Drew figured that he could count on getting a second salvo from everything before they started losing guns to general entropy.

Fortunately, they were big guns.

He'd never even seen a ship mounting fourteens. Or fifteens, which this might be close enough to call.

Great, BIG boom.

"Gunner, I am overtaking the target," Drew announced, watching two dots slowly merging.

It was all a theoretical estimate, right up to the moment when *Nubia* got close enough that the two fields canceled each other out and dropped them out of warp on top of each other.

Yaqub *wouldn't* be the one surprised when it happened.

"Counting down to engagement," Yaqub replied. "Sixty seconds plus. Gun teams, are you ready?"

"More or less," somebody replied.

Not like they were trained for this, but sometimes, you just needed warm bodies that could push or pull or poke something that wanted to balk. Big tools were good for that.

Drew adjusted his flight path a shade. Slipped to a lower plane while retaining forward velocity and direction.

All three turrets were on the top hull of *Nubia*, with smaller ones on sides and bottom for defense. When he dropped them, Drew wanted nine monstrous barrels all able to come to bear.

Wasn't fighting a cruiser or anything, but he didn't think that Dan was going to order them to heave to for a customs inspection or anything, either.

Sterling had sounded *pissed*. Never a good thing.

He checked his boards.

"All hands, contact in five, four, three, two, one."

FIFTY-ONE

Dan had found herself almost looking forward to this. The mental and emotional breakthrough of seeing a fight between squadrons of ships as just a bigger bar brawl meant that all her practice and experience was suddenly directly relevant.

All she had to do was redefine a few terms in her head. *Nubia* dropped that other ship into the real universe and suddenly she was on a dance floor with a drunk bully.

Except that he'd been a bantam cock. Like this one. The kind who only came up to her nose and had a chip on his shoulder about that.

And a bunch of other things.

Throw in a little racism at the color of her skin and she almost gave that other conductor a name. Except that then she'd have to explain that name. And the situation. And the memory.

Better to just call him *Dumbass*. It had a certain efficiency to it.

"Gunner, lock and engage with the fourteens," Dan ordered.

Uly and Sterling had wanted him *destroyed* as an example to the rest of the galaxy that the Warlord of the Spinward Reaches had placed Isann under his protection.

Under hers.

And records from Sterling showed that they had been at Bastion in the recent past, so they should have known better.

"Firing one," Yaqub replied.

On her console, it was just another dot detaching from *Nubia* and chasing down the other. Except that a 6dm was heavy enough to injure an old cutter like that. 14dm might crush it like an aluminum can.

Surprise didn't help, because he'd probably thought he was getting away.

Nobody escaped justice.

Today, Dan weilded the *Black Sword* herself.

Bantam cock *Dumbass* had just held up two drunken fists and asked the *washenzi* if she thought she was tough.

Right before she'd left his ass on the floor, out cold for the bouncers to carry off.

"Dan, I'm getting surrenders on channel nine," Haydar announced in a generic voice.

Right up there with a bored waiter telling you the day's specials.

"That's nice," she replied, turning eyes on his tentacles, just in case he'd missed something.

Dan supposed that Haydar could smell her anger from where he was sitting, after all.

"Duly noted," Haydar nodded and went back to what he was doing.

"Enemy vessel engaging our wavebolt," Yaqub said. "Pair of twos and a pair of ones, plus one Omnipulsar. Not going to be enough."

Bantam cock. Lessons to be taught.

"Give him a second one, Yaqub," Dan ordered, back on that dance floor with that drunk.

Let the bouncers carry him off later.

Yaqub flinched at her tone, but a hand went out and pressed a button.

A second wavebolt began tracking, like a pack of wolves coming for you in a dark forest, after running you down.

First bolt impacted. Electroshield Array absorbed it, after four defensive bolts had softened up the 14dm reasonably.

Wasn't enough.

Flash of light bright enough to be seen out the forward window, where she normally just had a view of stars. But that had been a small supernova in the distance.

On her screens, the bantam cock began tumbling, which threw off all of his defenses at really the wrong moment to have happen.

Yaqub looked back over a shoulder, like he was expecting an order to detonate the wavebolt before it finished *Dumbass* off.

Dan smiled at him. Watched the boy shudder and turn back to his boards.

Sometimes, you have to be the worst possible evil in the galaxy. Hopefully only once, after which people learn to leave you alone.

And keep their racist comments to themselves.

Defensive wavebolts tried, but they were in a bad situation, coming from the side instead of head-on.

That 14dm hit. Hard.

On her screen, the flash wasn't nearly as bright.

Then the scan showed what was left of *Dumbass* tumbling like a can she'd kicked.

"Yaqub, was that set to lance mode?" she asked.

"Affirmative, sir," he said, not looking back. "Figured that standard mode might simply annihilate them, while a spike might break them in two. Or blow one end off the ship, like this one seems to have done. Not opposed to hanging them after a trial back on Isann or Bastion."

Dan kept her snap of anger under control. She supposed that Yaqub was correct. Pirates could always be hung.

Or sentenced to twenty years to life and maybe they'd turn their lives around later.

And she hadn't ordered him either way, so Yaqub had used his best judgment. Which might honestly be better than hers at the moment, but she'd meditate on that later.

And talk to Suka Kuri.

For now, she opened a line aft to where Nasrin had been helping in the wardroom. She could cook, and was nothing but a strong back if they needed her in engineering.

"Monfared," she replied.

"I will have to remain in command here," Dan said. "You round up the team, assume tactical command, and prepare to board what's left of the pirate, capturing and retrieving any survivors to be transported to Isann for trial. Questions?"

"Negative," Nasrin replied, though Dan could hear dozens in her voice. "Activating Combat Team."

FIFTY-TWO

Nasrin looked around and wondered how the hell she'd gotten into this mess.

Except that she could track every single point along a long thread. Every decision. And she'd been with Dan the longest, in spite of being the youngest of all of them. Even Yanouk was older, relative to aging.

But Dan trusted her the most right now, which was just silly, considering that both Emro women were enough Sabre School to count these days.

As was everyone else, she supposed.

"Status?" Nasrin asked as Gennady finished handing out weapons and locked the armory up.

Solomon was back on *Corsac Fox*, so Uly had sent Gennady and Emil, understanding that the Combat Team was a separate command from the ship.

Even when Dan was in charge.

Everyone looked each other over as Gennady walked around touching shoulders and backpacks.

"All good here," he announced.

Gennady hadn't wanted to be an officer. Ever. He was still exceptional as a senior sailor handling duties that didn't involve making executive decisions.

That was Nasrin's job.

"Helmets on," she ordered. "Louvers open for now, but we'll close them in the airlock."

"Nasrin, this is Drew," the Pilot came over the radio. "Wreckage is forty meters outside your airlock, tumbling about once every three minutes, so fast enough that you will notice, but not bad enough that I needed to dock with a shuttle and kill their spin. They are on channel nine."

"Understood," she replied.

Nasrin slung her Omnibow over her shoulder and touched the Exoripper on her hip. The latter was her symbol of authority, but she doubted that the remaining pirates were going to be feeling all that frisky.

Not after the forward half of the ship had been *vaporized*. Someone had survived, because Dan had finally accepted their surrender.

And they would behave, or she'd happily leave them here. You honored your surrender, or you died ugly, and Dan had sounded ugly today.

The team followed her into the airlock, locked everything up tight, confirmed it one more time, then cycled out into space.

Backpack thrusters carried them across to the wreck. The parts she could see didn't even look that bad, until she turned to the front end, where it looked like a giant had torn a piece of paper in two.

She swapped over to channel nine with a tentacle and took a breath.

"Approaching your airlock now," Nasrin announced. "If I see anyone armed when we enter and everyone aboard dies. ***Everyone***. Am I clear?"

"You are," a male voice replied. "Only six of us anyway, with most of the crew off one of the captures. Got everything shut down and we're in the corridor outside the airlock in suits."

Nasrin nodded. That was the sound of shock still working its way through your system.

Sounded Zuath, which wasn't that surprising. They were barely the largest single cluster by species in the space between Z'Gosza and the Ononguli Sphere.

Dan had called them cockatrices, the first time she'd met one. Chicken-like heads with short beaks. Reverse hinged legs. Hexapod, with short wings that could barely slow your fall in low gravity.

Pirates, which was all Nasrin cared about. Fools who should have known better.

She rode her backpack to the ship, then let her magnetic boots lock her down.

"Ciah, in first as usual," Nasrin ordered. "Anari second."

Smallest and fastest up front, in case of trouble. Biggest and strongest next, with the rest of the team ready to pile on and start blasting.

Because those fuckers had been warned.

Into the lock. Cycle through, into an area that still had air and light. No gravity, but she had her boots.

And smoke, but not as bad as she'd been expecting.

Six Zuath, lined up in suits with their helmets on and locked. Two were supporting two others, but all looked mobile enough for her purposes.

"This everyone?" Nasrin asked, mostly to confirm.

"It is," the closest one replied. The one she'd been talking to on the radio.

"You lot go with these ladies," she ordered. "Anari, you stay with me. Yanouk, you take charge of them."

Six went into the lock with the her four and Nasrin watched the door close.

"Quick inspection," Nasrin said, turning to the big, Emro woman. "Mostly confirmation."

"Understood."

She led them towards the end that still existed. Corridors reminded her that most pirates got into the business because growing up and doing laundry regularly was too much effort, to say nothing of washing floors and painting walls occasionally.

Nasrin was happy to be on bottled air today. It smelled of her friends.

Engineering showed the same slack laziness. Grease smears. Oil stains. Random parts floating in the air that should have been strapped down tight enough to stay in place even without gravity holding them.

Nobody present. Nobody alive. Two corpses, one charred beyond recognition in such a way that the smoke smell would also probably taste like chicken.

At least the vacuum of space would clean a lot of that smell off her suit. And she'd make a point of scrubbing the rest instead of making Omid or one of her people do it.

"Are they always like this?" Anari asked.

Former *Auga* sailor turned pirate turned privateer turned *Corsac Fox* Combat Team.

Hell of a story arc for anybody, but Nasrin's still probably topped it, however little solace that brought her.

"Usually," Nasrin replied. "Folks join formal navies and get discipline. Not counting the Ononguli Horde, for whom the two are often one and the same, the rest get slack."

"This is just laziness," Anari announced with vinegar in her voice.

"You are not wrong," Nasrin agreed. "I've seen enough here. You?"

"Same," Anari replied, turning to go.

Nasrin clunked along in her wake.

"What do they get out of it?" Anari asked as they emerged back into the corridor.

"Most expect to live fast, get rich, go broke, and then die young," Nasrin said, wondering at how old and jaded she sounded, talking to someone half a decade her senior.

But it was the light-years, not the day cycles.

"Plus, there's no interstellar authority around here," Nasrin continued. "*Auga* controls their zone pretty well. Same with the Ononguli. The Khet are slowly catching up, but they won't get there anytime soon. Uly's creating a space where piracy gets crushed. Eventually, the pirates reform or go out of business. That's our job."

"And the prisoners?" Anari asked.

"That's up to the Isann, I suspect," Nasrin said. "I expect that they will have strong opinions, but I don't know how well these folks behaved when attacking. At least at Bastion, it was all stun weapons and apologies when the Isann realized that they'd grabbed a shark by the tail."

"Sounds rough," Anari said as she stepped into the airlock.

"Rough life," Nasrin agreed as she joined her.

FIFTY-THREE

Dan watched on her screen as ten bodies emerged from the wreck, four with guns and six Zuath holding onto a line and being pulled along by Ciah, from the size.

"Drew, you're in charge," she decided, rising and moving towards the hatch. "I'll be helping with the prisoners. And let the wardroom know we have guests."

"Will do," he said, but she was already gone.

Aft, she found Emil and Gennady watching the inside of the airlock. They were armed, but she didn't figure that six unarmed Zuath were going to be a threat, so she didn't worry about stopping to grab anything.

Her anger would be sufficient, if necessary.

The airlock cycled and opened. Ciah backed out and watched the prisoners. Two injured.

"How bad are the injuries?" she asked automatically.

"Walking wounded," Yanouk replied. "Possibly a broken leg that needs to be set, but that's medical's call. The other is jarred and heavily concussed, but cognizant."

"Good," Dan replied, then turned to focus on them. "Are any of you important?"

"Senior engine wiper, sir," one of them replied, stepping forward a little. "The only person in engineering that survived. Guess I'm senior. The rest are just crew."

Dan nodded. One with some skills. Five warm bodies. The lucky ones, unless their luck just meant that they survived long enough to hang later.

Pirate ships needed bullies willing to abuse captured ships and crews. Anybody with the mindset would do, leavened with a batch of trained experts that could keep the ship running as you captured others and stripped them or sold them off for cash to repair yours.

One of the reasons Uly had originally stolen *Wren* from the *Auga*, because it had given them a lot of supplies for free, plus things they could sell or trade with others.

Piracy, but war against the *Auga* authorities, rather than innocent civilians just trying to make a buck.

It was a thin difference, but one she'd come to accept.

"This way," she ordered, nodding the senior engine wiper to follow.

Dan took them to medical first. The machines all worked, though Blair was still on the *Fox* for the moment.

She took charge of the prisoners, getting them all scanned. The one had a hairline fracture that could be treated with a cast for now, so they got their right leg immobilized. The concussion showed nothing particularly bad on the scans she ran, beyond a hard life leaving a lot of older scars.

The other four were in better shape.

"What's next, ma'am?" their leader asked when she was done.

"Food," Dan decided. "We'll be back to Isann quickly enough, and I'd like you to be in better shape when the Corsac Fox meets you to decide your fate."

The Zuath nodded, already seeing the hangman's noose from the look in his eyes. The others shivered.

She got them to the wardroom. Still under guard, but none had offered any resistance and only the one had spoken.

Dan stepped aside and watched them grab what each of them obviously thought of as their last meal, from the way they approached it.

"From here?" Yanouk asked.

Nasrin and Anari had returned, but stayed to the back. Yanouk was in charge.

"Lock them in cabins that have a washroom," Dan decided. "Two per room so they have someone to talk to. Monitor audio for emergencies, but otherwise leave them alone. Uly will decide what he wants to do with them."

"Understood."

Dan left them at that and headed back to the bridge.

Her bridge.

Drew nodded when she arrived.

"No change here," he said simply.

Dan took her station. Looked over the notes and the scans.

"Yaqub," she said, getting his attention.

He looked up intently.

"Finish off the wreck," she ordered. "Then we'll go home."

FIFTY-FOUR

Uly surveyed the damage. The pirates had gotten lazy, thinking that as long as they stayed out of range of the stations' wavebolt launchers, nothing could harm them. Certainly, most of the ships in harbor had been much weaker, and Chief of Chiefs Usupov hadn't had time to organize a swarm to drive them off. Casualties would have probably been hideous in the process.

Four ships had been taken as a result, and had been in the process of being stripped in plain sight.

And then he'd arrived.

Or rather, Sterling had been unleashed on them.

"Mr. Huff, what is your status?" he asked.

"One probably did get away," the young lieutenant replied with a growl. "The other one has Drew on his ass, so that's just a matter of when *Nubia* returns. Three confirmed kills here, with boarding teams clearing them out."

"Sterling," Uly said sharply, causing him to turn and look back.

"Sir?"

"You have that ship's pennant, Sterling," Uly reminded him. "And the scan from when he was at Bastion. I'll be putting a bounty on the ship and the conductor significant enough that somebody will be making his life a miserable hell for me. Assuming we don't find him ourselves later."

"Aye, sir!"

Uly would let him have his anger today. It was the right kind. Indignation at bullies harming the innocent. The sort of thing that would turn him into a better officer tomorrow.

He found the line and connected.

"Lieutenant Wyndham," Solomon replied.

Like Sterling, young. Younger, as he was only eighteen today. And Security Officer for *Corsac Fox*. And would travel with most of the combat teams to *Nubia* shortly.

"It's Uly. How are you doing on prisoners and hulls?"

"Wrapping things up now, sir," Solomon replied. "I sent big enough teams to overwhelm them psychologically up front. And heavily armed enough to make my point. Surrenders and ransoms are being processed. We'll be ready to offload them from all three shortly. Are we hauling them back to the *Fox*, or turning them over to local authorities?"

"I will let you know shortly, Wyndham," Uly said. "Assuming the locals for now."

"Roger that, sir."

Uly cut the line and drew a breath.

"Del, connect me with Chief Usupov, please?" Uly continued.

"He's been on channel eleven when you have a chance," Del replied.

"I'll talk to him in my office," Uly decided. "Sterling, you have command."

Uly moved to his day office and settled. Kadyr was there on the screen a moment later.

"I'm sorry I didn't leave you better protected," Uly said even before the Isann could speak. "I'll be selling you some armed patrol ships for one Imperial Guilder each. Plus sending you some better wavebolt systems and plans you can use to build your own here. This was my mistake.”

Kadyr blinked. Blinked again. His eyes finally settled.

“Oh,” Kadyr finally managed. “How did this happen?”

“I’m guessing that your ship *Surly* made it successfully to Bastion and let them know the situation,” Uly replied. “News of a new trade connection got out, along with someone realizing that your local ships are not currently up to the standard of the rest of the galaxy today. Someone saw an opportunity to get in quick and steal a lot of things. It was only blind luck that I came back today, because from the looks of things, they’d have been gone in a few days more.”

“That was my impression, too, Uly,” Kadyr replied. “What next?”

“I’d like you to fly shuttles and teams to the three and take charge of the prisoners,” Uly said. “They attacked your system, so they get to be dealt with under your laws.”

“Thank you,” Kadyr said, then he paused. “What was that second ship that appeared? It was the biggest thing I’ve ever seen, short of the station I’m standing on.”

Uly nodded.

“In the *Karaŋgılıkka*, there is a chapter where Zamir Aytiev sails to the harbor of the black moon,” he began. “And saw a sword on the cliff, but couldn’t get to it because of the rocks.”

“I know the reference,” Kadyr replied in a quiet, awestruck voice.

“Turned out to be talking about a place, Kadyr,” Uly said. “My people were translating the *Karaŋgılıkka* and someone decided that those were sailing directions. My stellar cartographer figured out where they went. We found that ship, deep down in orbit around a black hole, where Zamir Aytiev’s ship couldn’t have safely escaped.”

“What are you doing with it?” he asked in a whisper.

“Turning it into my flagship soon,” Uly said. “There are a few surprises that I want Dan to share with you when she gets back, then I'd like your permission to recruit some crew for it. Aibek didn't think it would be a problem, and is already planning to have a long conversation with his wife about volunteering."

"That's almost enough for me to retire and join you myself," Kadyr chuckled. "Ten years ago, I would have, but we've only just gotten our shit together enough here to sail into darkness ourselves. What else is out there?"

"Those are some of the surprises, but I'd like you to think about assembling some crews that I could hire to do surveys for me," Uly said. "Sterling Huff has notes about places we should be looking and visiting. I think Isann sailors would appreciate the opportunity."

"We'd be honored, Uly," Kadyr replied, choking up.

Uly felt a little mercenary, but he also understood that it was these little things that would weld the Isann to his dream far better than even trade would, to say nothing of the *Auga* method of outright conquest.

The Auga simply squeezed until the mud ran through their hands.

Knowing the *Karaŋgılıkka*, Kadyr's people would drive themselves harder and farther than he could ever motivate them.

And it would anchor his rear flank, even as it expanded his network back into that darkness, and whatever might lay beyond.

"From there, I think I should stay in harbor here for a bit," Uly said. "Remind folks that any trouble they bring to Isann will run into me first. If I could convince you to carry a message to Bastion for me, then I can have Maks send you some reinforcements, as well as update them."

"*Surly* is here," Kadyr said. "Safe under the guns. I can send them back out as soon as you wish."

"Excellent news, Kadyr," Uly said. "Let's start building a new future in this region."

FIFTY-FIVE

Dan had had a chance to read the brief report that Sterling must have composed on the fly while shooting with one hand, given the amount of data he had included.

Pirate argosy that attacked Isann. Ships chased close enough to the stations to be safe, though a few had been taken for stripping. Two got away from Sterling. Only one got away from her.

Good enough for today.

"Drew, time to drop?" she asked, looking forward over his shoulder and the vast valley that the view always reminded her of, a trail down to a black sea.

"Two minutes," Drew replied. "Coming out a little high, just in case, and sending a message with our wavefront."

"Excellent," she said.

It was all even starting to make sense, though she'd only stay in this chair as long as she had to. Dan knew she could do it, but there were more important things not being done while she did.

Today's problems, stopping her from solving tomorrow's.

Corsac Fox was sitting high as well when they dropped out, rather than over close to the station. Orbital traffic had gotten serious again, with ships starting to move around instead of clustered fearfully.

"Message from Uly on channel two," Haydar said.

"Put him on the main screen," Dan replied, then smiled when he was there a moment later.

What the hell would she do without him? Carve some sort of something out here for the rest of her life? Sneak home and live under an assumed identity?

She had Uly.

"Success?" he asked immediately.

"Six prisoners for you," Dan replied. "The ship was destroyed when I was done with it. Most of the pirate crew was killed in taking it."

"Pirates," he said dismissively. "And folks that had come here from Bastion, so they absolutely knew better. I'll be posting bounties."

Dan shivered under his tone, then supposed that was how Yaqub had heard her.

That was what *ruthless* sounded like. She could almost taste it.

Uly could be the most wonderful, charming, friendly person in the galaxy, until he had to turn into that killer. Dan understood that to be something else they shared. Something that made them such an excellent team.

"What's our next step?" she asked.

"Kadyr will be sending the freighter *Surly* back to Bastion with a message pack from me," Uly nodded. "I need Maks to deliver some warships that can protect Isann, so we'll stay put here and start refurbishment and some of the repairs we need on site, with the rest waiting until we get back to Bastion and the *Watchtower* to complete."

"I'll need more crew," she said, then pause. "You'll need more crew."

Emphasis on *you* to remind him that he was supposed to be moving over and up.

"Understood," he grinned at her, acknowledging the subtle reminder. Another thing they shared, in that a look or a word could convey whole chapters of meaning. "I've talked to Kadyr and Aibek, and they don't think finding a bunch of sailors to join us will really be a problem."

"Not after they understand *Nubia*, no," she replied. "I'll need to spend time on the surface as well."

"Recruiting?" he asked.

"Altering the social construct of an entire civilization," Dan corrected him with a smile. "Isann sends the men off to have adventures, while the women stay home and tend the households. I presume that such a thing works for most of them. However, there will be ladies who will want to sail and have never been given the opportunity. That's changing. Now."

He nodded.

Uly understood. Dan saw herself as revolution. It could be polite, or not, but it was happening.

She would see to it.

"I've also let Kadyr know that you have some other surprises for them," he continued, smiling now. "All I've mentioned is Zamir Aytiev and the black moon. I figured it would be much more interesting if you told them about the Yarikh yourself. Especially as I intend to hire a couple of ships to explore some of Sterling's spots on a map to see who or what might be out there."

Dan nodded. Made sense. They'd come to Isann because it had been hiding back in the darkness behind Bastion. Instead, it had turned into the doorway to an even vaster and more interesting realm that someone would need to explore.

Every modern map simply showed darkness lit with stars. Sterling had taken copies of the astrogation records from her ship and was going to translate them.

And he was good enough. She'd seen that. Especially with Anari helping. Another good team.

Plus, if Sterling and Anari did get serious, Dan didn't have to worry about the young woman starting a family without a lot of planning, though she might start fostering.

An Emro and a Human raising an Isann child?

She needed to talk in much more depth with Suka Kuri, when they next had their regular tea. Things that had been purely theoretical for so long felt like they were on the verge of turning into concrete reality, and she needed to stay ahead of everybody else. Socially, just as Uly did politically and militarily.

Tomorrow wouldn't be tomorrow much longer.

"Give me a day to sort things here," Dan said. "You start shuffling some of the permanent crew over as soon as possible, so they can settle, then we can have Vahid and his crew fix Kadyr a formal State Dinner sort of thing. I think he and Aibek would like that."

"And I'll make sure they bring their wives and families," Uly grinned. "We're up to no good, you and I. We better make sure this is the biggest splash we can manage."

Dan grinned. She could see it taking shape around her.

FIFTY-SIX

Uly waited at the airlock as the shuttle docked. Dan was commanding from her bridge, because he wasn't about to take that away from her, even if she wanted him to.

Afterwards.

The hatch opened and Kadyr was there in the flesh. Shorter than he was in Uly's mind, where they were the same size, but Kadyr outmassed him significantly despite being half a head shorter.

A bevy of folks followed as Kadyr stepped up and bowed his head.

"Corsac Fox," he said formally, in spite of the smile on his face.

"Chief of Chiefs," Uly grinned back at him.

Behind him, Uly heard a slightly strangled yelp from Aibek, but only one and then nothing when he glanced.

"I took the liberty of expanding my invitation," Kadyr said, stepping sideways and gesturing.

Two Isann women, one matronly and one perhaps middle-aged, stood there, shepherding a pair of gangling Isann teens, an older female and a younger male, all eyes and shock.

"My wife and partner, Gulmira Usupov," Kadyr gestured to the older woman. "Madam Ainura Sulaymanov, and their offspring, Zhyrgal and Maksat."

Uly glanced back and Aibek was vibrating with energy, so Uly gestured him close and watched him hug his wife first, then his children.

Aibek had sailed off into darkness at the behest of his Chief of Chiefs, and brought back the Corsac Fox. It could have turned out so much worse for the Isann.

A few other Isann emerged from the shuttle and filled part of the chamber. Advisors, rivals, and explorers that met the requirements Uly had transmitted.

"Ladies and gentlemen, welcome aboard the vessel *Nubia*," Uly spoke up, silencing the crowd. "A dinner has been planned, with my favorite chef working with Chief Sulaymanov to create something that everyone should be able to enjoy. If you'll follow me, we'll head to the wardroom so that we can sit and break bread together as friends."

He led. Aibek only had two hands, but three people stayed close as they walked. Kadyr and his wife held hands and made quiet sounds as they looked at the swirls of the walls and other interesting oddities about the ship Uly had found.

With the help of a great many friends.

The sounds got even more interesting when they met the others in the dining hall. All of Dan's Combat Team, brushed and polished. Haydar dressed in his most formal civilian outfit, so that not everyone was in a uniform. Rabiu had done the same, but had to wear an entirely new suit made by Omid because he had ended up losing nearly half his mass over the last two years. Ethir almost looked distinguished, though anyone who knew him would be holding a hand on their wallet, seeing that smile.

Uly didn't think he was going to swindle the locals too badly, but he also knew that Ethir, Rabiu, and Piruz had put a lot of thought into trade treaties that they would propose to the Isann and anyone else they found out here.

Virgin territory, as it were, with all the first-mover advantages that those three could exploit. At least Uly and Haydar had reviewed everything.

Drew was flying and in command right now. Sterling had the *Fox*, parked nearby like a hungry hawk in case anyone misbehaved.

The Isann ooohed and ahhhed as they got settled. Water to drink, with various options available in tiny glasses for folks to sample as they explored. It helped that the Isann as a culture were explorers. Looking outward and wondering what was there.

The *Karaŋgılıkka*, after all, translated more or less as *Sailing Into Darkness* and formed the emotional cornerstone of their entire civilization.

Uly was at the low end of the table today, which was a fun enough change that he was already planning to make such a rotation permanent. Dan was still Commander of this vessel, and had Kadyr and Gulmira on her flanks, with the rest interspersed with his people, so everyone had someone to talk to.

Uly had both of Aibek's children close by, eyeing him at once nervously and curiously. As bread got served, the girl spoke up.

Zhyrgal Sulaymanov. Were she Human, he'd have guessed fifteen. She reminded him of his own sister Winter at that age. Winter would be twenty-three now. Occasionally, he wondered how her life was turning out.

"Human?" Zhyrgal queried, as if clarifying.

"That is correct," Uly nodded, sharing that body language.

"And all these others?" she asked, gesturing to Haydar, Suka Kuri, Nasrin, Kayta, Yeong-Suk, and all the other species present at this table.

"Dan and I went off on a grand adventure," he told her. "And got captured by pirates. When we escaped, the other prisoners came with us. Since then, we've accumulated a great many more friends from all over the galaxy."

"Where do the Isann fit in that?" she asked, sounding remarkably astute and grown up.

And, he supposed, as a mere child, she might be willing to ask those questions, when some of the adults down the table had turned sharply as if to intervene.

Uly smiled at all of them.

"You have a hunger to know what's out there," he said, gesturing with the hand not holding bread. "That is something our two species share, as I am so many light-years from the world of my birth that the number astonishes me when I stop to think about it."

"What is out there?" she pressed, her brother turning shy and wide-eyed, but absorbing every tidbit.

Uly gestured to the table.

"This is only a sample of the folks I have met," he said. "The Isann came to my new home at Bastion, but didn't turn out to be terrible people, once we sat down and talked. Like this. Your father convinced me that you could be great friends. Your Chief of Chiefs reinforces that. I'm looking forward to hiring ships and crews from Isann to explore that darkness for me, to see who else is out there."

He caught Dan's eye, longways down the table. And her nod. Much of the conversation had drifted off to quiet as other folks listened. And looked at the assembly of folks they were breaking bread with.

It was symbolic, but those sorts of symbols were important. Kadyr had turned from a gruff leader to a good friend, partly as a result of Vahid's cooking at the beginning.

And the *Karaŋgılıkka*.

That families had come aboard tonight was an even better sign.

"Who will explore?" Zhyrgal asked, eyes locked on Uly's face.

"Who wants to?" he countered. "Dan intends to go down to the surface, looking for women who wish to set out to see the galaxy."

His gesture caused Zhyrgal to turn her head the length of the table. Dan nodded to the woman, and Uly felt the message flow between them.

That the old limits would no longer be acceptable, because something new was coming.

Uly knew it to be the Corsac Fox, in his symbolic role, but he appreciated that it would likely let people like Zhyrgal Sulaymanov dream of something more than a good marriage and a family.

If she wanted it.

Some might not. That was acceptable as well, but Uly suspected that the Children of Zamir Aytiev would take a radically different look at their lives tomorrow.

Zhyrgal turned back to study his face.

"Anyone?" she finally asked.

Uly nodded as the next course of plates began to be delivered.

"Anyone," he confirmed.

FIFTY-SEVEN

Dan had taken the whole team down to the surface today. Suka Kuri had joined them.

The capital city of Naryn was having one of those glorious days that you normally only encounter in books, with the temperature a perfect twenty degrees under a cloudless sky.

Because of the *Karaŋgılıkka*, all of them were generally fluent enough to follow conversations, with Anari and Suka Kuri jabbering away happily to anyone who they met as they walked slowly through the souq, passing in and out of various arcades and by sidewalk cafes that left Dan almost a touch homesick.

Everyone was generally friendly, though there were a few frowns here and there.

Gulmira Usupov was their guide today, taking them to various shops and generally exploring without any goal other than to be seen. And to let the Isann know just how big the galaxy really was, when Human, Mazhin, Emro, Ononguli, Khet, and Guezal could mingle with the Isann as they shopped.

"Tea?" Gulmira asked at one point, an hour or so after a small lunch and a lot of sauntering.

She had a twinkle in her eye that told Dan she was up to something, but that it would probably be good. They'd talked quite a lot during dinner the other day. And since.

Another one, like Zhyrgal Sulaymanov, infected with radicalism.

Dan smiled.

"That sounds lovely," she replied.

Gulmira led the group through a smaller building with stalls selling possibly everything when Dan looked closer, then across an alley to a door that looked more like one where a shop took deliveries than anything.

Dan was armed. Everyone was armed except Suka Kuri, but she had her wits in an emergency.

Gulmira knocked, a code of some sort with an odd rhythm to it.

The door opened immediately inward and another Isann woman stood there, looking out at the group in the alley with hooded eyes.

The stranger nodded a moment later and stepped back. Gulmira followed, then Ciah, because she'd slipped ahead of Dan.

Short hallway, barely lit. The stranger held the door. Gulmira moved inward.

Darkness fell as the door got closed, but Dan could see a lit archway ahead, and followed Ciah into a larger space.

Turned out to be a courtyard, with two levels of balconies above, both currently empty. The floor felt like packed dirt under her feet, without any plants or paving stones. Several doors led off. Tables had been arranged into a square on one end of the space, with several Isann women of various ages clustered nearby.

And one enormous samovar off to one side of that.

Gulmira approached the group. Dan and the others followed, spreading out a hint but not much. Everyone she could see in this courtyard was female, so Gulmira was up to something.

The strangers all had nervous smiles and relaxed body language, so Dan concentrated on them, letting her ladies worry about flanks and overwatch.

Isann women generally tended to wear knee-length robes over pants in public. Darker colors seemed to prevail, usually embroidered or trimmed with brighter colors in ways that would have made Omid smile, had she been with them today.

Dan made a note to drag her out of her lair at some point and introduce her to Gulmira and her friends, as Omid tended to be as introverted as Nasrin was an extrovert.

The strangers wore the pants, but had removed the long robes, revealing T-shirts in black with a red logo and script over the heart and on both sleeves that felt formal and military, though none of these women gave off that impression.

"Dan Chastain, this is Elder Gulnaz Isakov," Gulmira said, moving to stand next to a woman who might be a cousin of Gulmira, from the resemblance. "Gulnaz Isakov, Sheridan Chastain, Commander of the vessel *Nubia* and Chief of Staff to the Corsac Fox himself."

Dan nodded. She and Uly hadn't done the formal hand-off of command, mostly because he would need to immediately turn around and promote Sterling, which would also entail renaming the old *Iron Wasp* into something new to reduce mistaken identity problems.

It would likely turn into something of a carnival around here at the time, because the Isann were sailors and had turned Uly and *Nubia*—and her when they came to understand that she was possibly Yarikh herself, as they might measure such things—into cultural heroes perhaps on a scale with Zamir Aytiev himself.

Sailing Into Darkness.

Isakov squared up and bowed formally. Dan returned it automatically, betrayed by her reflexes.

They stood facing each other for a moment.

"Welcome, Commander," Isakov began in a rich voice. "Has my cousin explained why you are here?"

"She has not," Dan said, turning to catch the immense grin on the woman's face.

"I suspected as much," Isakov turned a reproachful eye on her cousin. One that bounced off entirely.

Several of the younger women around the fringe also smiled now. Relaxing.

"My cousin is an elder and instructor of an ancient form of close combat called Karmap," Gulmira finally explained. "After talking to you about your Combat Team, I took it upon myself to bring you here that you might see it in the privacy of our dojo. No men are allowed."

Dan nodded. Gulmira had asked some off-beat and esoteric questions about the ladies over dinner, but Dan hadn't put it together until now. And they'd all been studying an ancient tome, instead of really going deep into modern Isann culture, at least as it had existed the day before Uly arrived.

"I see," Dan replied, smiling now. "Allow me to introduce my companions."

She did, in turn meeting a dozen of Isakov's students, all of them relatively senior, in spite of many of them only being young adults.

They sat and enjoyed tea. Or something close enough, served from that enormous silver samovar and enjoyed in small cups communally around the table.

After fifteen minutes of chatting, much of it driven by Gulmira and Suka Kuri like they'd worked it out ahead of time—they had, hadn't they?—Dan figured that she would rate Gulnaz Isakov as about a Fifth or Sixth Degree black belt. That point where one was expected to master every form the school taught, and be teaching it to others, including other teachers. At the same time, Gulnaz had spoken of her teachers, all more senior, as well as peers that studied and taught other forms.

Dan had never really done the formal dojo thing. The *Batyr* Navy taught classes in various forms of close combat, but they ranged across dozens or even hundreds of Human schools of thought on how to hit and injure people.

Since then, she had studied many things, as well as learning forms and techniques from Nasrin's Sunflower Fist to Ciah's Terrible Gaff to all of the sorts of things that Suka Kuri had picked up from her Sabre School friends over the decades.

She supposed that made her something of a peer to Gulnaz, depending on how you wanted to measure things, though she didn't have a single school of formal techniques codified.

Should she? Sabre School—of which Suka Kuri assured her Dan qualified as a mid-to-high level Adept—intentionally sought out new things to learn, so the whole of Sabre School slowly accreted things like an oyster making a pearl. Things got learned, refined, and handed down, then refined yet again, rather than maintaining a rigid curriculum.

They reached a lull in the various conversations going on around the table. Gulnaz drew all eyes to her with nothing more than the way she squared her shoulders.

"If it is acceptable, Dan, we would like to give you a demonstration of Karmap," she said. "Then perhaps prevail upon you for a demonstration of some of your forms, that we might learn."

Sabre School. Always learning new things. Meeting new people, just as Moss did the exact same thing.

Art, expressed in two different ways, but not all that different at the end of the day.

"I would like that," Dan said, understanding now what Gulmira was up to.

The Combat Team represented women of the various species —and cultures if you assigned Anari to Sabre and Yanouk to Moss as they had originally been—and provided Dan a team of experts who could each speak of their own civilizations with some level of authority.

Dan could generally guess at what made the Khet tick, but

Ciah could dive deep into the most esoteric details, because she was Khet.

Gulmira had understood that only a warrior could be part of what Dan was building, even as Aibek and his family were making arrangements to join the crew and family of *Nubia* on a semi-permanent basis.

Sailing Into Darkness with the Warlord of the Spinward Reaches. A grand sequel to *Karaŋgılıkka*, as it were.

Gulnaz nodded to one of the younger women at the table, who happened to also be one of the more senior students. Somewhere above that first black belt, where your rank merely demonstrated that you understood the forms and the school well enough to start learning it deeper.

Zamira Ismailov. A bit taller and lankier than many of the other women here, when the Isann, like the Khet, tended to be shorter and wider than Humans.

Gulnaz sat, while Ismailov led the others through a form that had remarkable similarities to Tai Chi Chuan, both in speed and in movement. Punches that could be grapples. Grapples that could be throws. Throws that could be punches, all done at a relatively slow and careful pace.

The group had a significant crispness to it, everyone stepping and turning as good as any dance troupe, with no more music than feet on dirt.

The whole form took about eight minutes to complete, and Dan could see sweat stains on bodies when they were done.

Sped up, it would be deadly. Just like many of the other forms that only looked like dance when you practiced them slowly.

"Excellent," Dan nodded as they came to rest.

She stood and removed her gunbelt, resting it next to Nasrin's Omnibow and various implements of death and destruction as she led her team to the space Zamira Ismailov's group vacated.

"Sunflower Fist?" she asked, looking around at them and noting that even Suka Kuri had joined in.

Dan had never gotten a straight answer from the woman about how many bar fights that woman had been in when she was younger, but Suka Kuri knew things that you didn't learn any other way. Dan could speak from experience.

"Lovely idea," Suka Kuri replied. "Not sure my knees are up to Terrible Gaff today."

They laughed.

Terrible Gaff was all about attacking the side of a Khet's head, going after large eyes and sensitive gills to stun then, then dropping to one knee when you had a good grip and face-planting your opponent before they could react.

Dan usually wore knee pads when she was going to be doing that at any sort of speed.

They began, and Dan fell into the rhythm of a sunflower, watching the dawn, proceeding through the day, then enjoying the sunset.

At least that was the philosophical bent. Nasrin had explained it as a form where the first punch has already been thrown and you must slip out of the way, while throwing the puncher into a wall. Or a buddy. Or a moving vehicle that happened to be driving by.

Gulnaz watched with a critical eye, while most of her students were merely studying the form and movements to see what they might steal for Karmap. Only Ismailov frowned like her Elder, watching closely whenever Dan happened to be facing that wall to see the reaction.

They came to rest and Dan felt the sweat, in spite of the coolness. She rejoined the Isann women and sipped some more tea.

"That form is—?" Gulnaz asked.

"Mazhin," Nasrin spoke up. "Something my people contributed to the Corsac Fox. Others have brought their own schools."

"You do not do much floor work?" Zamira asked. "Grapple then take them to the ground to control them?"

"Some of the motions assume a takedown, but the usual goal at that point is to either strike once while they are down, or simply withdraw to safety, having possibly thrown them hard into an immovable object," Nasrin nodded, using all of her tentacles in a way that seemed to mesmerize the Isann women. "Mazhin generally live most of their lives shipboard, or on stations, rather than on the ground. Because of Dan, I have already spent more days planetside than some of my elders, up on the ship."

That caused a polite ruckus.

"The Mazhin do not generally do planets," Nasrin answered one of the questions. Many of the them, all phrased slightly differently, all at once. "The clan or tribe lives and travels aboard a ship. The Corsac Fox has a small group that has been with him from the beginning, and we have been adding youngsters from other Mazhin ships as we travel, same as Katya is part of a larger Ononguli contingent or Ciah and the Khet. Only four Emro at present, but we are a long ways from their normal realms."

Dan approved. More seeds of revolutions planted, where Isann women could go into space and not have to give up everything to do it.

The men meant well as a people. It was merely that they'd lived sheltered lives to date, and needed to dream bigger.

But then, didn't everyone?

Dan settled in and enjoyed her tea, as everyone started to nerd out on the technical aspects of close combat training.

FIRE DIAMOND

FIFTY-EIGHT

It wasn't Tuesday. Lukyan had made damned sure of his navigation there, once Anna had gathered him and the rest up and ordered him to sail to Isann, where Uly had apparently done it again.

Because it was Uly. He got shit done.

And the Isann were already close allies in what? Three months? Something.

Surly had come out of warp with messages for Maks. Maks had called him. Lukyan had updated Anna, possibly almost as fast as Chervonya had, but Lukyan wasn't jealous that Maks had told Chervonya first.

Those two were on the verge of getting serious, if Uly ever came back and relieved Maks of the exquisite trap he'd put Maks Sobol in as Governor of Bastion and the *Watchtower*.

Hell of a way to ruin a guy's love life. Lukyan was just glad that he was generally single, odd weekends and occasional professionals notwithstanding.

Isann looked like a great many other remote and somewhat

isolated ports. Lots of small ships running around doing things. Two small stations. *Corsac Fox*.

"Boss, what the hell is that?" Dmytro asked, gesturing with one hand.

"Uly's new ride," Lukyan replied. "*Nubia*. I did warn you."

"You didn't say it was a Devastator, Lukyan," Dmytro grumbled.

Lukyan shrugged. Nobody had asked, and it was much more fun this way, watching his people politely freak out as that monster turned bow on like an arrow about to fly.

"We're being challenged," Oskar called nervously from his Gunnery station.

Lukyan wasn't surprised there, either. *Fire Diamond* had come in first, but there were already a half-dozen other ships behind him in argosy, like ducks flying south for the winter.

He found the switch and brought it up on the main screen.

Dan.

"Greetings," Lukyan said. "Uly asked for reinforcements. I brought 'em, and the *Vatazhko*. Been idling at Bastion for the last month waiting for you to get back."

"Anything critical?" she asked.

He didn't recognize the bridge, so she must be on *Nubia* itself. And in the conductor's chair from the way he saw Drew, Haydar, and a couple of others stretched out in front of her.

"News," Lukyan shrugged. "I'm just the taxi driver. Anna wanted to talk to Uly about something important enough to travel there, but Maks refused to negotiate anything important while you were gone. Anything interesting happen out here?"

Leading question, but it was Dan. Only second to Uly in most things because Uly. He'd still pick her in any fight. Especially with *Corsac Fox* sitting on one flank like a small shark eyeing your belly for a bite.

"We found the Isann," she nodded. "Then found and recovered an old warship that had been left for us. You probably know about the pirates that had attacked the local harbor while we were gone and didn't leave before we got back."

"Read the executive summary," he said. "Figured it would be more fun to get the blow-by-blow personally. Permission to sail into harbor?"

"Granted," she smiled. "And welcome. We've got a lot of news."

Yeah, he was afraid she was going to say that.

FIFTY-NINE

Anna had intentionally dragged Lukyan back to her office, instead of meeting in his. Both spaces would work equally well, but this made a statement that he was advising his *Vatazhko*, rather than her asking the conductor questions.

She studied the fellow. Unlike a lot of his peers, he was still in the sort of fighting shape he'd been in twenty years ago, and she had pictures from his files she'd compared. Lines in the face and a certain grimness that the youngster had lacked, but he'd been a successful conductor for a decade, first with *Compass Rose* and today on *Fire Diamond*, because she'd needed a reliable commander who knew Uly better than anyone else.

"How powerful is that ship?" she asked as they reached the business part of why she'd brought him here.

Lukyan paused and considered. Another reason she liked him. And valued his opinion. Most Ononguli men shot first then maybe decided if they wanted to aim later. Or not.

"I don't think *Storm Crow* could take it, one-on-one," he finally said. "Looking at the scans we've taken, I'm not sure any of your Devastators could, given that you'd be facing Uly, Sterling, and Drew as a command crew. No, scratch that. Sterling is on the *Fox*, so Uly's probably promoting him to command Adrian's old ship."

"Any chance he'd sell it back to us?" she asked, intrigued at the possibility.

Like *Scavenger Angel*, it could probably be more profitable as a floating hotel than a warship, given the provenance of the ship.

People will pay a lot to let a little bit of the legend rub off on them.

"Only if you swapped him for something bigger," Lukyan laughed. "And I'm not even sure then, since he has a nice patrol vessel to go with his big-bad-battleship. Sterling on his wing would be nasty to take. *Fire Diamond* might be able to take Sterling and the *Fox*. Maybe. On a good day."

Anna paused to consider that. She'd seen the logs of what Huff had done at Nyri, where a squadron of Interceptors led by *Corsac Fox* had shattered an *Auga* Heavy Striker with brutal efficiency.

And Uly had a Devastator now?

And what did it say that Lukyan Chayka freely admitted that his ship wasn't necessarily a match to something smaller? The only other Ononguli she knew with that level of self-awareness had just spent six weeks telling her that he wasn't about to negotiate any important deals without Uly being directly involved.

How had Uly so radically changed Maks and Lukyan that they didn't either of them feel Ononguli anymore?

Worse, was that infection likely to race across the rest of the Horde? And would that be a good thing?

That latter question kept her awake at night.

"Are you in any hurry to get back to Rayzian?" she asked, an obtuse non-sequitur, but a useful one.

She liked the way his eyes got cagey. Narrow. His ears even came forward a shade, locked onto her like a targeting scanner.

"Why?" he countered slowly.

And he could be gruff and short with her. They'd worked

closely on this voyage, grinding off those last few bits of formality that had been there before. Anna also knew that she could trust him, because he'd drag her into a quiet office and yell at her with the hatch closed if he thought she was doing something stupid. He had, twice.

And admitted he'd been wrong for one of them. And she'd been wrong the other time.

"Uly is likely to be turning this into yet another base of operations," she replied. "I've read the reports. Primitive planet only a few generations back to star travel and using old gear they were able to rebuild or crap that some traveling merchant sold them."

"The latter," Lukyan said automatically. "I recognize some Ugotha kit in the basic tech lines of their ships."

Anna filed that away for use later. If she needed to worry about it.

"Just so," she nodded. "And we brought four patrol cutters with us that Maks said were being sold to the locals for one Imperial Guilder apiece. Dead minimum crews, so those folks might be traveling home with Uly. Or staying here and training their replacements. That will still take time."

"Plus Uly and Dan need to recruit and train more folks to fill in slots on both ships," Lukyan nodded. "Maybe send *Surly* on yet another loop with a recruiting poster, next time they make a cargo run, so folks come here from Bastion and bring trade with them. Sneaky, because that turns the *Watchtower* into a true fortress, intercepting access back here, at least psychologically."

Anna absorbed that and nodded. She did politics and trade on Rayzian, capital of the Ononguli Sphere, while this conductor had spent a successful generation out on the periphery, where things followed much different rules.

And she could see Uly building up a completely new trade network with whatever other worlds he found back here, because even on her maps, there were none. Stars marked *Galactica Incognita*.

Here there be dragons.

And Uly had obviously set his mind to changing that.

"Are you ready to learn why I've been willing to travel this far myself?" she asked Lukyan, watching his flinch that never made it past his eyes. "Why I was willing to wait quietly and help Maks get things done, rather than return to Rayzian?"

"No," he said sourly. "But I don't suppose that will do me any good."

She nodded. Smiled even, just a little. Again, most conductors would jump at the chance to be involved in something directly with the *Vatazhko*. Certainly Maks had made a lot of money from his willingness to play along.

Lukyan Chayka didn't look at her like she was trying to grind his horns off, but he also didn't sugar coat things, either.

You got honesty from the man. And she doubted that he understood how valuable that was in her position.

"I took your advice," she said, just to watch that flinch turn into a twitch.

He watched her warily now. Anna relished it. Savored that intellectual dueling with this man, who had nothing to prove to her. Merely the mind to fence.

"Which bit?" he asked in a sideways kind of voice.

"Making Uly one of us," she said simply.

His eyes crossed as he furiously backtracked in his head to remember what he'd said.

Might take a while, as it had been years now. And a throwaway comment on his part that had slowly built resonance as she and her other advisors—like Chervonya—had thought about it.

"You can't," he finally said. "Everything the Horde uses as any sort of legal or social structure is built into the clans. Into blood ties and marriage and all that."

"Exactly, Lukyan," she smiled.

Anna really did treasure his ability to think clearly. To react with his mind first before his gut. And his willingness to bash horns with people when he thought they were wrong.

Even his *Vatazhko*.

"What am I missing?" he asked, further endearing himself. "How do you intend to finesse that in a way that doesn't piss off everybody and split the Horde right down the middle between the ones who see Uly as a way to start attacking *Auga* worlds and those who can't get past the lack of horns?"

"It took a while," she said, teasing him now, but teasing this man was a fun game they could both play. Adults, being comfortable in themselves. "And involved a lot of seriously vicious arguments behind closed doors, with an understanding that I would blackball the entire clan of anyone that leaked."

More flinch on his part. Every conductor went into space knowing that the *Vatazhko* could break them if they screwed up bad enough.

But to extend that to the entire clan...

Not even Adrian had ever screwed up that badly, though from some of the stories Maks had told, Adrian Sobol had tried a time or two. Probably just as well that the *Auga* refused to negotiate his release. Him and about a dozen other troublemakers that Anna didn't really miss today.

There were other firebreathers out there, and most of them would take orders better than the prior crew of the former *Iron Wasp*.

"And?" he finally asked, when it was clear that she would outwait him.

"And you were right," Anna said. "Then and now. The Horde would not accept him as he is, in spite of everything, because he's an alien. So we're going to make him one of us."

"How?" Lukyan asked, circling all the way back up to the top with a glower of discontent that she adored, because it was just irritation on his part at the verbal games, when they both knew they could skip them if they wanted.

"By offering him a marriage contract to an Ononguli woman of good family," Anna said simply. "Then he fits into the wider Ononguli network, has allies in the Horde as well as in the ones he brings to the table. He becomes one of us."

She'd never seen Lukyan Chayka at a loss for words. She'd seen—and heard him—angry enough to chew nails. Drunk enough to stop himself just short of making a pass at her. Philosophical about the unstoppable avalanche that was the Corsac Fox.

She'd never seen him struck mute, mouth hanging open for several seconds before his brain rebooted and he regained physical control.

"It's a damned good thing you didn't breathe a word of this to Maks," he managed in a quiet, grim tone Anna wasn't sure she'd ever heard from him. "That boy might have tossed you out of his harbor personally. I presume Chervonya knew and kept her mouth shut?"

"Yes, and you will as well," Anna ordered. "Am I clear?"

"As long as you aren't surprised later if I end up not picking your side, if push ever comes to shove," he nodded grimly.

"Picking Uly over me?" she snapped, but there wasn't much fire behind it. Curiosity, more than anything.

"Winning over losing, Anna," Lukyan growled. "I know better than to bet against Uly these days. Or Dan. You really don't understand their relationship, do you?"

Anna felt that first spike of dread take hold. What did Lukyan know that nobody, including Maks, had found out?

"Talk to me," she said. "We are in the privacy of my office, and everything that happens today stays here, am I clear?"

"Utterly, Anna," he said. "I have no intention of stepping into that firing line, even with orders from you. Uly and Dan might as well be one entity, *Vatazhko*. They aren't married in any legal sense because what they have been building is something they consider too fragile to let their personal emotions get in the way of it, if something went wrong later. Without Uly, Dan would still be an amazingly dangerous person, if you got her as an enemy. How do you think she'll react to this news?"

Oh.

Was there something there? Everyone had assured her that the relationship, even after this many years, must be entirely professional, down to the level of sleeping in two different cabins. Were they a romantic element and she'd missed it?

The *alienness* of everything jumped up and bit her on the ass as she studied Lukyan's hard eyes.

Humans. For all Uly came across as Ononguli in the important ways, he was still an alien. Had all of her *ONONGULI* advisors misread the situation?

At that moment, she was simply glad that she hadn't ended up bringing Halyna with her on this mission. She could still back off and never let this news see the light of day, because Maks didn't know and Lukyan's look promised that he would take this to his grave with him unspoken.

Might deny ever knowing her if pushed hard enough. Angry enough. And he might be.

Could Humans have that level of romantic relationship that was never the least bit public? That was alien to Anna, but she'd never married. Never found a male or female who was willing to accept second place behind her drive to power. To glory.

To *Vatazhko*.

Anna took two deep breaths as the silence stretched. Recalibrated everything all of her other advisors had told her, in light of someone who wasn't really Ononguli anymore, but still understood his people. He and Maks were half Human, folks had joked.

She'd joked as well, when she should have seen that there was a hole in her logic. In her advice.

In how she should move forward.

"How many people back home know?" Lukyan asked quietly as she sat silent. "In case you need to bury this information without ever bringing it up?"

Anna did the math. Considered the folks who actually knew. It had been kept as a remarkably tight secret, with the number who should know being under fifteen, now including Lukyan and Chervonya.

"Not that many," she said, pivoting to view Lukyan as a key advisor now, instead of someone she could talk about life with. "What would you suggest?"

Again, he came perfectly still and his eyes focused on a point a thousand light-years over her left shoulder for long enough that she'd wondered if he'd been turned to stone.

"Get Uly and Dan alone," he finally said. "Whatever cover excuse you need to use to do it. Nobody, including me, should know. Good thing you left Chervonya back at the *Watchtower* to keep Maks honest. You take Uly and Dan aside. You mention that it is an option. An OPTION, mind you, and not a requirement because that would probably piss them both off, even if they saw it as a good strategic move. Not that you'd done it, but that it became a *fait accompli* you dropped on them. Make sure Dan stays calm, because she can kill you with her bare hands so fast you won't know you're dead before you're in hell. Even you. Make sure Uly has an emotional and political opening where he can back off and walk away, if he needs to. Make sure you understand, Anna Shevchenko, that a *no* today might turn into a *maybe* in another year and a *yes* in three, so do not try to trap him. That's the best advice I can give you, because I don't know how they will react when you bring it up. Especially today, when Uly suddenly has a whole new set of allies in his back pocket, physically as well as metaphorically, plus a new flagship that wasn't there when you set out on this jaunt."

He stopped cold there and Anna controlled her temper. Her pique, that he'd had the audacity to issue her orders.

But they were in the privacy of her office. And he'd done this twice before, once when he was right, and once when he was wrong.

She suspected that he was right today, because he'd been up front that he'd pick the winning side over the losing one, and didn't necessarily expect it to be her.

And it was one hell of a risk, far beyond the immediacy that Lukyan had pointed out. A lot of the firebreathers back home would never accept Uly, even with an Ononguli wife. Even if she was a Bondarenko.

Anna might split the Horde right down the center at the worst possible moment, just when everyone predicted that the *Auga* were ramping up for their next invasion, however long Uly had delayed it by attacking Nyri.

But she'd done the math with her other advisors before coming out here. Had talked to Maks's mom in detail, because Halyna Bondarenko was her niece. Maks' first cousin.

Someone Anna had known since birth, just like her own niece Chervonya.

Lukyan's face relented.

"What do you need from me?" he asked.

"Keep me honest," Anna said. "And you'll be in the room with me when I talk to Uly and Dan, because nobody else knows them as well as you do."

His grimace was telling, but it vanished as quickly as it arrived.

"Okay," he said simply, acknowledging everything with one simple word. "I'll be there."

Anna nodded. She was going to rely on Lukyan more than she'd understood even as recently as yesterday.

SIXTY

Uly could feel it in the air, though he couldn't actually identify the scent. Maybe Nasrin or Haydar could. Possibly Piruz, or maybe Ethir, because it felt more like a scam than a difference in opinion.

In fact…

"Kossari," Piruz replied to the intercom with a bark and the grind of metal in the background fading.

"I need a Horse Thief," Uly replied. "Can you put out whatever you were doing and join me in my office?"

"It's not on fire," Piruz replied sullenly. "Made sure to remove flammables before I started working. Do I need a shower or is stinky okay?"

"Stinky is fine," Uly replied. "I'll only need you for a few minutes, then you can go back to the machine shop and play."

"Be right there."

Uly nodded and rose, putting aside the reader and reports he'd been absorbing. Maks had sent a voluminous report on trade and construction, including the part where the *Watchtower* was basically done except for painting and folks could move in whenever Uly or Dan gave the word and approved newcomers.

He moved to the sideboard and poured himself some fresh coffee as a mental and physical break from what he'd been doing.

Looking around, this conference space on *Nubia* was larger than the office he'd kept on *Corsac Fox*, even with Adrian Sobol's ego's demand for volume. The woman who had lived here had needed to hold big meetings. Probably planning sessions, as there was her desk at this end and a flat table with a built-in display and holoprojector closer to the hatch.

What kind of career had Selene Praxis had in command? And what had happened to her later, after she'd parked her ship and departed for all eternity?

Uly still saw *Nubia* as Dan's ship, but that was because every log he reviewed had her people looking back at him, darker and browner than the Turks who were his ancestors. Different bones in the face. Different eyes. Curly hair.

Many of them were attractive, but only Selene came close to as beautiful as Dan, and she'd been dead for at least three millennia at this point.

Who had she been?

Dan mentioned privately seeing Selene as an aunt, so Uly tried to frame her that way. To see the Yarikh in the light of folks from Aurtan.

And to see her as the kind of woman who had personally inspired the *Karaŋgılıkka*. That helped, because Uly didn't feel as alone that way, knowing that others had stood on the edge of night, looking out before setting sail.

The hatch opened and Piruz entered.

Uly gestured him for coffee and headed back to his desk, settling in as the Horse Thief got to work on his own mug.

They ended up facing each other across the space. Uly sat for a few minutes to let Piruz absorb his smell. His emotions. His surface thoughts.

"Do we know what's causing it?" Piruz finally asked. "You aren't the only person reacting a little hinky to Anna Shevchenko.

We've talked about it quietly, but wondered if it was just us. Of course, you're as close to being a Mazhin as someone born with ears could be."

"I don't know, Piruz," Uly acknowledged. "Anna is up to something. Maks makes note of it in his reports, but also spells out clearly that she didn't mention anything useful to him directly. Chervonya Borisov knew the secret, but didn't share. Maks read it by the way the woman changed after Anna arrived."

"Gotcha," Piruz nodded. "So the *Vatazhko* of the Ononguli is up to no good, but not necessarily in an evil way where we need to send assassins after her or ambush her with bandits. Yet."

"Something like that," Uly nodded. "I'd like you to maybe dig a little deeper. Ask other Mazhin to pay attention. Get Ethir and the cousins involved. Have Rabiu drag in some of the Khet. I doubt that anybody but Anna knows the truth right now, but she might have mentioned something to someone, as a way of preparing them. For what, I have no idea."

"We trust her?" Piruz asked, all of his tentacles forward now.

"She is an ally who has done right by us so far," Uly answered. "When she didn't necessarily have to. The *Watchtower* came together so quickly because she put up some resources and found us people, rather than me having to recruit more slowly and weed out spies for the *Auga*."

"Think the bill is coming due?" Piruz asked.

"That might be it," Uly shrugged. "If so, it must be something hugely important if she wouldn't tell Maks Sobol about it. Affairs of State, as it were, when he was only filling in as Governor while I was gone, because I'd asked and Maks owed me a lot of favors."

"The Ononguli are all about favors, right?" Piruz asked.

Uly thought about that concept for a moment, then nodded.

"Yes," he agreed. "The entire culture is connected that way, but the favors are personal things, rather than the sorts of business connections and economic profit that drives the Khet of Z'Gosza."

"And they span generations," Piruz noted. "I've heard some

rumblings from Maks about how his mother was the one with a personal connection to the *Vatazhko*, and how he didn't know that until she reached out to the Lord of the Endless Plains and said something. Or asked for something."

"Or fulfilled an old debt, yes," Uly said. "If we were home, I'd have you lean in on the construction folks for clues, but I get the impression that whatever she's up to will happen here, since she chose to come, even knowing that I'd be headed to Bastion in another month or so."

"Do you ambush her instead?" Piruz asked. "Get the Spatula to do something extra special for the three of you with Dan? Private quarters dinner without all us lessers running around eating cheese with the wrong fork?"

Uly laughed at the image. The Mazhin tended to have the best table manners of any group he knew, savoring meals with so many senses that everyone else lacked.

"Something," Uly agreed. "You grab Ethir and see what you can find out in the next day or so. If it turns out to be serious, that's probably about as long as we have, because she already bided her time at Bastion, helping Maks with various things, for more than a month, waiting for us. Her time might be up, because she'll have to return to the Sphere at some point."

"On it," Piruz said, rising and taking his coffee with him. "Keep Dan in the loop or bring it straight to you?"

"Whichever you think is appropriate," Uly said. "She'll find out soon enough if there is anything."

"I'm gone," Piruz announced, then fit deed to word.

Uly watched the closed hatch. Something was up.

But he'd set folks in motion to find out what.

SIXTY-ONE

Dan studied Lukyan's face as they settled on either side of her desk.

He looked tired. Possibly in better physical shape than the day she'd met him at Lacium, in spite of being into middle age, but worn right now.

"I'm going to start in the middle," Dan said, knowing that Lukyan was sharp enough to keep up with her in ways that even Maks found a little daunting at times.

He nodded, keeping his eyes shielded and his horns up.

"Uly invited Anna to a private dinner," Dan continued. "Them, plus me, so we could talk business at a very high level, since Anna had decided that there was something she needed to come all the way to Bastion to discuss personally. Anna insisted that you join us and make it a foursome."

He nodded warily, like a man waiting for the other shoe to drop. From the way he held himself perfectly still, Dan was willing to bet money that Lukyan knew what trouble Anna was bringing.

She also knew Lukyan well enough to know that she'd have to find some pretty awful and creative ways to torture him, if she wanted to actually drag it out of him.

It could wait. She had something more interesting she wanted to pursue. Dan even smiled.

Lukyan's hackles came up with his shoulders and the tips of his ears.

"So, are you and Anna an item?" she asked in a simple, blunt, friendly tone. Mostly to watch him politely freak out and nearly chew his lips off keeping his mouth shut.

Surprised, sure as hell. A whole wealth of other emotions in there, too. Like, all of them, if you wanted to snap pictures at sixty frames per second and then blow them up and catalog them individually later.

"What makes you say that?" he finally managed, in a voice that wouldn't even fool himself, let alone her.

"The way you watch each other, even when you don't," Dan replied. He deserved honesty, for all the good things he and Maks had done for her and Uly over the years. "The way you anticipate her motions and conversations. I've been watching in the larger groups."

"We had a long flight out from Rayzian," Lukyan shrugged. "And a lot of conversations where it was just us, because most of my mob aren't interested in dealing with someone that dangerous on a personal level."

"You don't mind," Dan pointed out.

"I know you and Uly," he countered. "Anna's wonderful people. I'd still rate her third most dangerous in that room."

"You're fourth," Dan observed.

"Not when Nasrin or Suka Kuri are present," he laughed harshly. "Maybe also some of your other ladies I don't know that well, but absolutely not those two."

"Which circles me back," Dan nodded. "Are you two an item? Maks and Chervonya are. Or will be, if we ever get back to Bastion. I've read enough between the lines that he's utterly smitten with the woman and won't do anything because he takes his responsibilities to Uly too serious."

"That he does," Lukyan chucked. "I pointed that out to Anna more than once."

He paused. Dan watched him closer, looking for those hints that she'd learned to read from him over the last few years.

"Maybe," he finally admitted, possibly to himself as much as to her. "Nothing's ever happened, but I get the feeling she's comfortable in my presence."

Dan laughed. Lukyan looked surprised.

"I've watched her with the other Lords of the Endless Plains, Lukyan," she said. "Including Harald, who she likes. Anna's not the least bit worried about you when she talks or when you do."

"I won't challenge her authority," he nodded, throwing in a shrug for good measure. "Not like a lot of other conductors. Even ones who know better still occasionally see her as a woman first and a hard-ass killer second. At least until they make their first mistake and she eviscerates them, metaphorically or socially."

"You're avoiding my question," Dan pressed.

"Because I don't want to admit anything, even to myself, Dan," he countered with a sigh. "I got no idea. She hasn't said anything to me and I'm in almost as bad a situation as Maks that way. Not something I can walk up and ask her. Dmytro did point out that I was a little drunk one night at Bastion and he thought I was about to proposition her. I have been stone-cold sober since then."

"You do look like hell," Dan noted. "Even Tuesdays haven't been this bad. Anything I can do to make your life less miserable?"

"Remember that I wouldn't be in the room with you, her, and Uly except that she made it a formal order to me," he answered, turning deadly serious. "She has a suggestion for Uly. I told her to walk softly and carefully in doing it, because I'm about the only advisor she has who knows both sides of the equation."

"If she fires you, Uly and I can always find you a new gig," Dan reminded him. "We tend to keep finding more ships than we have crews for them. That's why I'm still formally the conductor of *Nubia* at the moment. The Sphere's loss would be our gain."

"I'll keep that in mind, if I do piss her off enough next time," he grinned.

"Next time?"

"I've dragged her into an office like this to yell at her twice," he mused. "And apologized once when I was wrong. She apologized the time it was her mistake."

"See, she does like you," Dan smiled.

"She's still the boss," he shrugged. "I work for that woman, and remain employed at her good will."

"Or mine," Dan reminded him.

"If you still like me afterwards."

Dan let that one go. Anna really had spooked Lukyan, and he wasn't going to say anything more than he had.

She could read his body language. Maybe not as well as Haydar or Nasrin, but Anna had put the fear of something big into him, and he was honoring that. Honoring Anna.

If the woman did end up blackballing him, Dan would hire Lukyan in a heartbeat, because he'd made it clear that Anna's idea wasn't his. Or his fault.

Merely his load to carry in secrecy until it came out.

"So you keep being you," Dan said, rising. He rose with her and looked more relaxed than he had since he'd arrived at Isann. "We'll sort it out and I won't hold you responsible."

"That's really all I can ask, Dan," he said, seeing himself out without another word.

Dan considered saying something to Uly, but he'd mentioned his misgivings about Anna already, though he didn't know what. And it would come out over dinner.

How bad could it be?

SIXTY-TWO

Uly had showered, shaved, and even gotten his hair cut, a concept that the Mazhin still found a source of endless amusement, but they only had the finest body hair from what he'd been told. Not even eyebrows.

He'd dug out the nice uniform that Omid had hand-sewn for special occasions. Medium blue, trimmed with scarlet and a pale green she'd called mint. The heavy black boots with a matte finish. The pants baggier than he was used to, but they breathed better. T-shirt tucked in under a button-up jacket with rank tabs on his neck and shoulder straps for a weapon, should he feel the need to strap something on.

Dan matched him. Anna and Lukyan had gone equally formal, in the lime they wore: tunic, shirt, and jacket, trimmed in white, rose, and black. They'd even arrived with the opera-style cloaks that were part of the outfit, in spite of being on a starship, where there was no weather.

But she was the Lord of the Endless Plains herself. The *Vatazhko* of the Ononguli, with the silver Rayed Sun of Rayzian on her shoulders, even as Lukyan had the solid circle in rose gold of a conductor marking his place.

Anna's right hand tonight, even as Dan was his other half in all the ways that mattered.

Maybe all of them.

Nasrin had met them at the airlock and conducted them to a small dining room not that far from those kitchens that Vahid had taken to like a duck takes to water. They even shared a bottle of *Danumash* wine from the badly-depleted stocks that Uly had inherited from *King Hewitt II*.

Not many of those left, but Piruz and Ethir had found a yeast that could be used by others to make something similar. As long as you didn't expect to be a connoisseur of such things.

This was to make it that extra level of formal, as everyone had been a little brittle on arrival. Lukyan because he didn't want to be collateral damage. Dan with him, expecting something that Anna was afraid might piss him off enough to ruin the formal relationship between nations.

Lukyan seemed worried that Uly or Dan would throw them off the ship.

Uly's mother had raised him to never shirk from his duty, no matter how painful it might be. He supposed that stubbornness had gotten him where he was today, so Uly wasn't about to take anything out on Lukyan. That man was here because Anna had demanded it.

How bad would it get?

"Should we eat first or deal with your news, Anna?" Uly asked as everyone got settled.

Anna and Lukyan had watered their wine, but all held glasses, as if prepared to toast.

"Dinner first," she replied.

Dan nodded and sent Nasrin off to let Vahid know. They spoke instead of news of Bastion and the *Watchtower*. Things that Uly and Dan had learned from the Isann and the Yarikh, which turned out to cover several courses of dishes Vahid had selected from local ingredients to impress the *Vatazhko*, having known the various Ononguli of the crews for so long.

Finally, they finished a dessert tart pastry containing a jellied local fruit. Vahid, rising to the occasion such that Uly considered licking his plate clean, manners be damned.

But things had grown formal again. Almost brittle, in spite of the good food and two hours of companionable conversation with friends.

At least he hoped they would still be friends when it was all done.

Uly set his wine down and stared at Anna.

She took a sip and nodded to herself. Lukyan had gone perfectly still. Dan was keyed up like combat was imminent.

Hopefully not.

"Talk to me," Uly instructed Anna. "We are all friends here. Affairs of state might impinge, but never forget that."

"It helps, Uly," Anna replied. "I have a proposal for the Corsac Fox."

He liked the way she was so easily able to divide him into two people. Ulysses Fortier and The Corsac Fox. A Human many many light-years from home. The leader of a new star nation in the process of being born, here in the vastness of the Spinward Reaches.

"I will preface by suggesting that Lukyan Chayka commented years ago that the Ononguli Sphere didn't really have a mechanism by which the Corsac Fox could become one of us," Anna continued. "That everything in our system presumed that you were either Ononguli or an outsider, with no middle ground."

Uly nodded. Ethir, Rabiu, and Piruz had actually found that, looking at various contract language Lukyan had provided at Lacium, because *Iron Wasp*'s command safe had been emptied by the *Auga* when they captured Adrian Sobol.

He watched the *Vatazhko* closely for body language,

wondering if she knew how much she was broadcasting. Or maybe it was all the time he had spent around the Mazhin, learning how to listen with all his senses instead of just one.

"My advisors have come up with a solution that might—MIGHT, I remind you—bridge that gap," Anna said. "Lukyan insisted that the entire conversation be handled by the three of us, but I required that he accompany me because he and Maks understand you and Dan better than just about anyone I could ask. I trust his judgment. He also insisted that it be done in this privacy, in case you found the proposal objectionable and wished me to bury it and pretend like this conversation never happened."

Uly turned to Lukyan. Today was not Tuesday. That was not an accident, but Uly appreciated how superstitious Lukyan could be about the subject.

And he liked the fellow. Many people he respected. Few he liked.

Lukyan nodded exactly enough to convey that he hadn't been replaced by a statue, and no more.

Uly turned back to Anna and nodded at her to proceed.

"It would be possible to make you one of us, Uly," Anna said, her voice dropping to just above a whisper. "If you wished to be brought that deep into Ononguli politics."

Uly let the ghost of a grin play across his face. He'd had monumental arguments with Lukyan, early on, in similarly private settings, where voices could be raised and issues settled without going outside that space.

Because he had stolen *Iron Wasp* from the *Auga*. Because he had brought a chunk of Adrian's crew with him, however augmented by everyone else either then or now. The Ononguli Horde expected him to be Ononguli himself.

And he wasn't. Thus, everything slammed into a bulkhead that it was not prepared to avoid, because the Ononguli had NEVER had to deal with a similar situation, going back millennia.

"And your proposal?" Uly asked, matching her tone with his own quietness.

"A political marriage," Anna answered. "A woman of the Bondarenko clan, as your wife under Horde law, thus making you a blood-ally of the Bondarenko, and a close ally of the Shevchenko."

Uly was impressed. Lukyan might be carved from red granite. Dan had gasped once, then fallen silent.

"Maks's mother is Bondarenko, if I recall correctly?" Uly asked, probing.

Anna nodded.

"Lyra Bondarenko Sobol," Anna said. "Her niece is at the top of my list. Maks's cousin. And no, he has no idea, because he refused to even entertain discussing affairs of state with me at Bastion."

"Smart boy," Dan breathed heavily.

"Oh, I agree," Anna gestured to her. "The connection to his mother goes back well before he was born. I've known who he was forever. And learned to trust his judgment and his brains when Lukyan here brought him back from Khet space."

Uly nodded. Lukyan had had his own reasons for remaining away from the Ononguli Sphere, but Maks had allied with Anna more recently and made a lot of money doing it. And held his honor more dearly than his wallet, so Uly had made him Governor of Bastion, at least for now.

Only for now? Something else to consider.

Uly drew a breath to say something, and Dan's hand on his arm stalled him.

He turned to look at his partner in all things. Waited for her to nod to him, then she turned to Anna.

"We'd need to see a proposed marriage contract," she said simply.

Uly felt all the air want to rush out of his lungs, but managed to keep everything still. Almost like Lukyan.

Was Dan seriously considering such a thing?

And he couldn't ask her now. Not in front of strangers. Even these two. Perhaps especially these two.

Anna had frozen. Probably expecting the sharp edge of someone's tongue.

As she should, given the circumstances.

What had Dan seen or known that he had missed? Obviously, she was as smart as he was. And more cunning, because she'd lived in harder places that the son of an Assistant Deputy Secretary of the Party might never imagine outside of books or vids.

And he trusted her completely, so Uly kept his mouth shut and let Dan negotiate. Whatever it was that she was after.

"I have such a thing I could transmit," Anna said quietly. "Obviously, this was not a situation I could easily prepare for, without an endless array of options, most of which would be superfluous."

"Understood," Dan replied. "What will the Horde say, if this were to happen?"

"Lukyan suspects a fracturing," Anna admitted, nodding to the man. "Those willing to accept the Corsac Fox because of everything he's done, up to, including, and beyond Nyri. Those others who will only see the lack of horns and be unable to get past that."

"I'm familiar with the feeling," Dan said so dryly that Uly wondered if somebody should be bleeding as a result.

Anna flinched. Lukyan grimaced exactly enough to register, but remained locked in tight on himself.

"How quickly did you need an answer?" Dan pressed, like they were dickering over points on a currency arbitrage contract with a Khet Trade Factor.

Uly kept his utter shock inside, next to his wonder, his surprise, and his anger. Where nobody could see it.

"If the answer were to be an immediate no, that would be sufficient," Anna said, relaxing some as Uly watched. "If a solution is negotiable, then knowing that simply means that my people need to be locked in a room with yours to discuss all those details. This would bring the Horde in on Uly's side."

"And draw the Corsac Fox into our wars," Lukyan pointed out. "Bondarenko will gain new enemies, even as it grows in stature and profitability."

"We'd sic the Khet and the Mazhin on them," Dan said, chuckling musically.

In the same way that a rusty razor blade can be said to be *artistic*. It all came down to how you used it.

Uly was lost. How could Dan even be entertaining the concept?

Except that she was. That much was obvious from the way she spoke. Held herself. Smiled professionally, even.

What would it mean between them, if the Ononguli suddenly contracted him with a wife?

Uly didn't know.

Still, the person he trusted above and beyond everyone else seemed to have a plan.

That was enough for him.

"At this juncture, I think it would be beneficial to everyone if we withdrew to our ship," Anna said, rising. "You'll have to discuss such things with your advisors in depth, and then review contract language and make the first of what I expect to be a series of counter-offers. I understand, and look forward to news."

Uly rose with them. Saw them to the door, where Emil had stationed himself as a guard and steward, escorting the two Ononguli down the corridor and out of sight.

He turned to Dan, saw the emotions roiling her now. Uly closed the hatch with them alone inside, then locked it and studied her closely, even as she did the same.

"Do you trust me?" she asked.

"Completely," Uly replied.

SIXTY-THREE

Dan studied his face. Always, she compared this man to Lieutenant Dupuis, her former boss, back in the bad old days of *Marshall Castillon*. Always Dupuis was found lacking in her mind. As a person, as a boss, anything.

Because Uly trusted her. Completely. Believed in her. Would do whatever she instructed, trusting her judgment.

She couldn't help herself. She grabbed him and pulled the man into a kiss that surprised him almost as much as it did her.

Wasn't much, as first kisses went, save for the promise behind it. Still, if felt like everything she'd ever hoped it might be. Dreamed of. Dreaded.

He gasped as she let him step back, but he didn't go far. Stayed right up where they were breathing on each other. Where she was certain he could hear her heart pounding. Like she could probably hear his.

There was a cliff in front of her, and their toes were right at the edge of it.

If she dared to jump. To fly.

"I have an idea," she said in a whisper. "It's not a plan yet, but it will be, once I talk to some people about a few details."

He nodded, watching. Silent.

Trusting.

She could suddenly see clear to the bottom of his soul. See the pain there, where he thought that having an Ononguli wife might suddenly come between them and he'd lose her, because the affairs of state would be more important than the happiness of two people.

She wouldn't allow it.

"You keep being you," she told him.

"Whatever you need," Uly replied.

Dan wondered if it was possible that he could endear himself even more to her soul, but he kept finding ways, for all that had been the first time they had ever taken any sort of step like that.

"I need you to trust me," Dan repeated.

"Yes."

Gods, could she have found a better man? A better partner?

She could see that in his eyes.

Yes.

"We will see what kind of contract they offer," Dan breathed, working out details even as she spoke them aloud. "The Ononguli Horde is not sufficient to stop the *Auga*. They never have been, but the *Auga* have been patient enough to bite off individual chunks and chew them up before proceeding to the next one."

He nodded. Listening.

How many officers had she ever known—how many men— who *listened* to her? Saw beyond the color of her skin or the gender of her uniform or the rank stripes and actually expected her to have a sound, solid, rational, useful opinion? On any topic?

None, save one.

"In order to defeat the *Auga*, the Ononguli will need friends," she continued, unrolling all these ideas and tasting them as she did. Sweet. Bitter. Fire. Ash. Glory. "Except that they cannot have friends, because everything they do was always them against the rest of the entire galaxy. The Corsac Fox upsets that, even if they do manage to make him one of them by connecting him to the Bondarenko clan as a blood ally."

"Does Anna understand that I will bring all of the Spinward Reaches with me?" he asked, falling into a political discussion rather than an emotional one.

Because he trusted her.

"I think she is counting on it," Dan answered. "That the others might not realize how many worlds and people that will be, when the Corsac Fox raises his banner and calls on *everyone* to rally to his side to fight the *Auga*. Anna knows. The other Lords of the Endless Plains might have to discover that yet."

She watched him nod, absorbing her ideas and accepting them without comment, because he had tasked her with building up the political side of the Corsac Fox. With creating that thing that would have him as the leader everyone acknowledged, even as he was counting on her to run it, while he continued to charm folks like the Isann.

Though she might be the one that brought the Yarikh on board, once someone took Sterling's grand map and sailed to those places to find them.

Dan nodded back.

"The devil, as they say, will be in the details," she continued. "I intend to put points and vesting in for Rabiu, Ethir, and Piruz, so we can guarantee that they will go over and above everything they did to the folks at Z'Gosza. Or Lacium. Or even *Taeli Station*."

She grinned as his eyes crossed a little in confusion, trying to parse that, but this was just a different kind of treaty. The Khet of Z'Gosza worshiped business, so they had raised contract law to a holy text.

The Ononguli saw themselves as warriors astride the Endless Plain. Dan could use that against them just as well.

He nodded again. Acceptance. Trust that she would do this right, and he could believe in her to accomplish it.

She grabbed him again for a second kiss. Longer. Held it as she finally allowed herself to enjoy this man. His touch. His kiss. His soul. It was filled with the promise of things she couldn't even say right now, because she didn't know. Needed to work out a few details that had never occurred to her until this moment.

Uly relied on her. On her.

Dan had her team, but she had Uly. He would do what she told him was for the best.

They broke and he smiled at her.

"Your orders, Conductor Chastain?" he asked with a bright, teasing smile.

She kissed him a third time, mostly to make up for the years when they had danced silently around this topic. Hadn't allowed themselves the joy and hope of taking that next—that final—step into what they could become. How much love they could express.

Could share.

The dancing was done, because Anna Shevchenko had put them into a situation where there would have to be hard decisions made.

"We need to settle Sterling," she stated, gasping a little as her breath refused to stay normal. "I appreciate that you wanted to wait on that topic, but I think affairs of state interfere at this point."

"Agreed," he said simply. "And I need to free you up from commanding *Nubia* to handle more important things, but I'm glad we did it this way. That you got to be there, to see it done and do it yourself. That will make a lot of things easier for both of us later, because nobody can *ever* challenge you on those grounds."

Again, he was thinking of her instead of himself. Of how her time commanding a flagship like this in combat put her at least on a par with any other conductor that came along later.

Just one of the many reasons she loved him. And understood,

watching him, how much he loved her, and how desperately frightened he was that he might lose her.

You will never lose me, Uly. But I can't give you all the details just yet.

She smiled. Kissed him again with promise.

"Back to work?" he asked.

"Back to work," she agreed. "How soon do we tell the others?"

"When you drop a printout of that contract on the Legal Department and instruct them to make it better," he grinned, taking her hand in his and drawing her to the hatch.

Because he trusted her.

She wasn't about to let him down.

SIXTY-FOUR

Suka Kuri listened to Dan's entire explanation without comment. It was a skill she had developed over long decades of learning, that ability to silently absorb everything, then repeat it back years later, down to the specific inflections, that she could pass on those stories and keep them alive for the Moss School.

Finally, Dan wound down to silence, but it had taken nearly an hour. A whole second pot of tea brewed and consumed.

Silence stretched. Dan watched her fearfully. Why fearful, Suka Kuri had no idea, but perhaps it was just nerves at the raw audacity of what Dan proposed.

Because Commander Sheridan Chastain—Conductor Chastain—never did things small.

"Thoughts?" Dan asked in a tiny voice.

Suka Kuri laughed, which seemed to be the last thing Dan was expecting from the way her face scrunched in.

"Dan, I continue to be so happy that I lived in the current era and had the opportunity to know you," Suka Kuri replied. "Uly as well, but he will be as famous as Zamir Aytiev in his own way.

Nobody will ever understand how dangerous you were as an opponent.”

“Lukyan knows,” Dan said absently.

“That just goes to show that he’s smarter than he lets on,” she nodded. “Hopefully, Anna Shevchenko realizes it and doesn’t let that one get away.”

“You think she will?” Dan asked, whiplashed sideways again, but that got her loosened up enough to think.

“I will make a point of suggesting it to her at some point,” Suka Kuri replied. “What good is it being an old woman, if I can’t get up in the faces of youngsters and speak truth to power occasionally?”

“You never have with Uly or me,” Dan noted.

“I’ve never needed to,” she beamed. “Both of you listen and pay attention to what is going on around you. The *Vatazhko* might have overlooked the man because he’s too close to her, most of the time. It will be my job to fix that.”

“How?”

“Oh, I’m wilier than most people give me credit for,” Suka Kuri noted dryly, causing Dan to laugh.

“As to your plan, Dan, I agree wholeheartedly,” Suka Kuri turned serious. “It builds on everything you and I have already been up to before this, and creates an entirely new thing in the universe, at a time when this galaxy might have gotten a little stale and full of itself and risks turning stodgy when it wasn’t looking. And I’m an expert on avoiding *that* silliness.”

“It will change everything.”

“Good,” Suka Kuri laughed. “Those old farts need to be shaken up. Or shaken to their very cores. Whichever thing will break them out of their thinking best.”

“Oh?”

“Dan, what did you and Uly do to the Khet?” Suka Kuri probed.

She’d never heard of this Socrates fellow until recently, but Suka Kuri approved. He’d have been an Exemplar of the Moss

School, were he around today. Possibly Sabre as well, since he'd been a noted warrior in his youth, however incredibly long ago that might have been.

That Humans still carried him with them today merely spoke to the truths he had been willing to confront and challenge in his own time.

At any costs.

And Suka Kuri loved calling it the Socratic method, even if she'd been using it for many, many decades before this.

"We made them give up piracy," Dan replied.

"You made them become an entirely new *civilization*, madame," Suka Kuri said haughtily.

Then started giggling. The Khet of Z'Gosza had deserved no less.

"Lacium is a nice place now," she continued. "Because Uly showed them a completely new way of living from anything they had ever tried before. There are other places on that list, because Uly infected a number of worlds with *civilization*, but it wasn't Uly alone. He brooks no argument that he couldn't do any of this without you, and I agree. The rest of us help in our own way, but you and Uly have it in you to change the galaxy. That might involve bringing down the *Auga*."

"As opposed to?" Dan asked, suddenly intrigued and leaning forward.

Suka Kuri paused to find the right words, aware that she had suddenly stepped into a nexus point in history itself with this woman.

One of those moments when future history books would either begin or end with this exact conversation, just as many would start with the day that *Marshall Castillon* captured *King Hewitt II* and sent over a young officer to take command as a prize ship.

Or Uly, sailing the *Fox* into Z'Gosza and offering the Khet the deal of a lifetime. If they were smart enough to take it.

"The Khet were set in their ways, Dan," Suka Kuri said, knowing that she would need to write all this down later and transmit it to both Yanouk and Anari, for each of them to convey to their own students when they became Exemplars in turn. As they would, if they survived long enough.

The entire galaxy would eventually need to know—to absorb —this day. Everyone, down through history.

"The Ononguli were set in their own ways," Suka Kuri continued, drawing Dan's mind down into a new way of seeing things.

Not Moss nor Sabre. Starfare, perhaps, where war was simply the continuation of *diplomacy by other means*. Dan would need diplomacy to pull this off.

And friends, but she had those.

"The Isann were set in ways that were framed entirely by the *Karaŋgılıkka*," Suka Kuri noted. "*Sailing Into Darkness*, because they wanted to see what was on the other side. Most cultures see the Other as people to be conquered or exterminated, but not the Isann. Not today. Ulysses Fortier has taken his place next to Zamir Aytiev in their pantheon, and he's really only getting started, Dan."

Suka Kuri watched the woman. Saw the new stresses, but also saw that relaxation where Dan and Uly had finally admitted the truth to each other.

And themselves.

Good.

"Uly, before he is done, may be able to so radically impact the *Auga* that they become something else," Suka Kuri pronounced. "Something better. I do not know today what it would take, but I understand that Uly might be the only person I have ever met or even heard of with that potential power in him. You, Dan Chastain, need to keep in the back of your mind the understanding that the *Auga* do not have to be *destroyed* in order to defeat them. They can be changed for the better, if they have the right example put before them, and decide that they want it enough."

Dan had stopped breathing. Suka Kuri as well, but she had

bigger lungs. She watched this precious youngster draw a single breath and something broke.

A chain. A collar.

A *limitation.*

Possibly something that even Dan hadn't been aware of, but it was gone now, freeing her to be even more than she had been yesterday.

Any yesterday.

A seed had taken root, and would grow in fertile soil.

If nothing else, this moment alone made everything else Suka Kuri had ever done in her life pale by comparison, because she had just changed all of civilization's future history with these words.

And it would be good, even if she'd likely grow old and die laughing at Death Herself before she had a chance to smell that flower bloom.

It would still be good.

"Thank you," Dan whispered.

Suka Kuri smiled and nodded, seeing what Dan herself would look like in another few decades, when she became Exemplar herself.

Because Dan had that in her, as well.

This future was going to be so much fun to discover.

SIXTY-FIVE

Uly studied the uniform that Omid had modified for him.

Until today, he had arrogantly worn the rank of Captain (O-7). A solid black ring around each cuff, with a broken black ring above that. He had considered taking the rank of Fleet Captain for himself today and making that second ring solid as well, but Dan had put her foot down and refused.

And she'd been right. As usual.

Omid had taken the black off entirely and replaced them with two solid rings in gold cloth, each as wide as his thumb. Dan wouldn't even settle for the single ring of an Echelon, the lowest of the Flag ranks back home, but had insisted that he take upon himself Vanguard. Two rings.

Presumably, assuming he survived, he would add a third and fourth as he grew his fleet and this new nation Dan was helping him build. Marshall and Fleet Marshall.

And then?

Perhaps, someday, he would create a new Commander-In-Chief position as civilian executive of everything, along with Head of State, but his State today consisted of two ships and a station.

One system that directly called itself his, along with a vast trade network of independent places that acknowledged him in some form or another.

Warlord of the Spinward Reaches. Whatever the hell that actually meant.

The Ononguli would have opinions, because Dan was moving forward with having the Legal Department review and make a list of suggestions that she would approve.

Tomorrow's task.

Today, something far, far more important.

He emerged from his quarters and found Emil and Gennady there to escort him, both in their best and as cleaned up as he could remember either of them being.

And that said a lot with these two men.

But they agreed with the day.

And that said everything.

He nodded. Both returned with smiles.

As a trio, they walked aft, eventually boarding a shuttle and making the short trip across to *Corsac Fox*.

Yuriy Kovalchuk greeted them at the airlock, also dressed in a crisp blue that looked good on the man, especially when Uly thought back to the *Iron Wasp* pirate engineer that had been randomly put in the same cell as their prisoners when the *Auga* had captured Adrian and his ship.

"Permission to come aboard?" Uly asked formally.

"Granted and welcome, Vanguard," Yuriy grinned, more or less all pretense of solemnity gone.

Uly shook his hand, then got led forward through corridors that had been scrubbed and painted. Cleaned and refreshed, even from the high level that Uly had maintained when he had commanded from his deck.

The bridge was crowded when they got there. Packed almost as full as it could safely be, with the blowers running all out to keep the air clean and the temperature down.

Yuriy moved off to one side, standing formally next to Vitali Havrylyuk and Bello Temitope. Sterling rose from the command station and turned to look at Uly with nerves visible in his eyes, but nowhere else.

Again, Uly remembered those first days. The quiet midshipman who had only wanted to be a stellar cartographer, just learning his craft on a civilian slave transport under the iron command of an asshole like Lord Tevin Winter, *Danumash* Captain and younger son of a baron.

Who could have imagined that they would come to this day?

Uly smiled to reassure him, then turned in place to study the crowd along the walls. All of the Humans, originally from either *Marshall Castillon* or *King Hewitt II*. All ten of the Mazhin who had been prisoners on *King Hewitt II* that fateful day. Slaves being carried from one facility to another. Everyone who had been in that cell block aboard this very ship after Adrian Sobol had captured them. Suka Kuri, Hiko Seiichai, and Yanouk Miyoshi. Ethir Ewin, Waltin Gysby, Ralphye Byne, and Hobse Baldo. Uly even saw several Ononguli folks who had been in the cell with them on an *Auga* Prison Barge, awaiting *processing*, because they had chosen to join Uly and Dan on this adventure. All of the Combat Team.

All here today. It was good.

"Lieutenant Huff, you will step forward," Uly said, causing the room to fall to utter silence save for those fans.

And smiles. Lots of smiles.

Dan stepped out from the crowd and fell in on his right. Omid joined on his left. The others all crowded back, opening up a space roughly three meters across.

Sterling moved close and came to attention, shoulders back, head up, feet together, and unshed tears in his eyes. Uly nodded and smiled.

"When we first met, you were my enemy," Uly pronounced slowly. "A *Danumash* midshipman aboard a captured vessel, striving to keep the ship itself from being destroyed. You worked with me to keep the ship and crew alive, Mr. Huff. To see that we got someplace safe. Since then, you have gone over and above time and again that I lack the ability to properly reward, because we don't have enough ribbons to mark it, save that I consider you a friend."

Sterling's flinch was obvious, as was the pained smile on his face, eyes locked on a spot over Uly's left shoulder and eternity. Tears wanting to come, but continued being held at bay by that same tremendous force of will that marked everything about Sterling Huff.

"We gather today to offer you some small reward, Mr. Huff," Uly continued. "A mark of that esteem that conveys to everyone we meet that you speak for me. That you command a vessel in my fleet and in my name. Previously, you have been a lieutenant commanding a warship in service. It is my unbridled pleasure to promote you formally to the rank of Commander, Mr. Huff. Madame Adl?"

Omid gestured to Roshan, standing nearby, and a bag was produced from somewhere. She opened it and drew forth a new jacket, even as Sterling unbuttoned and removed the one he had been wearing. This new one had a solid black stripe on each wrist to replace the broken ring he'd been wearing previously.

Commander Sterling Huff.

More important to Uly was the name sewn on the right breast, opposite *Huff* over his heart.

They had spoken about the need to formally rename this vessel, once Uly took command of *Nubia*. The big ship would retain that name in service, honoring Dan and the Yarikh who had once flown it.

But *Corsac Fox* would continue to confuse people once Uly no longer flew aboard except in rare circumstances.

He beamed at Sterling got the new coat buttoned up and smoothed down. Omid ran her hands down the front, smiling at him with her tentacles, then stepped back with an even bigger smile on her face as she nodded to Uly.

"Commander Chastain?" he turned to Dan next.

Quintin Butcher stepped out of the crowd on Dan's side, the quiet, honest banking assistant who had inherited the job of payroll and finances when the Bursar of *King Hewitt II* had been killed. He reminded many people of a loyal dog, quiet and steadfast while getting the job done and not making hardly any fuss at it, even as he had been subsumed into the Legal Department by Haydar, Ethir, Piruz, and Rabiu. Always there, always correct in his sums.

Always.

Today, he handed Dan a scroll tube with a slight bow, then stepped back.

Dan took it and opened the tube, pausing to read the thing silently before handing it to Uly to read.

He had already approved everything, so this was formality and show, but it was a good one. Butcher stepped up with a clipboard and pen, and Uly signed it, dating it according to a variety of systems: Human, Z'Gosza, Ononguli, and **Bastion Founding**.

"Commander Huff, your orders," Uly announced, handing him the document and stepping back.

"By command of the Corsac Fox, be it known that Commander Sterling Huff is hereby appointed commanding officer of the Heavy Interceptor *Batyr*, the renamed *Iron Wasp* in Corsac Fox's service," Sterling read in a voice that cracked with emotions, even as others around them showed the same. They had all been through a lot together. And there would be more. "All vessels and conductors will accord him the honor and respect of that position as they remain in Bastion service. Dated and signed by the Corsac Fox himself, Vanguard Ulysses Fortier."

He stepped back, crying, but that was okay. The uniform was waterproof and he wasn't the only one.

"Yuriy Kovalchuk, Vitali Havrylyuk, and Bello Temitope, you will step forward," Dan announced.

Two Ononguli and a Khet stepped into the space Sterling stepped out of, himself moving to stand next to Omid.

Butcher produced three more scroll tubes, but Dan signed each of them this time, before handing them to the three men.

"You three have each been promoted to the rank of Lieutenant in the Bastion Navy, aboard the warship *Batyr*," she announced. "First Officer, Gunner, Pilot. Omid?"

The three's uniforms had blank sleeves. Omid stepped up and wrapped a broken black stripe around each wrist. It had a sticky back that would hold for several days, and Omid herself intended to sew them permanently in place, just as she had made Sterling's new uniform.

The audience clapped finally when Omid was done.

"Commander Huff?" Uly asked with an unstoppable smile when the noise fell.

"Vanguard," he nodded. "There is a reception aft, where we have invited a much larger group to help us celebrate, but it was decided that this ceremony was best handled here, with those folks that had been there from the beginning. If efferyone would begin making your way to the main wardroom, there is food, drink, and desserts awaiting."

Folks began to drain out of the room, but Uly grabbed Sterling before the man could escape and engulfed him in a tremendous hug. Commander he might be, Sterling was still only twenty years old.

But he could handle the responsibility. He'd proven that.

As had they all.

SIXTY-SIX

Nasrin tasted the emotions on the air currents as they moved through the corridors. All of the crew could not join them, but representatives had been picked, occasionally by lottery. And Uly and Dan had made sure that everyone who had been there the longest was here.

Not that the newcomers were somehow lesser, but she still remembered the quiet midshipmen that Sterling Huff and Solomon Wyndham had been four years ago. Hardly younger than her, relative to age span.

How far they had come.

She wasn't the first into the big reception room, but her senses were there as soon as the hatch opened and air blew out, along with noise from folks who had been watching on monitors as Sterling took his rightful place.

He deserved this. She could say that, because she'd known the man longer than Uly had. All of the ex-slaves had. None of them had bad things to say about him. Or Drew. Quinton. Marlowe and his trainees. Even Blair Mitchell had been accept-able, because the others had been worse, though she did occasionally pause and wonder what had become of Leith Masters, left behind in the jail break because he'd been treating Doctors Spence and Atwater.

The addition of new Ononguli scents wasn't even that big of a note, because it was mostly Anna Shevchenko and Lukyan Chayka, plus a few aides who hardly ever spoke around Nasrin, probably afraid that she could read their minds.

Wasn't their minds she was reading, but she didn't bother enlightening them.

The Isann were the most interesting flavor to the room. Perhaps forty in total, including the Chief of Chiefs, plus Aibek Sulaymanov and his family. They had chosen wisely in adopting the future that Uly and Dan represented.

And Nasrin did think of the two of them as separate entities now. Uly and Dan. She could smell the one on the other in ways she hadn't before. Perhaps not the final step, but they'd finally moved to admit things to one another.

Nasrin approved. Uly was simply amazing, and Dan was exceptional.

She moved off to one side and found a glass of juice to drink. Haydar ended up standing next to her not long after that, tentacles flowing and communing in ways that the others simply lacked the vocabulary to understand. No words today. Just emotions.

Haydar was working his way through a series of advanced training programs and syllabus notes for Starfare. Nasrin was backing him up as an editor, so she would end up auditing most of the curriculum, though she had no interest in commanding starships. Might still be necessary at some point, so it would be a useful skill to add to her catalog.

Dan broke loose from the crowd at one point and walked directly towards Nasrin, an unreadable smile on her face.

"Could you pardon us for a second?" Dan asked Haydar.

The old, wet hen grumbled gamely and moved off, but that was Haydar being a grouch.

Dan leaned in like two Humans would whisper in one another's ears, though it was unnecessary with tentacles.

"I have a proposal for you," Dan said so quietly that Nasrin had to practically taste it.

She nodded to the woman.

"I've had a chance to talk to Suka Kuri," Dan continued. "And the rest of the Combat Team, though that might turn out a bit different in the long run. It also might not, and nothing has to be resolved today."

Nasrin found it terribly rude, the way Dan had her hanging on pins and needles, because she'd apparently been left out of some secret by the other ladies.

Scanning the room with her tentacles, everyone else was in on it, because they were all watching her discreetly from wherever they were standing and talking to others. Uly had Anna and Lukyan going on some topic, possibly the marriage contract from the way Ethir's hands gestured.

Nasrin found her head coming around to make eye contact with Dan, in spite of herself. Dan's grin was terrible.

"This is what I intend to place before Uly and Anna," Dan said, then proceeded to explain it.

Anari's smile across the way redoubled when Nasrin felt all of her tentacles go perfectly, painfully straight for a beat, before attempting to tie themselves into knots that might take fingers to unravel later.

Nasrin's eyes were all the way around, staring at Dan. She blinked, processing the words. The concept.

The utter audacity of it.

She'd known Humans before she had met Dan or Uly. *Danumash* had been her jailers for years. Longer, for many of the men that had been there that day.

None of them compared to Dan.

"Will it work?" Nasrin whispered.

This was a chunk of Human history that she had never

encountered before. And there wouldn't likely be much available. And what there was would be tainted by mostly being *Danumash*, because Uly and the others had largely brought nothing but their bodies and their suits aboard *King Hewitt II*.

Nasrin turned to Suka Kuri and semaphored a question at the elder. The Emro woman lacked tentacles, but could read them. And nodded. Not that Nasrin was surprised, because this had her scent on it, for all of Dan's audacity.

Dan Chastain had likely thought it up. Suka Kuri probably wasn't getting enough credit for her part.

Or blame, whichever was appropriate. Nasrin wasn't sure.

"What changes?" she asked Dan.

"Everything, and nothing," Dan nodded, understanding the leap of faith she was asking.

But Nasrin was the last one being asked, not the first. All the smiles around her from the Team promised that.

Because she'd been with Dan the longest? Likely. Dan's Second-in-Command of the Combat Team. And perhaps her closest advisor, in spite of being the youngest of them.

Because yes, everything would change. And not that much, presumably, because what Dan was asking was for Uly. And all of them.

Suka Kuri smiled. That brought Nasrin comfort.

"Yes," she told Dan. "Sounds like an adventure. Are you making an announcement?"

"Not everything," Dan answered solemnly. "This is Sterling's day and we're celebrating that. At the same time, I'd like to be able to send Anna and Lukyan home as soon as possible. Possibly with Ethir and Piruz to keep dickering details while making some sort of round trip to Rayzian."

"Is the galaxy prepared for what you and Uly are about to do?" Nasrin asked.

"Gods, I hope not," Dan grinned finally. "If they can't figure this out, they can't get ahead of me in their planning. It's like Sterling and Drew in combat, only this is in the conference room."

Nasrin nodded. It had that feel. Or a bar fight, of which she'd lived a much more sheltered life than Anari or Yeong-Suk, though she had absorbed their stories of such things.

And knew how to handle herself if one broke out.

"I've got your flank," Nasrin assured her.

"That's why I saved you for last," Dan nodded. "Now, let's go drop a bomb on the Ononguli."

Nasrin fell in and stayed on Dan's right. The woman was left-handed, when most Humans were not, so she was on that side as they moved close.

The Horse Thief knew she was coming. He stepped to one side, drawing Ethir's immediate attention by opening a space for Dan to slide in next to Uly.

Lukyan eyed her carefully and took a half step back. Not like a man about to throw a punch, but moving himself closer to safety and letting Anna Shevchenko bear the brunt of what was coming.

Nasrin nodded understanding to him and focused on the *Vatazhko*, even as Piruz asked questions she wasn't about to answer today.

None of his damned business.

Uly paused to glance at her and Nasrin smelled the center of gravity of the entire room shift. Maybe the whole system. Around her, people took note and conversations fell off quickly to silence.

Dan waited. Anna waited. Uly watched.

Nasrin held her breath, but maintained her stoic equilibrium in front of anyone who wasn't a Mazhin. Or an Exemplar of the Arts.

Or Uly.

"I wanted to give you an update," Dan began in that quiet tone that caused folks without tentacles to lean in and turn their heads.

Like *Vatazhkos*.

"Oh?" Shevchenko asked, feeling the gravity generators possibly meandering a bit.

"Ethir and Piruz were asking about some of the more esoteric points of the contract proposal," Dan nodded. "Haydar and Rabiu have both gone over it to their satisfaction."

Nasrin suppressed a snort at the level of fanatical devotion that document had engendered as everyone tore apart every single subphrase and detail, parsing them with nigh-religious fervor.

And Dan was about to pull a fast one on *everyone.*

On all the men, anyway. And the *Vatazhko,* but she could fall into that group.

People **not** part of Dan's Inner Circle. The Combat Team, including the Elder.

Dan paused, so others got the pins and needles treatment, too. Nasrin felt better.

"On the whole, we find the contract generally acceptable," Dan pronounced, setting off a quiet explosion of sound.

Mostly gasps. A few profanities. Somebody dropped a shatter-proof cup that bounced twice off the deck before it got caught.

Anna Shevchenko blinked too many times, and then realized that she'd missed some critical detail from the way her eyes got narrow and cagey. Her scent changed, but Piruz was probably the only other person who noticed.

Besides Uly.

"I see," Shevchenko replied carefully.

"I'd like to send Piruz and Ethir with you back to Rayzian," Dan said. "Plus a few other folks along as support and such. That way, everything can be nailed down tightly by the time Uly arrives at Rayzian to formally sign off on the contract."

"When did you think that might occur?" Shevchenko asked, still wary about deeper traps.

"You'll need time to load up and prepare at Bastion," Dan said. "We have some business to conduct here yet, then we will follow along. At Bastion, if we can convince Maks to remain in office for a time, we can turn around and follow you in a few weeks."

Nasrin caught the flinch from Lukyan on Maks' sbehalf. As Governor, he didn't dare allow himself to become personally involved—intimate—with the Ambassador to the Ononguli Sphere, much as he might want to. Alternatively, the construction was done, so technically, he was supposed to return home aboard *Treta Envoy*.

And he might not. Somebody would have to take the job if Maks left, but Nasrin was hard-pressed to think who Uly might trust that much and be willing to leave there.

Then she smiled.

Of course.

Anna and Lukyan caught her look and got distracted. Dan shifted around. Uly turned and studied her in ways that had Nasrin blushing, but he could probably read and understand her as well as Piruz and Haydar.

That was going to matter soon.

"You had a thought?" Dan asked.

"Maks," Nasrin replied. "Governor Maks, at least until we get back."

"Until?" Uly asked, suddenly watching her sharpest of anyone in the room. Like he could see her soul, in spite of lacking tentacles.

But it was Uly.

"The *Vatazhko* likely needs him back, now that construction is done," Nasrin pointed out. "Technically, his contract with you ends at that point. Should Commander Huff step in instead?"

Everyone else had opinions, but didn't voice them. Like that mattered to a Mazhin, but she kept her mouth closed and her tentacles casual as she listened to the room.

Uly saw it immediately. His smile was almost frightening, the speed with which he absorbed her comment, internalized it, parsed it, and agreed with it.

"I believe I have taken advantage of Maks a bit, yes," Uly

nodded, turning to the *Vatazhko*. "Anna, I'll send *Batyr* and Sterling with you as soon as everyone can load up supplies to sail, and that lets Maks off the hook to return to the life I so rudely interrupted. And thank him for me personally? I'll send a note, but I might be tied up here and not get the chance to see him until we get to Rayzian."

"I will," Shevchenko nodded, still sidelong, like she might bolt if somebody made a loud noise right now.

Nasrin understood the feeling. She was watching the galaxy change.

And participating.

Luckily, she trusted Dan.

And Uly.

SIXTY-SEVEN

Uly opened the hatch when it beeped and smiled when he found Dan standing there.

"Join me?" he asked, stepping in and sideways. "Was just having some hot chocolate. I mean, it's not, but it has many of the right tastes, at least for a guy, where I lack some of the receptors you have. Figured I should find something else to drink, to stretch the supplies as long as possible."

She smiled and stepped into his cabin, pausing to kiss him lightly as the hatch closed, then moved to the couch and sat, curling her legs sideways in a way that he would have found painful.

Uly moved back to his chair and picked up his mug. He held it out and she had a sip, but it wasn't real chocolate, so she handed it back.

Uly drew a breath, held it, and released it.

"Today went well, I think," he offered, mostly as an opening.

Sterling promoted. *Batyr* formally commissioned into service. Anna dealt with as well as possible for now.

It helped that Halyna Bondarenko was an attractive woman.

At least as a Human might see an Ononguli. It helped when he thought of her as just like any other woman.

Any other person.

Uly supposed that a lot of people wouldn't be able to make that emotional and psychological leap, would they?

Dan had a plan. He trusted it. Hopefully, she'd even tell him what it was at some point.

He looked at her expectantly.

"Today went extremely well," she agreed, nodding. "Sterling will make a good temporary governor at *Bastion*, though I've been giving thought to the need to hire a civilian administrator to execute things, since it will be important for you to be elsewhere for extended periods. Might call on Rabiu or the Bondarenko to suggest folks."

Uly nodded. Rabiu was technically still employed as part of Trade Factor Bitrus's organization, though he was largely a free agent these days. And the Bondarenko would become even closer allies once...*things happened*.

Uly just had to trust her.

"What about Anna?" Uly asked.

Dan smiled that secret, dangerous smile that told him she was up to absolutely no good.

And that it was aimed at someone else, which was even better.

"I've put the fear of a variety of pantheons into Rabiu and Ethir," she grinned. "As have Piruz and Haydar and several other folks, now that everyone understands that we'll be moving forward. And probably quickly."

"How quickly?" he asked automatically.

They were going through with it. That much was certain. Contracts like this were going to be handled like treaties between nations.

He hoped that someone had taken Halyna aside and asked if she wanted to be a pawn on Anna's game board, but couldn't just ask. Not without giving a lot of unnecessary offense.

Even the Ononguli crew he had asked, Katya and others, had more or less shrugged when pressed. Maks would probably be gone before Uly could question him, but he'd been gone to sea for a long time, and might hardly remember his cousin. Lukyan had looked like a man willing to go to the gallows without talking.

Uly had to trust. Fortunately, it was Dan.

"It might go fairly quickly," she answered. "The Horde don't generally drag out engagements like this. Historically, you might meet her for breakfast, marry her after lunch, and ride off on the Endless Plains after dinner."

He wanted to shudder, but she was grinning at him, enjoying his discomfort.

But duty was duty, and if this was what it took to bring the Horde in on his side in the greater war with the *Auga*, Uly would do his duty.

This was bigger than him. Possibly bigger than the Corsac Fox, whatever that meant.

"What am I missing?" he finally asked her bluntly. "You're smiling far too much for my peace of mind."

She laughed. It was a lovely laugh, full of joy and mischief.

"You are the Corsac Fox," she replied, sobering but still filled with mirth.

"I am also the Corsac Fox," he corrected her. "*We are*, when you get right down to it."

That stilled her. She blinked blankly for a moment, then her smile redoubled.

"Just be you," she whispered.

"I'm trying," he nodded.

"The Ononguli Horde have offered you a political marriage," Dan explained, calmer now. Almost businesslike. "A connection that directly links you to the Bondarenko Clan and their allies, which is Maks, his mom, and her people, among others. More importantly, it draws the *Vatazhko* in on your side, because the Bondarenko are close to the Shevchenko, especially useful here because Maks's mother and Anna sailed together when they were both young."

"Did they now?" he asked with wonder. "Nobody has mentioned that."

"Not loudly," she agreed. "I pushed Maks into a corner and got the truth out of him at one point, and knew that we could trust him from the way he pushed back on some things and not on others. Highly developed sense of ethics for a pirate."

"He got that from Lukyan," Uly pointed out.

"Yes, and he's solid," Dan said. "Anna rewarded him and his mother for things they did quietly in the background. You've drawn him in as ally already, so the Sobol and the Bondarenko are well disposed to support the Corsac Fox."

"Yes, and you are evading my question," he pointed out.

Dan grinned. Cheshire Cat grin he considered kissing. Leaned over and did, before she could escape. Not that she put up much resistance.

"You understand the Combat Team in a theoretical sense," she said, turning back into his Chief of Staff when they were done.

Uly nodded.

"Suka Kuri suggested at least one woman from each species we've encountered as something more than merchants in harbor," Uly said. "Two, given the pair of Emro, but they are technically Moss and Sabre anyway, so they are distinct cultures. And you already have an Ononguli in Katya Zehlennko. Were you planning to add Halyna to that? I was not aware from the notes that she had the level of combat training you required?"

"I doubt that she does," Dan said. "If necessary, we could train her up. Yeong-Suk had hardly anything initially, save for a willingness to step up when she saw the opportunity."

"Okay, so what am I missing?" Uly asked, knowing that she had a point and was enjoying torturing him getting there.

He'd come to know her that well over this long.

"You will have a wife of the Ononguli," Dan said. "Halyna

Bondarenko, cousin of Maks Sobol and niece of Lyra, Maks' mom."

"Yes," he agreed. "That's your plan."

"Who says that the Corsac Fox must be limited to only one wife?" she asked.

Uly wondered if he'd fallen out of his seat. Had he been standing, he might have. He put the mug down before he was wearing it, using the sort of care one developed when exceedingly drunk.

He wanted to say something pithy, but it came out as a garbled moan of confusion, which just made her smile all the more.

Then he saw it. Saw the conversation. Saw where she'd been guiding him.

"All of you?" he whispered hoarsely, eyes utterly *HUGE*.

"All of us," she smiled. "It was my idea, but Suka Kuri immediately agreed with it. Each species has a pattern now by which they can ally with the Corsac Fox, by marrying a woman into his household."

Uly felt his fingers slipping off words again and again. Finally, he managed one.

"Children?" he asked.

Dan nodded.

"I'm the only one you might directly impregnate," she replied. "The others, if they wish, can pursue quiet means artificially. Or adopt and foster, which we intend to do anyway."

"Anari and Sterling?" he asked.

"They make a good team," Dan agreed. "I've worked hard to get him over the last little bits of *Danumash* in his head. As the Corsac Fox will have multiple wives, she might end up with multiple husbands, but that's not a problem to deal with immediately, as she's only older physically. Emotionally, Sterling is more mature. They'll need time, and they will get it."

"You are the most dangerous person I've ever met," Uly whispered flatly. "I'm just sorry you haven't met my parents to understand how high a bar that is."

"One of these days," she smiled.

Yes, one of these days, if he could ever set the Corsac Fox aside long enough.

Because it wouldn't be possible to sail into harbor at *Gralbo* and pick them up. Either he'd need a fleet big enough to make the locals behave, or he'd have to sneak a team in to kidnap or rescue them. And he had exactly three Humans that he could use, plus a lot of aliens he could call on.

"Suka Kuri is more dangerous," Dan started to say, but Uly's laugh interrupted. "Okay, maybe it's a tie."

"At best, woman," he smiled. "At best. When were you going to spring this on Anna and the Horde?"

"I thought we might arrange for Chief of Chiefs Usupov to accompany us to Bastion," Dan grinned slyly. "Wherein he could officiate a wedding for the history books."

"It feels wrong to have a harem," Uly said. "Even knowing that the folks involved to be acceptable must be smart and beautiful by any standards."

"It's not just a harem, Uly," she said.

"Oh?"

"It will be something that the Mazhin understand," she nodded. "And something that other places will grasp quickly enough, if they want you as an ally. It will be The Congress of Wives."

Uly considered it. Considered how he *Spoke* for the Mazhin he had inherited, then collected more along the way. And how that species organized themselves into a lower house called the Hall of Voices and an upper house dominated by the women who were the various clan leaders.

The Mazhin Convocation itself.

Yes, what Dan was envisioning would work.

And he could trust her.

That was all that really mattered.

READ MORE

Be sure to read the rest of the Corsac Fox series!

https://www.knottedroadpress.com/product-category/science-fiction/corsac-fox/

ABOUT THE AUTHOR

Blaze Ward writes science fiction in the Alexandria Station universe (Jessica Keller, The Science Officer, The Story Road, etc.) as well as several other science fiction universes, such as Star Dragon, the Dominion, and more. He also writes odd bits of high fantasy with swords and orcs. In addition, he is the Editor and Publisher of *Boundary Shock Quarterly Magazine*. You can find out more at his website www.blazeward.com, as well as Facebook, Goodreads, and other places.

Blaze's works are available as ebooks, paper, and audio, and can be found at a variety of online vendors. His newsletter comes out regularly, and you can also follow his blog on his website. He really enjoys interacting with fans, and looks forward to any and all questions—even ones about his books!

Never miss a release!
If you'd like to be notified of new releases, sign up for my newsletter.

http://www.blazeward.com/newsletter/

Buy More!
Did you know that you can buy directly from the KRP website?

https://www.knottedroadpress.com/shop/

ABOUT KNOTTED ROAD PRESS

Knotted Road Press publishes dynamic fiction set in exotic locations and unique non-fiction voices in genres such as autobiography, business, cookbooks, and how-to. Our authors cover a wide range of genres including science fiction, fantasy, mystery, literary, and poetry, appealing to all readers. We offer both DRM-free ebooks and print books for a global readership.

Knotted Road Press
www.KnottedRoadPress.com
www.KnottedRoadPress.com/Shop

www.ingramcontent.com/pod-product-compliance
Lightning Source LLC
Chambersburg PA
CBHW051121300726
48981CB00021B/501/J